The Looking Glass

The Looking Glass

JANET McNALLY

HARPER TEEN

An Imprint of HarperCollinsPublishers

HarperTeen is an imprint of HarperCollins Publishers.

Library of Congress Cataloging-in-Publication Data

Names: McNally, Janet (Janet M.) author.

Title: The looking glass / Janet McNally.

Description: First edition. | New York, NY : HarperTeen, [2018] | Summary: A copy of
Grimms' Fairy Tales sends Sylvie, a sixteen-year-old ballerina-in-training, in search
of her runaway older sister amid strange happenings, such as a women leaving a shoe
behind while running.

Identifiers: LCCN 2017034545 | ISBN 978-0-06-243627-6 (hardback)

Subjects: | CYAC: Ballet dancing—Fiction. | Sisters—Fiction. | Runaways—Fiction.
| Supernatural—Fiction.

Classification: LCC PZ7.1.M4645 Loo 2018 | DDC [Fic]—dc23

LC record available at https://lccn.loc.gov/2017034545

Typography by Jenna Stempel-Lobell

18 19 20 21 22   PC/LSCH   10 9 8 7 6 5 4 3 2 1

First Edition

To the Lady Nation: my daughters, Juno, Daphne, and Luella, and my nieces, Orlah, Faye, and Charlie. Always be brave and fierce and kind.

When you walk,
the soles of your feet take turns on the ground,
but the rest of you is in the sky, enveloped in sky.
As you move through it, you make a tunnel
in the precise size and shape of your body.

from "Sky" by Maggie Smith

PART ONE

Once Upon a Time

What Ballerinas Do

HERE I AM, BAREFOOT ON a stool in the wardrobe room, trying as hard as I can to stay still. There are masses of tulle around me on the floor, piled like drifts of cotton candy. I'm floating in a pastel sea. I'm a very small, very fidgety boat.

It feels like every molecule in my body is vibrating, electrons pinging around in my atoms, shaking my soul loose. This is what I've been like lately. My problem right now is this: if I don't stop wiggling, our seamstress, Miriam, is going to kill me.

She looks up at me, eyes narrowed, mouth full of silver pins. She's been making costumes for forty years, so she's pretty good at talking with sharp things in her mouth, but right now she doesn't bother. She just *looks* at me and I feel like a five-year-old caught misbehaving. I understand why she's mad, though. Today is our last class, and she's trying to finish before we leave so I can dance after a dinner for donors in August. And I'm not helping.

This will be my gravestone:

Here lies Sylvie Blake, who had a pretty good run until Miriam killed her with a sewing needle.

"Sorry," I say to Miriam. "I don't know what's wrong with me."

Miriam shakes her head, but I can see a hint of a smile in her eyes, even if it hasn't quite made it to her mouth yet. I know I'm one of her favorites, so she lets me get away with things, up to a point.

"Spine straight," she says through half-closed lips, jabbing a pin into my pearl-gray tutu. "Unless you want your skirt crooked." Even though I don't really care if my skirt is crooked, I try my best to pull my spine into a straight line. My Level Three teacher Miss Inez used to tell us to pretend we were fastened to a thread hanging from the ceiling: *head, neck, backbone, tailbone,* all in a row. *Femur, patella, tibia, fibula,* each pointing straight down to our feet. I imagine it now: the string fastening me, all those bones hanging, completely still, but it doesn't work. Miriam clicks her tongue.

"You're just like your sister," she says, half to herself. "She could never stay still either."

At the sound of this word—*sister*—all the molecules in my body move just a little to the left. I stand there, my tiniest parts swirling imperceptibly. Here's what I'm thinking: I'd give almost anything lately to stop feeling like an actual galaxy.

Walt Whitman was right, I guess. *I contain multitudes.* And Julia is the one who did it to me.

Today is my birthday, and it was supposed to be different. Today I was going to figure out how to leave it all behind, be something other than a sad sack or a celestial event. But instead, I'm standing on this stool, feeling so suddenly dizzy that I press my right thumb lightly to the inside of my left wrist. There's nothing but my own skin in the spot, but this is exactly where my sister's tattoo is. I was there when she got it, holding her right hand in my own. The ink spells out three words in swooping cursive:

Twenty-six bones

With my fingers on my wrist I can feel the tiny thump of my pulse below my skin, the way it marks how hard my heart is pumping. Even broken hearts keep working most of the time.

That's still the most surprising thing.

"Sugarplum," Miriam says. That's what she always calls me, and it makes me think of *Nutcracker* songs, fake snow under stage lights, man-sized mice. The ever-present weirdo beauty of ballet.

"Are you all right?" she asks.

I glance down at her and see she's looking up at me, sharp dark eyes under her crown of silver hair. I shrug before I can stop myself. I expect Miriam to chastise me and say, *Ballerinas don't shrug*, the same way she often says, *Ballerinas don't slouch*. But she doesn't. She smiles. She gives me her hand for balance and helps me get down.

"Go have a good last class," she says. She slips the tutu down over my legs and I step out of it carefully, without letting its new pinned hem touch the floor. It's as delicate as a spiderweb, lighter than air. But that doesn't really matter. It would fall to the ground the same as anything else.

There are rules in this world, or at least there are supposed to be. To be honest, Julia always seemed exempt. She was magic. She broke the laws of physics, slipped past the reach of gravity every day. She was made of sparkle and shimmer and grit. But the truth about magic is this: it's hard to keep believing in it once it's gone.

Whipped

"WE NEED TO TALK ABOUT gravity," Tommy says. At least that's what I think he says. His voice sounds really far away.

Right now, I'm turning fouettés so fast I must be throwing sparks. I'm finally able to move the way my body wants to, and I'm making up for lost time. The room streaks around me like an Impressionist painting left out in the rain, but I'm spotting the window frame hard so I'm not dizzy. A warm honey-gold feeling rises in my belly, fueling me. It might be sorrow. It might be fossilized hope. Either way, it keeps me spinning.

Fouetté means "whipped," and that's what I'm doing to the air. Just making my own weather, my own personal cyclone. And it's all going beautifully until I hit forty-eight turns. Then the ticker-tape count in my head switches off and my ankle falls out of orbit like a faulty satellite. I stop spotting and sputter to a stop, put both feet on the floor to catch myself. The room whirls.

And there's Tommy, a dozen feet away, one hand on the barre. His posture is perfect, all vertical lines, the muscles of his arms so defined they might be cut from marble. Old Marble-Arms, we call him. Well, not really. But still, he might as well be half Greek god, half fairy-tale prince.

(It's my job to break the hard news to the princesses: he's looking for a prince of his own.)

"I saw that," Tommy says. The studio slows and tilts a little, then rights itself. Blood swirls in my veins.

"Saw what?"

His voice goes all deep and dramatic like a nature-documentary narrator. "Here we see the elusive dancer," he says, "threatened in her natural habitat." I roll my eyes, but he doesn't stop. "Much like the puffer fish and its poison sting, or the squid, which expels a cloud of ink, the young ballerina has her own method of defense."

"I don't know what the hell you're talking about," I say. Which is true, but it doesn't stop him.

Tommy gestures his hands toward one another, fingers curved like they're about to wrap around a neck.

"Someone was going to strangle me?" I say.

"No," he says, faux-exasperated. "Yuki and Rachel were coming over to hug you goodbye. You didn't see them? I assumed that's why you turned into a spinning top."

I shake my head. "No," I say. But I can't help looking across the studio toward Yuki and Rachel. My friends, or at least they used to be, when I knew how to talk to them. When they knew how to talk to me. I used to be like them at the end of each year: dripping with last-class nostalgia, standing with the rest of the class in a cluster near the doorway. It's clear more hugs are in the forecast.

There are my classmates, floating around as sweet and wispy as cotton candy, sugar spun to air. Lately I'm feeling more like a Lemonhead: tart and sharp and hard to chew.

"Ballet dancers aren't supposed to be cuddly," I say to Tommy. "We're supposed to be beautiful. Elegant." I arrange my arms into fifth position and pose.

"Bitchy," Tommy says. "I get it."

I roll my eyes. He points across the room to Emma, who, unbeknownst to her, plays the part of our nemesis when it seems fun to have one. Her cider-colored hair in a perfect bun, no strays escaping but also no sign of hair spray. *It's a conundrum,* I always used to say (a little-known Nancy Drew title: *The Mystery of the Immovable Bun*), and then Tommy would answer in a stage whisper: *Dark magic.* I'd believe it. After all, her grand jeté is pretty otherworldly, and she's just the type to sell her soul.

"You want to be like She Who Must Not Be Named?" Tommy says.

I shake my head. "Not particularly."

Tommy flips up his palms, triumphant. "Then let yourself be hugged once in a while."

"Okay," I say. "*You* can hug me whenever you want."

Tommy smiles. He tips his head to the side. "Let's talk about the fouettés," he says. He raises his eyebrows. "Forty-eight. Pretty stellar."

Because of course he was counting too. None of us can stop. It's a disease.

I shrug.

"Come on, Sylvie," Tommy says. "It's way more than you'd need for *Swan Lake*."

He's right. To dance Odette/Odile you have to be able to do thirty-two fouettés in a row. Not exactly easy, but I can do it. I mean, I better be able to do it because I've been practicing all year. In the beginning, I think part of me believed that there was some number I could hit and everything would feel okay again. That if I spun long enough, my molecules would settle back into their proper places.

And then my sister would come home.

But at this point, that's not going to happen. Julia's been gone since my fifteenth birthday and today I turn sixteen. A year is long enough, right? It's time to stop hoping and try to move on.

I cup my foot in my palm and straighten my leg above my head, toes pointing toward the ceiling. If I were anywhere else this would look like showing off, but here it's nothing special. So utterly normal it's almost boring.

"Screw *Swan Lake*," I say.

"My thoughts exactly." Tommy leans back against the barre, head tilted. James Dean in tights. "Waterfowl have absolutely no place in ballet."

"Damn straight," I say. I try not to smile.

Tommy and I have grown up together, here in the studio. We've been friends since we were seven. Tommy's mom was a ballerina herself, first in Buenos Aires, where she was born, and later in New York. She quit when Tommy was born, but as she tells us, she knew he'd be a dancer. *It's in his blood*, she says.

It was the same for me, I guess. I followed Julia to the Academy. When Tommy and I were younger, we'd sneak into her classes and sit cross-legged against the wall, watching the older dancers. We learned to be invisible in our sweatpants and ballet slippers, still trembling with warmth from our own class down the hall. The rooms smelled of wood and sweat and rosin, and they smell the exact same way now. It's disorienting, actually. It leaves me breathless sometimes, the way the past comes tumbling into the present, forcing me to remember.

If it would only stay where it belongs—in the past—this would all be much easier.

Now I turn and look at myself squarely in the mirror. When we were younger, Miss Inez used to warn us that we couldn't depend on mirrors to tell us if we were doing things right. Reflections are flipped around and far away, locked somewhere behind the glass. We perceive them differently. "You have to trust your own body," she'd say, in her raspy Barcelonan accent. "You can't trust a looking glass." I don't know why she called it that, if it were an accident of translation or a purposeful renaming, but it made us all remember. I still do.

I step forward, rest my fingers on the barre. It's smooth and cool and still, an object fixed in space. I swear, just the steadiness of it is enough to make me cry.

What the hell is wrong with me?

"You seem a little jittery," Tommy says, reading my mind. "Are you having an early quarter-life crisis?" He rubs his shoulder. "Sixteen is the new twelve, I assure you."

"Good to know," I say. I turn around and fold at my waist, pressing my forehead to my legs.

"I'm serious, Syl."

"I'm fine," I say to my knees. I hope they believe me, because it's unlikely that Tommy will. I'm not ready to explain things to him. I don't want his Eternal Optimism™ shining in my face. Not about this.

"Okay," Tommy says, his voice floating down from above me. I stay folded.

My pinkie toe stings, and I wonder if my blister has opened. I wiggle my toes inside my pointe shoes and feel an electric twinge of pain. I won't be surprised if my new tights are bloodstained when I take them off. *Baptized*, Julia used to say.

When I stand up straight, Tommy is still there, his brown eyes watching me.

"Let's get out of here," he says. "I think you need a break. And the faster you go to dinner with your parents, the faster you can come have cake with Sadie and me. She's been baking all day."

"All day?" I say. "For one cake?" I picture an eleven-tier wedding cake, covered in sugar flowers. Sadie in a frilly apron, her hair powdered-wig white, dusted with flour.

Tommy shrugs. "That's what she says. Let's just hope it's edible, because either way, we have to eat it." He gives me a gentle shove toward the hallway. "Go get ready. I'll meet you outside."

He walks over toward Rachel and Yuki, to be taken into their candied embrace, I'm sure. I don't wait around to see. Right now, it sounds so good to get out of here.

But my escape plan needs an escape plan, because as soon as I set foot in the hallway I hear someone call out my name. It's Miss Diana, my favorite teacher and Julia's too, the only one in this whole place besides Tommy who hasn't acted like my sister never existed at all. I know I should be comforted by seeing her, but instead— inexplicably—panic spreads through my blood like heat. It only gets worse when I see her lift a small white package in her hand like she's on a ship, signaling to shore. Signaling to me.

I don't know what makes me do it, but I make like a squid that's run out of ink. I just hightail it out of there, leaping down the hallway before I can stop myself.

Running from what I don't want to know.

How to Stay on the Ground

I DON'T GO FAR. THERE'S a door next to me—the bathroom—and I pull it open, fold myself inside, shut it. The whole time, I'm holding my breath.

The bathroom lights are off and I don't turn them on. I just stand there in the soft light from the window, planning the rest of my life in case I have to stay in here forever. There's water, obviously, and a toilet, though nothing in the way of nourishment, which is a problem. I think I have a granola bar at the bottom of my dance bag, but after that I'm out of luck.

I pull off my sweaty dance clothes, trading them for a black jersey dress I had rolled up in my bag. Then I lean on the white porcelain sink and look at myself in the mirror. If you look quickly, I could be any other dancer: brown hair pulled back in a tight bun, black leotard, pale pink tights. That's the pleasing thing about ballet, sometimes, the corps mentality where you get to look like every other girl. Where you're *supposed to* look like every other girl, down to your smile, your perfectly pointed toes. Ballet may be all about story, but the corps dancers' individual stories get obliterated. Unless you're me. I look enough like Julia that sometimes I'll pass a company member in the hall and she'll do a double take. When Jules was still here I used to like it, but now it just makes me feel like a reflection instead of a real girl.

My heart is still beating so hard that I barely hear the knock at the door, muffled and rhythmic as a heartbeat of its own. But it keeps coming, that low knocking. I turn the water on and off once, twice, watching it splash in the sink. Then I open the door.

Miss Diana's out there in the hallway. She's wearing a black dress and sandals, her blond hair in a braid wound into a knot at the crown of her head. Her signature Heidi hairstyle. There's an old publicity photo of Miss Diana in a hallway somewhere here at NBT, smiling in the bright red costume she wore when she danced the Firebird, her gold braid in that same bun. She's always seemed like someone who lives and breathes ballet, who might not exist beyond the studio or the stage. I've seen her at Starbucks, though, and once, in the subway station at Astor Place. I'm pretty sure she's a real person, at least sort of. As much as a former principal dancer can be.

"Hello, Sylvie," she says now, smiling.

"Okay," I say, which makes no sense. Then I manage a more fitting "Hi."

"Are you all right?" she says. "I thought you were running away from me."

"Sorry about that," I say. "I really had to pee."

Miss Diana nods. She holds up the envelope. "This came for you."

She hands it to me. I can see now that it's white and padded and has no return address, just a smudged postmark in red ink, and a label with the postage on it. My name written in neat black Sharpie letters on the front, *c/o Diana Sparks, National Ballet Theatre*. In handwriting I know as well as my own.

Of course I know it. And I think Miss Diana knows it too.

My heart flutters behind my ribs like a bird in a cage.

"Are you getting your mail delivered here now?" she says. Her voice is light, but I hear something heavy below it, a lead-weight shadow.

"I guess so," I say. As I reach out and take it from her, a thousand sparks go off in my fingertips. In my hands, the envelope is flat and firm, not too heavy. I picture my sister printing out my name and then Miss Diana's. I picture Jules in line at the post office, in a room full of strangers. No one there would know who she is. She would just be ordinary. I can barely imagine that.

I look up.

"Must be a birthday present," Diana says, holding my gaze. "I hope yours is the happiest. You deserve it."

"Thanks," I say, though I'm not sure what she means. I deserve a nice birthday because I'm a nice person? A hardworking dancer? Or because my virtuosic sister overdosed on painkillers and then left town?

Any of these is possible, I guess.

Whee. Bring on the cake.

"I'll see you in a few weeks?" Miss Diana asks. At those

words, my heart seizes a little. Intensives start just before the end of the month, and before that, I'll be spending a week at what Tommy and I call Fancy Dance Camp. We'll get massages and do yoga and drink smoothies. We'll do just a little dancing, but once intensives start, that's pretty much all we'll be doing. Again.

Miss Diana is watching my face, so I say yes. It feels like a step in a complex routine, something someone else is telling me to do. Because the truth is, I could use a real break.

When I came back to the Academy after everything fell apart, the studios hushed every time I entered them. It was pure choreography: the dancers turned toward me, paused two beats, then scattered to the edge of the room. They'd try to smile but it came out as a stage grin, full of teeth and no real happiness. I just stood in the center of the room like the lone surviving character from a ballet where everyone dies, of consumption, maybe, or being stabbed. I was still living in the old world, but the rest of the company was hard at work building a new universe where Julia never existed. Which, for a while, was fine with me.

It's amazing, though, because before her accident, Jules was the kind of dancer teachers talked about in hushed tones, their cheeks flushed with excitement. A star from the beginning. I was too, I guess, but a smaller star. If she was a red giant, blazing scarlet, I was a white dwarf. Just a tiny pinprick of light, burning near silent in the way-off black. But now that she's gone, everyone seems to expect me to be the red giant. They want to forget about the first Blake girl and let the second take her place.

It's exhausting.

Miss Diana is still watching me, her lips pressed together. "I know you miss her," she says. She puts her fingers around my wrist and squeezes. When she lets go, I feel like a balloon. Like

I   just   away.
      might   float

Straight up to the ceiling, over to the window, and out across the bright blue sky. Miss Diana must see something in my face because she starts to shake her head.

"You know, Sylvie." Her voice is soft. "It's okay to talk about her. We can say her name."

If that's true, I want to say, *then why doesn't anyone?* Even Miriam didn't, this morning. She said *sister*. It's safer, I guess. But in the next moment, Miss Diana surprises me.

"Julia," she says.

She says it like it's the answer to a question, and I guess it is. I expect the whole world to crack open or at the very least, the plaster of the ceiling. But nothing happens, at least not that I can tell.

The moment stretches out and hollows, and there might be space in it to finally tell someone what that day was like.

(Everett holding Julia in his arms in the lobby, waiting for the ambulance to come.)

(The sound of the siren filling the room until I couldn't breathe.)

(Red-and-blue lights sparkling across white marble.)

(My nails biting into my palms, leaving half-moons on my skin.)

16

But I haven't been able to tell that story—or any of the others—to anyone else since Julia left. I can barely tell them to myself.

"Sylvie," Miss Diana says. I look at her. She's the one who taught us *twenty-six bones*. She says it at the beginning of every class like a mantra, to remind us that we have to work as a collective to make something beautiful, the same way the tiny bones in our feet work together. Twenty-six bones hold us up on our tiptoes, just a little lamb's wool and cardboard separating them from the floor. Any dancer can tell you how hard it is to defy gravity, because in the end, the earth just wants to hold you down.

I wonder now if Julia ever showed Miss Diana her tattoo. Or if she meant to, but didn't get the chance. I want to know, too, why everything feels harder today. I open my mouth to ask, but the words feel like feathers stuck in my throat. They won't come out.

Miss Diana smiles at me anyway.

"She's okay," she says. "I know it. And you will be too." She tilts her head, keeps looking at me. "We've seen how hard you've been working. It's wonderful."

I make myself nod. My voice is gone.

"Take care, Sylvie," she says, resting her hand on my shoulder. Then she turns and walks down the hallway, heading into the office at the end. I go in the other direction.

When I turn the corner, I catch sight of an empty spot on the gallery wall. There's still a small nail here, a dark speck on the pearl-colored paint. I reach up and touch it like I always do, like it's a good-luck talisman. In the picture that used to hang here, Julia was Sleeping Beauty, asleep on the stage floor, cheek resting on her arm. Her tutu was a frothy pink flower around her waist, her cheeks flushed with blush. She looked like a dream. Like she might never wake up, and she didn't even mind.

I've wondered a lot where the picture went (Nancy Drew #35: *The Case of the Disappearing Photo*), but what I really want to know is if it was the teachers who took it down, or one of Julia's friends. Grace, or Henry, or Irina, maybe. Did they discuss it first or did one of them just slip the frame into a dance bag one day, hook and all? Where did they put it afterward?

(At the bottom of a drawer.)

(In a box in the company's archives.)

(In the trash.)

In the end, it doesn't matter. I don't need the picture to remember Julia pretending, convincingly, to be in a sleep as deep as death. I saw her do it onstage. Then I saw her do it on the couch in our living room, when she wasn't pretending. When she nearly died for real.

She didn't die, but she's a ghost anyway. Memories come to me in flashes, like projections on blank walls. I lean into the doorway of the last studio and I see her, gone and not-gone, film-flickering in this room full of pale gray light. These mirrors held Julia once, and if I look hard enough, I can still see her, spinning her magic, balancing on all the small bones of her feet.

My Great Escape

OUT ON THE STREET THE sun is so bright the whole world shines white. I've shoved the envelope so far down in my bag that it's totally hidden by my dance clothes, but I feel like it's sending out a radio signal from inside the canvas. A distress signal: *beep beep beep.*

I had a plan, I want to shout. I was going to leave this stuff with my sister behind. And instead I'm carrying it with me. Literally.

I pull the hair tie from my bun and let my hair fall over my shoulders, crinkly at the ends. I look around. My first unfortunate discovery is that Yuki and Rachel haven't left yet. They're on the sidewalk right now, turning their huge smiles toward me like stadium lights, too bright to stare at directly. I feel dread begin to grow in my belly like a fire started on kindling, but then Emma appears in front of me in her cat-footed, ghost-spy way and I startle before I can stop myself.

"Hi, Sylvie," she says. I wave, which I know is weird since she's standing right in front of me.

She looks at my lifted hand and blinks. Her hair is still pulled back in its perfect bun, dark-magic smooth. She tilts her head like she's hearing a sound I can't (dog whistle, approaching earthquake, message from the aliens).

"I hope you have a great summer," she says. Her voice is caramelized sugar, deeply sweet and burnt in spots. Her loose T-shirt is pulled down over one shoulder, her tights the dark black of brand-new spandex. Tommy and I have watched a lot of dance movies, and Emma is basically every antagonist in every one, with her perfect *look at me I'm a dancer* street clothes and her sweet-burnt voice. And the way she appears out of effing nowhere when you least want her to.

"What?" I say. "I'll see you in a couple of weeks. At intensives. And, you know, at camp."

"Oh," Emma says. She puts her hand just below her delicate collarbone. She's a picture of concern, like some kind of *well, bless your heart* Southern woman in an old movie. Except that my freshman-year English teacher was from Alabama, and I know what Southern people mean when they say *bless your heart*.

"I heard a rumor that you weren't coming back," Emma says.

"Why wouldn't I be coming back?"

"Oh, you know," she says.

I look at her. "I don't," I say. Which isn't really true. But if we're having this conversation, I'm going to make her say it.

She winces a little, theatrically, as if it pains her to say this. "Because of Julia," she says. In Emma's mouth, my sister's name comes out as a whisper.

Well, bless your heart, I think. What Emma wants, of course, is for me to get out of her figurative way. She wants the solos, all of them. She wants to be the best, and I'm the competition.

Take the damn solos, I want to say, but instead I shake my head. "Nah, I think I'll stick around."

The wind blows my hair into my eyes and I let it stay there for a moment. I feel my own heart then, steady and quick and ready to burst out of my chest.

This is when Tommy saves me. He can't have heard what she was saying—he was half a building away, talking to Mikhail (cute, new, Russian) by the curb. But he must have seen something in my face or my body language, so here he is. He sweeps around behind me and I feel his hands on either side of my rib cage, lifting me up. I raise my hand in a wave again (*hello, goodbye*) but I don't look back at Emma.

"Excuse us," Tommy says. "Sylvie has birthday business to attend to." He holds me straight up into the air so I levitate over the sidewalk. This is one of my favorite things about ballet—being able to fly without trying. Of course, you need a partner for that, and it's not exactly easy to be lifted either. You can't be floppy or else your partner won't be able to hold you up. You do half the work.

I feel my heartbeat slow. I angle my neck to look over my shoulder.

"Life would be so much easier," I say, "if you just carried me around all the time."

Tommy smiles, still watching the sidewalk ahead. "I'm not sure you could afford me."

I can feel his arms shaking a little, but he keeps holding me high. A silver-haired woman with a cane gets out of a town car to our right. She's wearing a navy-blue suit with a coral necklace, and she looks utterly delighted at the sight of us.

"Hi," I say.

"Hello," she answers, smiling and shading her eyes against the sun.

Tommy sails me past her and keeps going.

"Well, now you're just showing off," I say to Tommy.

"I'm providing an important function," he says, squeezing me a little.

"Saving my ass?"

"Entertaining the world," he says. "But I'm only taking you to the corner. I'm happy to rescue you, but you have to get to the restaurant on your own."

"Deal." I can see sunlight in the leaves of the trees above us, and happiness bubbles in my chest. I glance down and there's a little girl on the sidewalk in front of us. She has light brown skin and huge dark eyes and she looks totally amazed.

"Can I get a little arabesque?" Tommy calls.

I point my toes in my sandals and lift my left leg behind me. I'm careful not to kick Tommy in the head. This is especially hard when you're floating in the air. I raise my arms over my head in a perfect oval. "Pretend you're holding the moon," my first teacher used to tell us. We were five. We had no idea what was coming.

The little girl on the sidewalk is clapping, and her father, tall

22

in a gray suit, red tie, and dreadlocks, joins her. I look down at Tommy and I can see he's smiling, a real smile, shining out the kind of joy that comes with a perfect performance.

We are ridiculous. A spectacle. I don't know what I want anymore, but I know that if I could figure out how, I'd stay up here forever.

I'd never ever come down.

This Message Will Self-Destruct

WHEN TOMMY SETS ME DOWN and gets on his train home, I go straight into secret-agent mode, all hush-hush and furtive. I know I need to open this envelope before I go to dinner, and I have to find a secure place in which to do it. When I see a tiny corner park, I dash across the street and lean back on the iron fence in the shade. Lush green leaves touch my shoulders through the fence. I take a deep breath, and then I slide the envelope out of my bag.

The handwriting on the front of the envelope is precise and even, stark black. I look more closely at my name, printed neatly across the front. Then Miss Diana's, and the Academy. I remember this handwriting from the bedtime notes Julia used to leave me when I was a kid and she was going to be out late: my sister's perfect writing on a notepad shaped like a flamingo. She'd write in black ink up the bird's slender paper neck: *good night/sweet dreams/see you in the morning.*

The ticker tape in my head starts up again, counting something.

(The number of days since she's been gone.)

(The number of times I leaned in the doorway of her studio and watched her dance.)

(The number of minutes it took for the ambulance to come.)

I don't even know why I'm waiting. Maybe I need a password (*open sesame*) (*swordfish*) or an incantation for good luck. Maybe I'm just terrified. But a taxi honks its horn loudly, right in front of me, and I snap out of it. I open the envelope gently, as if what's inside is fragile as a robin's eggs or seashells, or dangerous as poison powder. There's extra Bubble Wrap on the inside, and when I pull it apart, it lets out little pops in protest. Then the envelope is open and no one dies. At least not right away.

But everything is . . . different.

It's just a book: small, old, hard-covered, with a matte dust jacket, edged with filigreed gold. I breathe in its scent: that old-book smell of vanilla and almonds and crushed flowers, dead and dried for years. The title is printed across the cover in raised gold letters. *Fairy Tales of the Brothers Grimm*, it says. *Abridged.*

I know this book. It used to be mine but I lost it, on vacation in Montreal when I was eleven years old. I left it in the drawer of the hotel's bedside table and didn't realize until we were three hours away in Quebec City, the next stop on our maple-syrup/ski-lodge vacation. I never saw it again, until now, when it slid through space and time, apparently, to land in this envelope, in my hand.

I open the cover to the title page and there it is, just like it used to be: the title crossed out in black ink and another one written above. I recognize those Sharpied letters right away. Julia wrote them, of course, three words just as important as *twenty-six bones*. I run my finger over them now, slowly, touching every single letter. This is what they spell:

G-I-R-L-S
I-N
T-R-O-U-B-L-E

I remember.

_L R R H_

JULIA WROTE IN THIS BOOK half my life ago. I was eight and she was fifteen. She'd just been given the lead in an abridged Academy production of _Cinderella_, even though she was still in Level Six and the Level Seven girls were pissed. She was in the studio all the time, coming home every night sweaty and exhausted.

We still lived in our old apartment on Riverside and shared a room back then. One afternoon, I came into our bedroom to find her sitting on my bed with our fairy tale book in her lap. When I was small she'd read to me from that book all the time, telling me about Snow White and Briar Rose and the Goose Girl, but at that point she hadn't picked it up in years. I had, of course. I still loved how magic made the forests in the stories go all glittery and other-worldly, and how ordinary animals turned enchanted and gained the ability to talk. I loved that the parents were usually gone, the kids left to their own devices, and the heroines had to prove their goodness or their bravery to get what they wanted in the end. The world of fairy tales made its own kind of sense, and I found it satisfying. I thought Julia did too. And even though I could have read the book to myself that day, I wanted my sister to read it to me again.

Instead, Julia opened the book to its title page, pulled out a marker, and crossed out the title. I may have gasped. It seemed so wrong to write in a book, especially that one and in permanent marker. I leaned forward and breathed in the harsh, chemical smell of the Sharpie, a foreign scent in our room. Julia pressed her lips together as she wrote.

"What are you doing?" I asked.

"Giving it a new title. A secret one." She held the book out to me. I looked at the words for the first time: *Girls in Trouble.* "This makes more sense," Julia said.

"But why?"

She shrugged and stood up, crossed the room toward the door. "Because at least then the reader knows what she's going to get."

She left then to take a shower, and I held the book in my hands for another minute, studying the words. Julia had talked about "the reader," but the only readers of this book were her and me. Who was the message for?

I could have asked her, I guess, could have waited outside the bathroom door for her to emerge in her bathrobe. But I didn't. I put the book back on the shelf and tried not to think about what it meant, and the way the book felt different with its rewritten title. Heavier, like a thin layer of silver had been added to every page.

Full of a specific, sparkling kind of pain I didn't understand.

Now, here on the sidewalk, I can hear the swishing sound of traffic and a jackhammer somewhere a few blocks away. I run my pointer finger across the words Julia wrote. The page is completely smooth. I can't feel a thing.

I flip through the pages, stopping to read the first line of each story.

Once there was a man and a woman who had no children, and this made them impossibly sad.

Once upon a time, a daughter was born to a mother who had wished for her.

Once there was a girl who had to travel through the woods.

A shiver moves through me like a current of electricity. The cars keep passing, sunlight reflecting off their hoods. It feels as if the world's been run through an Instagram filter. It's golden and high contrast and lovely, but it's all hurting my eyes. (*Once there was a girl who was overwhelmed by the absolute terror and beauty of everything.*) I turn my head and that's when I see her.

Little Red Riding Hood is coming up the street.

Or not Little Red Riding Hood, exactly, but a pale-skinned, dark-haired girl in a white dress, with a billowy red shawl draped over her head and shoulders. And a wolf—or what looks like a wolf—at the end of a leash.

The wolf, dog, whatever it is, skims its nose along the curb, sniffing. He crosses the sidewalk and makes a beeline for the fence next to me. The girl smiles. She's used to this.

"He's friendly," she says.

The dog bumps my hip with his nose. He *is* friendly, panting, his long pink tongue hanging from his mouth. His white teeth are impossibly sharp and long.

"Sorry," the girl says. She's still smiling. "He doesn't know how to respect people's personal space." She tilts her head. "But you look like a dog person, anyway."

"I am," I say. "But mine's about three percent of the size of yours." I put my hand out and the dog sniffs it, then slides his head under my palm, determined to be petted. "What kind is he?"

"Malamute," she says. "It's a little warm for him out here today. He's built for the tundra." She lifts one edge of her shawl with her non-leash hand. "And I'm trying not to get sunburned."

I smile. "Summer averse. You're a good match."

The dog swings his enormous head down toward the pavement, starts sniffing again.

"He looks like a wolf," I say.

She laughs, and it sounds like tinkling glass. Her eyes are violet, or at least they look it in this light. The color doesn't quite seem real, or not normal, anyway.

"Do you think so?" she asks.

I nod. And, honestly, I'm mostly fine with the whole situation until the thing that happens next.

"All right, dude," the girl says to her dog. She's smiling,

ruffling the fur behind his ears with her fingers. Her nails are painted black. "We have to get to Grandma's house."

"What?" I ask, but she's already turning away, starting off down the street, her shawl fluttering like a cape behind her.

Cellophane Girl

How do you come back to the real world when you've fallen out for a bit? I have no idea. All I know is when I get to the restaurant, I'm breathless. This is probably because I ran the last few blocks, just took off as soon as the red-shawl girl was out of sight. The West Village didn't know what to make of a sprinting girl with a hot pink dance bag slung over her shoulder (Nancy Drew #54: *The Case of the Runaway Ballerina*), so they mostly ignored me as I dashed by. Now I fling the restaurant door open and stand there in the swirling air-conditioned air. There's a hostess at the podium across from me, wearing red lipstick and a green silk dress and an expression like she wishes she had a security guard standing by.

"Hello," she says, and it sounds like an accusation.

"Um, hi," I say. "I'm meeting my parents." I crane my neck and peer around her, and there they are, at the back of the restaurant, sitting in front of a pearlescent rice-paper screen. My mother in a black dress with an asymmetrical neckline, my father in a gray suit and bloodred tie. They look like they're onstage, an example of a Beautiful and Important Couple with No Real Problems in Their Lives. And maybe they are. We never talk about Julia at all, and my dad, at least, barely mentions my brother, Everett. I might as well be an only child.

"Sylvie!" my mom calls. She puts her hand up in the air and waves like a beauty queen on a parade float. I wave back, and somehow, I make myself cross the restaurant toward them.

When I get to the table, my father stands up to hug me. His watch snags on a lock of my hair.

"Hi, Dad," I say, pressing my face into his shoulder.

"Birthday girl," he says, and lets me go.

Before I sit, my mother takes my face in both her hands and pulls me down so she can kiss me on my forehead. She smells like gardenias and amber, the way she always does. So many other things changed in the last few years, but that didn't.

"Hi, Mom," I say.

"Happy birthday, sweetheart," she says. Her blond hair is twisted neatly behind her head. She looks perfectly chic, as always, and here I am with after-dance-class hair and a wrinkled dress. And, oh yeah, wondering whether I just hallucinated.

"Sixteen," my father says, as if that's a proper sentence and not just a number. He clears his throat.

"Yep," I say. This is the kind of one- or two-word conversation we have all the time. (Really, I should be happy that it doesn't have to do with the weather. *It's raining/Cold today/Look at that wind*.) I know my father loves me, but it often feels like his powers of speech are rescinded when I'm around.

"We have tea," my mother says, "but we haven't ordered our food yet."

She pours some of the jewel-green liquid into my blue handleless cup, and I lift it to my mouth without waiting for it to cool. It burns my tongue and tastes like fresh-cut grass.

We sit, looking at our menus. Or rather, my parents look at their menus and I look at my parents, because I'm not really hungry anymore and I can never figure them out. They love each other, I know, but sometimes their love feels like theater. My mother is the faculty wife, the gracious counterpart to my father's intense economics professor. She shakes hands firmly yet gently and remembers everyone's name. She throws parties with kick-ass crudités and serves on the boards of three nonprofits. But she barely uses her own master's degree, which is in French literature. Well, she speaks French with the Haitian doctors trained by one of those nonprofits, but that's about it.

"How was the last class?" my mother asks.

"Fine." I try to wrap the whole experience up in that one word, but it comes out sounding flat. She doesn't notice.

"On to Level Seven," she says, her eyes shining. I nod.

"Yeah," I say.

The server comes back to the table then, bearing a tray of appetizers. He sets down brown ceramic bowls of steaming miso soup and white porcelain spoons, then a big bowl of edamame still in their pods. I must just look confused in general, because when he catches my eye he smiles and tells me what they are.

"Magic beans," he says. I flash to *Grimm's*, to Jack and his beanstalk, the cranky, murderous giant up at the top. My mind keeps spinning.

"What?" My voice is sharp, and the server looks a little startled.

"Green soybeans," he says. He looks down at the table. "They're . . . green soybeans."

"Oh," I say. I fully know what edamame are, but I don't see how it would help at this point to tell him that. "Fantastic." I pick one up, then put it back into the bowl.

The whole time we're eating miso soup and, later, tempura and avocado rolls, my brain keeps thinking, *Julia Julia Julia*. Of course I don't say my sister's name out loud, but I worry that my mother can hear it echoing around anyway. My father doesn't hear half the things I say with my actual voice, so I'm less worried about him.

My mother takes a sip of her tea, watching me.

"I thought you liked edamame," she says.

"I do."

Her forehead crinkles. "Then why aren't you eating them?"

Because stories about magic beans never end well for the characters in them, I think.

"I don't know," I say.

She looks at me and nods slowly. "Okay."

I slip the *Grimm's* from my pocket and pass it across the table to her. The gold letters on the cover glint in the rice-paper light.

"Do you remember this book?" I say. She smiles.

"I do." She looks up at me. "I remember you lost it when we

were in Montreal." She flips it to look at the back cover. "But this can't be the same one."

"No," I say, though it is. At least, I think so. "I can't believe you remember that."

"How could I forget?" Her eyes are sparkling. "We were in Quebec City by the time you figured out you'd left it. You fell apart, just dissolved into pieces on the floor."

I remember how upset I'd been, how I couldn't express why it bothered me so much to lose the book. Part of it was that I was convinced that the next guests in the room had it, and that, somewhere, some other kid was being read *my* stories before she went to bed. The other part of it was that Julia was in that book. She had defaced it, or renamed it, anyway.

She'd done it, I thought, for me.

"Your dad drove back," my mother says. "Do you remember that?" She looks over at him now but he's scrolling through his phone flat on the table, his eyes glued to the screen. He doesn't hear her.

"He did?" I ask. I don't remember this. I remember the whole city strung with fairy lights, dusted with snow like powdered sugar. At night, all that white snow reflecting the light back into a pinkish-gold sky. I remember cross-country skiing until my nose was frozen. I remember my despair when I lost the book. That's all.

She nods. "Hours. He never found it." She smiles. "Though I don't think he minded being alone on the road in the Canadian countryside." She hands the book back to me. "Where did you get this one?"

Anonymous package from your long-gone daughter, I think.

Though who knows how she got the book back in the first place.

"I told Tommy about it once," I lie. "He found a copy for me."

"That's so sweet of him," she says.

I want her to be suspicious, to know Julia sent it, the way I do, but her tone is too easy. And anyway this is when my father zones back into our conversation, like he's just now found the right frequency to pick up the transmission.

"Are you dating Tommy?" he asks. His brow is furrowed. I don't know what bothers him about the idea—if it's that he suspects Tommy isn't straight or that he has another plan in mind for me. Maybe one of his colleagues' kids. Because Julia's relationship with Thatcher turned out *so* well.

My mother rolls her eyes at me and grins.

"Tommy's gay, Dad," I say. "We're friends."

"All right," he says. He clears his throat.

"How thoughtful of Tommy," says my mother. "Really." She turns the book over in her hands again, but she doesn't open it. I want her to. I want her to see the title page with its *Girls in Trouble* and help me figure out what it means. Why did Julia send this? Does she want me to know she's okay? Or is this her way of telling me that she's the one in trouble, that she's trapped in the tower and the dragon is closing in?

It was my mother who first bought the fairy tale book for Julia before I was born. She should know. Instinct should tell her where this came from. Why it's here.

But she doesn't say anything else about it.

Here's the problem: half the time when she looks in my direction she sees right through me—as if I'm made of cellophane. She never looked at my sister like that. My mother always seemed to *see* her. Now she looks at me and sees . . . I don't know. Julia, Version 2.0? (*New and Improved, Now Without Painkiller Addiction!*)

A few months before Julia got hurt for the first time, she was profiled in a *New York Times* article about standout members of the National Ballet Theatre corps. She posed for a picture with six of her fellow dancers, including Grace, who had been her best ballet friend since she was five. I can still call up that photo in my mind: Julia in white tights and a scarlet leotard and sheer skirt, leaning on her friend Henry's shoulder. Grace in the center with her gorgeous half smile.

My mother cut the picture out and put it in the middle of the fridge. She had half a dozen other copies that she stored in a box in her closet. This is what she always wanted: a beautiful, talented daughter who ends up in the *New York Times* for all the right reasons. If I can do the same, maybe it'll make up for that whole thing going so spectacularly wrong.

Now my mother sets down her chopsticks. They're dark blue and glossy, not like the disposable bamboo ones in the paper packets that Tommy and I use when we get takeout. The chopsticks at this restaurant look like weapons.

"I wish I could drive you to camp," my mother says. "It's too bad we have to leave before you. Though if I'm honest, I don't mind going to Paris." She looks at my father and he smiles back. "Good thing your dad has that conference."

"That's okay," I say. I wonder if my mother wants to go to Paris because that way she can actually use her French. She can walk into a bookstore and read any book on the shelf. I half-heartedly took

French lessons when I was younger, but the ability to speak another language still seems miraculous to me. It's my mother's superpower.

"Dessert?" My mother holds the slim menu toward me.

"Sadie baked me a cake," I say. "I should probably wait."

"Okay," she says. She sets the menu back down on the table. She looks disappointed.

"I'm sure they'll have dessert at your party." A party with a bunch of economics professors and banker types, where my mother will pretend she's just someone's wife.

"But not special birthday dessert. It won't have candles." She shakes her head mock-sadly.

"I'll bring you home a piece of Sadie's cake, if it's edible," I say. "No promises on that last part."

My mother smiles and her face goes half-happy (mouth) and half-sad (eyes). Same as usual.

I wonder if she's remembering my birthday last year, when we had chocolate cake on the roof of our building, but Julia didn't eat any of it. She was still in withdrawal and too sick. She just leaned against the terra-cotta pots that held our neighbor's tomato plants, the leaves a green cloud behind her head. She stretched her long legs out in front of her and tried to smile. Her collarbone poked against her moon-pale skin; her thin wrists looked like they'd snap if she leaned on them wrong. My parents and Everett were there on the picnic blanket too, the five of us sitting together in a lopsided star shape. But I was the only one who could bear to look at Julia. And then, a few hours later, she left for good.

I slip the book back into my bag and button the flap.

Let Down Your Hair

Out on the street, my father puts fifty dollars into my hand. I didn't even see him pull out his wallet, so I'm actually considering whether he keeps folded bills in his sleeve or maybe loose in his pockets. He's a mystery.

"Take a taxi," he says, embracing me. "And be safe."

What does "safe" mean to my father, I wonder?

Possibilities:

1. Don't drop out of college to become a comic-book artist. (Everett.)

2. Don't get hooked on painkillers. (Julia.)

3. Don't get run over by a bus. (Someone, probably.)

4. Don't date any of his colleagues' asshole sons. (Julia again.)

"Okay," I say.

My mother pulls me into a hug so tight it hurts.

"Happy birthday," she whispers, and then she lets me go.

I stand on the corner and wave as the town car pulls away from the curb, heading crosstown. When I see it disappear around the corner, I pocket the fifty and head in the direction of the subway. Julia taught me to do that a long time ago, and I've always followed her advice. That first time was my thirteenth birthday, and we were on our way to the Museum of Natural History. "Never take a cab," Jules said, pulling me in the direction of the subway. "We can spend Dad's money better than that."

We did. We bought a velvet bag of sparkling, split-open geodes and a stuffed triceratops, even though I was probably too old for stuffed animals. The only gift I wanted was to spend time with my sister, who was a member of the studio company then and barely ever around. We looked at dioramas of wolves under a painted-on aurora borealis and bison on a fake-grass plain. We stood underneath the life-sized blue whale in Hall of Ocean Life, and I wondered, as I always did, why the whale was positioned to seem like it was flying. Later, we waited for a train home in the 81st Street station.

We were standing together on the platform, I remember, and Julia was humming. Prokofiev, I think, something from *Cinderella*. I wasn't surprised at first when she started to dance.

She'd done it before, danced ballet in strange places, out in public. She'd go arabesque in Washington Square Park, leaning on the fountain, or plié low and then lower while hanging on to a wrought iron gate on the street. It was a little weird. It was Julia. I think she was sending a signal: she was a dancer before she was a human being.

In the subway that day, she swept her arms toward the ground as she lowered herself into a fifth-position grand plié. She leapt across the platform, spending more time in the air than should have been possible, then landed gently. Jules rose up on the balls of her feet, not on pointe because she was wearing sandals, but close. By then she was on the absolute edge of the platform, balancing. It seemed like a breeze could push her over, make her fall on the tracks, but if there was anything my sister understood, it was gravity and her own power over it. I stood there frozen by the white-tiled wall, holding my stuffed dinosaur. I felt like a kid.

People clapped. Over the sound of applause, I could hear the train approaching, half a station away. It sounded like the sea, like a tsunami approaching. When the glow of its headlight appeared, my sister gave a little bow and stepped toward me, away from the edge, away from the tracks and the place where the train would be in moments.

The people on the platform smiled at her and then watched the train pull in with its great rush of air. They didn't look afraid. I couldn't blame these strangers for not understanding what was going on, because I was her sister and I didn't understand it either. Not until much later.

Today, I walk three blocks to the A train in the gold light of evening, still feeling a little shell-shocked. I'm about to go down the stairs to the station when something holds me at the top for a moment, like I'm suspended in a spiderweb. This is when I see her.

Not Julia, of course, but a girl near the bottom with the longest hair I've ever seen, flowing past the backs of her knees, shining like spun gold in the lamplight. It nearly touches the stairs behind her as she walks.

Like Rapunzel's.

"Hey!" I say, my voice sharp in the white-noise rush of the train leaving the station below. I don't mean to yell—the tone of my voice is a surprise to me too—and as soon as I do I clap my hand over my own mouth. She reaches the bottom and turns around, looking up the staircase at me. I can't explain it, the expression on her face. It's something between curiosity and fear.

She turns away then, around the corner and out of sight. But before I can stop myself, I'm running down the stairs, my right hand skimming the guardrail. I do this before I can decide if she's something I even want to chase.

When I get down there she's already gone in. I have to swipe my MetroCard three times to get it to work, and then I push through the turnstile. I can hear the train pulling into the station below, brakes squealing. I run down the next set of stairs to the uptown tracks, my sandals pounding on the concrete, and jump the last three. I land hard on the pavement, my bones rattling as the earth pulls me down. Then I take off again.

By the time I make it to the platform, the girl is gone.

Foxy Lady

I TEXT SADIE WHEN I come up from the train station, and to my surprise she greets me at the corner of Cabrini and 181st Street. Her honey-colored hair is wound into a knot at the top of her head and she's wearing a pale blue sundress. There's no sign of any cake flour on her body or her clothes, though I don't have much time to check because she throws her arms around me and squeezes so hard my ribs creak.

"Happy birthday, my favorite!" she says.

"Thanks," I say. I try to make my voice sound normal, but I still feel jittery and strange. Sadie lets me go—holds me at arm's length, really—and looks at me.

"What's wrong with your face?" she asks.

I blink. She smiles.

"I mean, you're beautiful, obviously, always, of course, but you're making a Face of Pain."

This is a Sadie-ism that I'm used to. I know exactly what she means, but for some reason I can't bring myself to tell her about today. I don't even have words yet.

"I'm fine," I say. "Long day. Long dinner."

"I get it," Sadie says. "Parental drama." She rolls her eyes.

Sadie has been my best friend since we were eight years old and her mom started working for my family a few times a week as a personal chef. Renata used to bring Sadie with her and we'd sit on the counter stools in our kitchen and watch Renata cook. She'd feed us raw red peppers and green beans, strawberries with their tops cut off. She'd whirl around the kitchen, her method for making dinner like another kind of dance.

In the weeks before Julia left, when she was sick because she'd given up the pills, Renata made lemongrass broth and tortilla soup and baked macaroni and cheese. Every comforting recipe from every cuisine she'd ever studied. Julia ate it, sometimes. Or she didn't. But Renata still tried, and I'm grateful for that. And also for the fact that since I met Renata's daughter, we've always been Sylvie-and-Sadie.

Now Sadie links her arm with mine like we're gal pals in some 1950s movie (*Damsels in Dismay*, now in glorious TECH-NICOLOR!). We walk in silence for a few moments. The air is cooler now that the sun has slipped behind the buildings, and I feel like I can breathe again, finally. Half a block from Sadie's building, a cat runs out from beneath a bush, a blur of orange fur. I stop walking, but I lean toward it a little. It's rare to see a cat loose around here.

Except it's not a cat.

It's a fox.

It walks toward me tentatively, sniffing the air. I can see the white fur on its muzzle, the black fur of its paws. When it's almost to my feet it looks up at me, and then it sits down, curling its fluffy tail around itself. For some reason, I'm not afraid.

"That is a fox," says Sadie. She's inching away from me, backing up toward the giant maple tree behind her.

"Yes," I say.

"I've never seen a fox in Washington Heights."

"Well," I say, "I think there's at least one."

"Do you think it's rabid?"

I look a tiny bit closer. Mostly, this means I lean forward slightly and squint hard at the fox. It's not foaming at the mouth, and I don't know any other signs of rabies.

"Um," I say. "No?"

"So what is it doing here?" Sadie flaps her hands at it as if to shoo it away. It tilts its head to the side, listening, maybe, or just watching Sadie act like a weirdo.

"I have no idea." Which is true, but it's getting to the point where the strange things that are happening can't be explained away. They can't be explained at all, at least to another person.

"Well, get rid of it!" Sadie is backing away as she says this.

"I'm not a fox expert, Sades."

But I am, maybe, at least in comparison to Sadie. I look over my shoulder and see that she's practically behind a maple tree now, peeking out from behind the slate-gray bark. So I turn back to the fox and try to channel the narrator of every nature program I've ever watched. (Though they seem disproportionately to have Australian accents. Is this necessary? Preferred? I'm not sure.)

"Go home." My voice is calm. It's all I can think of to say.

The fox looks at me, its eyes like amber beads in its pointy face, its ears small satellites angled toward me. It listens. Then it turns and goes, streaking off into the underbrush, its white-tipped tail the last thing I see.

Static on the Line

"HAVE YOU HEARD FROM EVERETT yet?"

We're up on the roof of Sadie's apartment building, side by side in matching Adirondack chairs. Headlights sparkle ahead of us on the George Washington Bridge. The sun has already set, and the leftover light at the horizon is silver and pink. Streaks of red cross the sky like spent flares. It's quiet up here, except for the *shush-shush* sound of traffic and musical-note soup of birds singing over the river. My heart is still thumping harder than normal, but I feel safer, somehow, up here. It feels like nothing can get me here, closer to the sky and away from all the weirdness. Or at least away from all except the particular weirdness of my best friend.

"I mean, I'm just wondering," Sadie says. Her voice is purposely nonchalant. She's the fiercest person I know, but whenever she talks about my brother she gets a little moony.

"He called earlier," I say. "I have to call him back."

"Well, do it!" She leans forward, her hands pressing down flat on the arms of her chair. "Maybe Liam will get on the phone with a special birthday wish for you."

I've had a crush on Everett's indie-musician friend Liam since I was in seventh grade. He's completely oblivious to that fact. He ruffles my hair when he sees me and sometimes recites obscure rock-and-roll facts tailored to my own musical tastes (like a lot of '80s girl groups), but he's only ever going to see me as Everett's little sister. And I'm okay with that. I guess.

Next to me, Sadie's making kissy faces.

"Clearly you'll be celebrating your own ninth birthday soon," I say. "Or is it your tenth? I forget."

"Come on," Sadie says. "I'm just teasing. And you know I'm in the same boat. My love for your brother is undying." She presses the back of her hand to her forehead like a dramatic nineteenth-century lady and flops backward into her chair.

"*My* brother, on the other hand," she says, "is currently being a complete jerk. He doesn't want me to go visit our dad."

"Why not?" I ask this, but I already pretty much know the answer. Sadie and Jack's dad left when they were small, but three years ago he came back into their lives. He's a pretty famous chef now, with a Michelin-starred restaurant in Richmond, Virginia. I guess he'd gotten his career to a place where he felt like he had time to have actual contact with his children. He sent birthday cards first, to Sadie and then to Jack, and a few months later he got their cell phone numbers from their grandma and started calling. They both let it go to voice mail at first, but eventually Sadie started answering. Their dad said he'd made a mistake in leaving when he was young. He said he wanted them in his life.

They've seen him a few times since then, mostly for fancy, uncomfortable dinners when he's in New York for work. The chefs come out of the kitchens to chat, bringing elaborate complimentary dishes to the table. Their dad can talk about food, Sadie says, but not much else. There's a lot of silent chewing. But Sadie wants to keep trying. For some reason, it's easier for her to forgive than it is for Jack. Maybe it's because Jack is the older one, or maybe it's because he's generally harder to please. I know this from personal experience. Jack has never been much of a fan of me.

"Jack says he's an asshole." Sadie tilts her head thoughtfully. "I mean, whatever, Jack's right, Dad used to be, but I really think he's changed. Not a complete transformation but"—she pauses— "an *incremental* one."

"Nice vocabulary word," I say. "Ms. Kobayashi would be proud."

Sadie smiles, then just as quickly her smile fades. "You know, in the end, I'd still like to have a dad. Even if I only see him one week out of the year."

"Yeah," I say, poking her. "It's like a Dadfest. Dad-a-palooza."

Sadie's smile comes back. "Burning Dad," she says.

Out ahead of us, the lights on the bridge get brighter as the sky darkens. The cars and trucks could be toys sliding across the span, the suspension cables strung with lights and glowing like strands of stars. I tap my foot on the wall's grating, pointing my toes.

Last year, Sadie and I were up here just after someone jumped off the bridge. We didn't know that it had happened, but when we came up we saw the police boats in the water and the blue-and-red flash of officers' cars on the bridge. We stood there, silent, for a minute, and then Sadie took my hand. Someone had been alive an hour ago and was dead now, and the evidence was right in front of us. We didn't stay to watch whatever else was going to happen.

Sadie pokes me in the shoulder now.

"Start talking to me," she says.

"About what?"

"Whatever's going on." She leans farther back and looks at me. "I know there's something you're not telling me."

Who's the real Nancy Drew? Sadie, probably.

"It's hard to explain," I say.

Her gaze is still steady on me, some kind of interrogation tactic, I'm sure. "Try."

I take a breath, sigh it out. "It's Julia. She sent me a book." I bend down and pull it from my bag. "Fairy tales. We used to own it but I lost it years ago."

"Wow," Sadie says. "She actually made contact." She says this as if Julia is an extraterrestrial, someone whose existence is only rumored, not confirmed. Which actually isn't all that inaccurate.

Sadie opens the book and does the same thing I did, runs her fingers over the words *Girls in Trouble*, like if she touches the ink on the page, it'll tell her something more.

"Well, this book is a message," she says.

"Yeah, but what does it mean?"

Sadie looks at me. "It means she's sorry, I guess." She flips through the book. "That's enough, right?"

No, I think.

"I guess," I say. "But how did she get it? I lost it in Montreal when I was eleven."

Sadie shrugs. "Who knows? Weird things happen every day."

I nod, probably too emphatically. The girl speaks truth, even if she doesn't fully know it.

Sadie's phone chimes in her lap.

"Tommy," she says, looking at the screen. "I'll go let him in. We may be a minute. I have to make some final touches on the festivities." She circles her arm through the air. Then she points at me. "Call your brother."

I hear the door to the stairs slam shut behind her, and then I pull out my phone and find my brother's number. I took the photo that comes up with Everett's name a couple of years ago. He and I had overpriced fruit pops by the river one day after my ballet class, and I snapped his picture while he leaned against the guardrail. Behind him is blue sky spiked with clouds, rays of sun spinning from a hole in one of them. His head is turned to the side, the pop dripping red juice down his hand. He looks happy.

Now he answers on the second ring.

"Happy birthday, kiddo," he says. I can hear the radio-static sound of a crowd behind him, plenty louder than the shushing traffic on the bridge.

"Thanks," I say. "Where are you?"

"I'm at the arts college in Nashville," he says. "If you can believe it, they invited me to be a speaker in their summer program for illustrators." He pauses. "Which is pretty interesting, since I'm not exactly a poster child for higher education."

This is a sore point with my father, that Everett dropped out of college when, with the faculty discount, he could have graduated from Columbia for next to nothing. But he never liked his classes, and when things started to go wrong with Julia he decided he'd had enough. He was just going to draw, he said, and do freelance graphic design work to pay the bills. Everett lives in Nashville now, and draws a comic called *The Square*. It's about a bunch of skater kids (three girls and two boys) who live in Washington Square Park. Not *by* the park but *in* it, because Manhattan has been mostly abandoned due to rising sea levels. The East River and the Hudson are moving toward each other, and the whole borough has fallen apart. It's a cautionary climate tale plus old-fashioned orphan story. Or, come to think of it, fairy tale: all the parents are dead or gone. *The Square* sounds a little out there, I know, but it's so good. He drew the early versions and copied them himself on the machine in our father's office at Columbia. Then he got picked up by a good indie comic publisher, and things have gotten better from there.

"I'm going to DC next week," Everett says. "There's a conference on graphic novels at Georgetown. They asked me." He says this like he almost doesn't believe it.

"Wow," I say.

"I mean, they're making me take the train and stay in the dorms." I can hear him smiling. "But still."

I picture him now just offstage in a college theater or a large lecture hall. Wearing a worn-out band T-shirt (Neko Case or the Weakerthans, maybe), with a bunch of those black-ink pens he likes in the pockets of his ripped jeans. I feel an ache behind my rib cage. If he were here, Everett would help me figure this out.

I hear a low voice in the background, then my brother again.

"Liam says to tell you he's going to listen to the Bangles later, in your honor," he says.

I let myself swoon a little. "Liam's there?"

"Yeah, I told him I've gone to enough of his shows. He should come to some of mine."

"Cool," I say. "Tell him I'll listen to the Bangles too."

He tells him. I hear Liam laugh.

"And the Go-Go's," Liam says. I hear it through the line.

"Okay," I say, a little too loudly. "I wish you were here. Both of you."

"I do too," he says. "Or maybe that you were here. You should see this crowd."

I smile. In the past few years, it's so rare to hear my brother happy. I decide to tell him about the book Julia sent, but just as I'm about to, the crowd noise on his end of the line gets louder. They're clapping, I think. I say it anyway.

"I got something from Julia today," I say. "In the mail."

"What?" Everett says. "They're about to introduce me, Syl. I can't hear you."

I know he can't. The noise on the line sounds like a thousand people each crumpling a sheet of paper into a ball. But I keep talking anyway. "I saw Little Red Riding Hood. On the street. And Rapunzel in the subway. She looked scared."

"I'm sorry, Sylvie," Everett says. "I know you're talking but I can't understand the words. Can I call you back later?"

"Okay," I say.

"Syl? I'm assuming you're saying yes. Love you, kid."

The crowd noise stops with a click and I'm left with the near silence of the roof and the sky above me, now fully charcoal-colored. It feels different up here than it did a few minutes ago, when Sadie was here. More lonely, sure—there's nothing like being the only girl on a roof in the middle of New York City—but there's something else too.

Above me, there's a fluttery racket as a flock of pigeons appears out of nowhere. They land in a semicircle around my lawn chair and start a sort of feathery muttering, pecking at the roof. They move closer, one peck at a time.

"Um, hello," I say. The birds tip their faces up toward me, first one with white-edged feathers by my feet and then the others. They stop cooing. They stop moving too.

It's like they're pretending to be bird statues, or they're waiting for me to say something. But I have no bird-worthy pronouncements.

"I don't know what to tell you," I say to them. "Except that this is getting ridiculous. A bit over the top, if you ask me." I look up toward the sky, toward the rest of the universe spreading out there somewhere, and I wave my hand a little like I'm trying to catch someone's attention. Who, I have no idea.

"If you're trying to tell me something, just say it! Quit sending weird omens." The pigeons start cooing again, agreeing or disagreeing. I don't want them here, staring at me with their beady bird eyes, so I look down at them and whisper, "Shoo."

They're unmoved. This is basically the fox all over again. I say it louder, in what I think is a slight Australian nature-show accent. Then I straight-up shout it: "SHOO!" I stand up and wave my arms and they scatter across the roof, then take off all at once into the near-dark sky.

I pick up the fairy tale book and follow them to the edge of the roof, where I face north and watch the river disappear toward the Bronx. The Hudson flows in both directions, Sadie told me once. I don't know how that works, but I'm glad something else is as confused as I am.

I lean against the scratchy stone wall and open the cover. I flip through the pages and land on the back endpapers.

What I see makes me gasp. There's a sketch I've never seen on the final page, a five-petaled flower drawn in pencil. And on each of the petals, a name.

Starting with mine.

Sixteen Candles

Sylvie IS SPELLED OUT IN Julia's perfect script, tiny letters filling in the top petal space.

I don't know how I didn't notice this earlier, but I must have never opened to the back endpapers. I mean, why would I? There was nothing in this spot when I used to own this book. I've been through every page at least a hundred times in my life. The endpapers used to be blank except for the pale gold filigree tracing the borders. They were just clean paper, empty space. And now they're not.

I look at the other names.

Grace

Rose

Thatcher

Daniela

My heartbeat picks up speed, thumping in my chest. Grace, Julia's best friend and fellow dancer. Rose, our cousin and Julia's childhood partner in crime. Thatcher, her idiot ex-boyfriend. I don't know who Daniela is.

Let's review, Junior Detectives. My sister left a year ago, hasn't called since, and now has sent me a book from my childhood—a book I lost in another country (Canada, fine, but still) five years ago—with some weird flower list in the back.

What does it mean?

I have no freaking clue.

I turn my face upward, above the tops of buildings. I want to stare at the blank New York sky, see nothing for a few minutes. Clear my head of all the Julia. Light pollution will take care of all that. But when I look up, the sky isn't blank. It's full of stars, and not just random ones. They're a constellation, my favorite one: Ursa Major, the Great Bear.

It's named for Callisto, a mortal girl from a Greek myth who got into trouble in a way that was completely not her fault (the asshole king-god Zeus fell in lust with her, and she didn't want anything to do with him). She was turned into a bear, and then, later, when she almost got shot by her son (long story), she was saved by being transformed into a bunch of stars. My mother used to tell me that story when she'd take me out to look at the stars, and I loved it, even though it was sad. The Big Dipper is inside this constellation, so it's easy to find. I can see it now, handle and all.

There's another Adirondack chair over here, and before I think twice I drop the fairy tale book on its seat and step up onto its flat armrest, first one foot and then the other. From there it's easy:

I step straight onto the foot-wide guard wall. I want to get closer to the stars. The ones that have been put here just for me, maybe.

My bones are humming. I don't look down, though I know the penthouse floor's narrow patio is below me, and beyond that a thirteen-story drop to the grassy lawn. I look out over the blue-black river toward New Jersey, the shadowy trees on its shore. I look at Ursa Major, which isn't even twinkling, just burning straight through the black sky. I balance. I breathe. My bones go quiet, my heart shifts down a gear. It feels as if I've cast a spell. I haven't felt this calm in months, but I'm not like the people who jump off the bridge. I don't want to fall. I just want to stand at the edge.

My sister was the one who taught me how gravity works. She came to my ballet class for a demonstration when I was ten, maybe, all of us Level Threes dressed in identical black leotards, our legs like long petals in our pale pink tights. Julia was seventeen and had just joined the studio company after eleven years at the Academy. She stood in front of the mirror, making two Julias back to back, each in an ivory leotard and sheer pink skirt. Her friend Henry smiled next to her, a head taller, so handsome he practically glowed.

"Here's what you need to know," Julia said. She paused and looked at us, and we all leaned forward. We were holding our breath, waiting for her to tell us.

"The thing that lets us dance is gravity," she said, and her words sounded like a poem. "Everything we do is completely dependent on it. We need to be tethered to the earth"—she pliéd then, sweeping her arms toward the floor—"in order to leave it." Henry stepped behind her, placing his hands on either side of her rib cage. He lifted her straight up in the air.

She slowly raised her arms to fifth position and smiled. "Dancers, if you can get gravity to work for you, you're golden."

Henry lowered her down so slowly that she might have been a chiffon scarf dropped from a skyscraper.

"You can also do it on your own." She smiled right at me and took a running start into a grand jeté. When she leapt into the air she moved as fluidly as a boat's white sail in the wind. She made no sound when she landed. The girl next to me breathed in sharply. I think my classmates were still naïve enough to believe that Jules was magical, that she really did do this effortlessly, but I had seen her sweat through enough technique classes to know the truth. As breathtaking as she was as a dancer, it wasn't effortless. It was hard. But somehow, for me, that made it even better.

"Gravity is a force," Julia said, "but it's also a promise. As in, *What goes up must come down*. It lets you know what will happen next." She smiled her slow-as-syrup smile, and my classmates clapped.

Back then I accepted what she said as truth, but now I wonder what she meant. Sure: if you drop something, it'll fall. But if Julia could have seen her future, wouldn't she have found a way to get a different ending? Wouldn't she have made gravity promise her something else?

The sky now is lead-colored, dull except for those bear stars. Below them, the world tilts: the river, the shadowy trees, the lights suspended over the bridge. The door creaks open behind me now, across the roof, but I barely notice. I hear the swish of traffic on the bridge but I don't move. I can't move, maybe: I'm balanced here so perfectly on the twenty-six bones in each of my feet. Gravity, it turns out, is the one thing you can depend on.

"Syl." This is Tommy, somewhere behind me. His voice is like a trapdoor opening, an offer of escape that I'm not sure I want. "I'm going to get you down," he says.

"All right," I say. I don't really have a choice.

He puts his hands on either side of my rib cage just like he does in class. I close my eyes as he lifts me up a few inches so my feet clear the wall, then lowers me to the roof.

It's only when I feel my bare feet touch the roof that I start shivering. It's like my bones are vibrating, my cells shaking loose, and I'm not sure what I'm afraid of. What I just did—what could have happened—or the fact that I liked it?

Tommy wraps his arms around me. I let him.

"What are you even doing?" he whispers right into my ear.

"I don't know," I say. And then, "Balancing."

Tommy takes a long breath, lets it out slowly. "Please don't," he says.

I want to say something—*I was fine up there* or maybe *I think there's something wrong with me*—but instead I just say, "Okay." Over Tommy's shoulder I can see the stars in Ursa Major wink out, one by one, leaving the sky charcoal gray and blank. Tears fill my eyes.

I don't know what any of this means.

The door creaks again, I hear Sadie, across the roof. Tommy lets me go. I turn toward Sadie and see that she's carrying a flaming cake.

"Way to abandon me, Tommy," she says. "It was a bitch getting the stairway door open after I lit the candles."

"Sorry," Tommy says. His voice sounds wrong. Crooked, like a door hanging off its hinges.

Sadie looks at me, her brow furrowed. She's trying to figure out what just happened, but for some reason, she doesn't ask. It's like none of us can manage to talk to each other about the things we don't understand. Our voices might as well have been taken by a sea witch somewhere, or given to an enchanted bird. Everything is off-kilter, messed up.

"Well," Sadie says. "Now she needs to take care of these candles."

"I can do that," I say. I step close enough that I can feel their heat on my face. There are sixteen candles, their fires flickering in the wind.

"Make a wish," Tommy says. He's standing close to me.

I wish the same wish I've wished for a year. I wish the thing I was going to stop wishing, the wish I was going to give up. Because if the world is going magic, I might as well lean into it. I bend over the tiny flames and blow.

Heartbeats/Hoofbeats

MY MOTHER KNOCKS ON MY bedroom door early, when I'm still asleep. I hear the knocking as pure rhythm, and I start counting the beat in my head. I feel my tiny dog Pavlova stir next to my head. When I open my eyes, my mother is right next to my bed in slim black cigarette pants and a blue sleeveless shell. She sits on the edge of the mattress, the picture of elegance.

"We're leaving for the airport," she says, smoothing my sheet with her hand. "What do you want me to bring back?"

I answer, "Chocolate," at the same time she says, "Postcards?" She laughs.

When I was small, my mother would bring back a stack of postcards for me from wherever they traveled, and I'd tape them up on my wall. They're still here, actually, behind my open closet door: white horses in Irish fields, the headless white-marble statue

63

of Nike in the Louvre, an azure-blue parrot in a Costa Rican forest. Every once in a while, the tape comes loose and one of those vacation spots flutters to the floor. Sometimes I stick it back up and sometimes I don't.

"Maybe a little of both," my mother says.

Pavlova steps across me to settle in my mother's lap. My mother pets her absentmindedly.

"Be careful while we're gone," she says.

"Okay," I say. The memory of last night floats up, the terrifying freedom of standing at the edge of the roof. I will it away.

When my mom was pregnant with me, the doctors were scared because I wasn't gaining weight the way I was supposed to. In the month before I was born I had to have my heart rate monitored once each week. My mother leaned back in a recliner as soft as a cloud, she's told me, and the nurse strapped a belt with a little box around her belly. Julia came with her sometimes. She was seven years old then, and my mother told me she'd sit on the arm of the recliner and together she and my mother would listen to my heart thump.

"It sounded like galloping," my mother told me once. "Like hoofbeats in an old Western. And when I sat there, hearing that, I knew you were safe."

Here's what I want to ask her now: *Is there anything I can listen to that will tell me we're safe?*

The fairy tale book is on my bedside table, and my mother places her hand on its cover. *Open it,* I say to her silently. She doesn't.

"You'll have a good time at camp, right?" she says.

This is a question, obviously. And I should answer it honestly, tell her that I don't want to go, that I'm not sure I even want to dance at all anymore. At least not right now. But then she says that same thing again, this time without the question mark. She answers herself.

"You'll have a good time," she says.

"I know," I lie.

She hugs me. "I love you, Sylvie."

"I love you too, Mom." I take a quick breath, let it out.

My mother smiles at me and presses her palm to my cheek. Then she leaves, shutting my door with a gentle click.

My lie stays in the room with me.

Someday My Princess Will Come

I'M LYING FLAT ON TOP of my comforter, staring up at the weird crack in the ceiling that's shaped like a mountain range. After yesterday I'm in no hurry to go outside. Maybe ever again. I have St. Vincent on the stereo, soundtrack for the world's dazzling peculiarity. I'm planning to stay in this position for quite some time, or at least until my Thai food delivery gets here.

My phone rings.

"Let's go," Sadie says when I answer, instead of hello.

"Go where?" I say.

"Out." She says this as if the answer is obvious. "Let's take a walk in the park, and then we'll go to the High Line. Aryanna and Amal will be there. And maybe some other people. Plus," here she switches to a stage whisper, "I texted Tennis Dude and he said he'd come."

Tennis Dude is Sadie's latest crush, a guy who, it would seem, plays tennis. (Maybe I do have detective skills.) I haven't had a conversation with him yet, but I have seen him carrying a racket. So he lives up to his name.

"I don't know," I say. "I wasn't planning on going out today." Next to me on the couch, Pavlova rolls over on her back and groans. She agrees, clearly.

Sadie sighs. "You only have a few days left before you're off to camp, and then intensives. This is your summer, Sylvie. It's about four days long."

She's right. But I feel safer inside my apartment, away from the pigeons and the foxes and the strange maybe-magic girls.

Sadie's still talking. "If you don't meet me," she says, "I'm staging a rescue. I'm just going to break in."

"To my building?"

She waits. "Well, Rafael and Tony would let me past the lobby, right?"

Our doormen love Sadie, because everyone loves Sadie. "Probably."

"So really, I just need to get into your apartment," Sadie says. "I've been working on my lock-picking skills, so it shouldn't be a problem. I'll drag you out by your hair if necessary."

I sigh theatrically. "Great."

"Seriously," Sadie says, "I don't know what is up with you lately. I'm just trying to save you from yourself."

"My hero," I say. And then, "Sorry."

"It's okay," Sadie says. "Just get ready. I'll be out in front of your apartment in an hour."

"Just enough time to eat my red curry," I say.

"Go for it," Sadie says. "But be ready."

When I hang up, I lean back on a pillow and look at the ceiling. If Sadie were here right now, and I told her what was going on, she'd look for clues. She'd look at the fairy tale book. The list. That's where she'd start. With a visit to Grace, maybe. Or by asking Rose.

I take out my phone and type a text to my cousin.

Have you seen Julia since she left here last summer?

I stare at the words for a moment like they're an incantation, a spell that could solve this whole thing.

Then I press Send.

If the Shoe Fits

THERE'S A GIRL ON THE path in front of us, and she's running. She appears from behind some shrubbery in a hydrangea-blue dress and silver heels, followed close behind by a guy in a suit. I see the flash of his violet tie before they turn and run, laughing.

When I see her, my skin prickles as if someone just tossed a handful of glitter down my shirt. Sadie and I are wandering through the park, half-heartedly heading to the High Line. Or at least I'm half-hearted about it. Sadie actually wants to go.

"Race you to Strawberry Fields!" the girl calls.

"Too far!" says the guy, but the girl is still booking it, her red hair streaming behind her like the tail of a comet. She stumbles a little and loses one shoe. He passes in front of her. She keeps going.

A few steps later she takes off her other shoe. She keeps that one in her hand, pumping her arms as she sprints barefoot across the lawn, catching up with the guy. The other shoe stays where she left it, in the grass.

I blink. A blue dress? A lost shoe?

Oh my god.

"Ah, young love," Sadie says, next to me. "Lucky bastards." Tennis Dude didn't answer her second text, so at the moment, we're not sure if he's coming out or not. She's *angerpointed*, which is a Sadie-ism for being angry and disappointed at the same time. I understand.

I walk toward the shoe, and when I get to it, I kneel down to look closer. It's a spike-heeled silver slip-on with crisscrossing straps.

"What are you doing?" Sadie asks.

I don't know, I almost say. "Don't you think it's weird that she left it?"

Sadie shrugs. "It's hard to run in heels."

"Yeah." I'm not convinced.

"Maybe she just really wanted to win that race." Sadie starts walking forward again, away from me. "I mean, *I* wouldn't run through this park barefoot, but to each her own."

I pick up the shoe and stare at it. Frankly, I'm considering putting it in my bag. Why?

1. To run chemical tests on it.

2. To see if it disappears at midnight.

The problem with that method is that I'm fresh out of chemicals, and Cinderella's shoes inexplicably stuck around even after the clock struck.

Well, that's one of the problems.

Sweat prickles under my arms. I feel that there's a good chance I've lost my hold on reality. I take a deep breath, then another one. I drop the shoe in the grass.

"All right," I say. I take a few quick steps to catch up with Sadie.

She's looking back at me intently.

"What?" I say.

"You know what," she says. Then she shakes her head. "Forget it."

We walk along next to each other for a while. I try to forget about the shoe.

"So," Sadie says. "My brother might come meet us tonight."

"Really?" I try to sound excited or at least neutral. Sadie has always tried to make Jack and I friends, but it never takes. We little sisters idolize our brothers, but at least mine has a personality.

Sadie shrugs again. "He said maybe."

"Okay," I say.

"Do you think I'll survive a week in Virginia? Like, with my dad?" Sadie asks. I sneak a glance at her. She's looking straight ahead.

"Sure," I say, even though I'm not. I mean, yes, she'll survive, but it's hard to say what will happen with her father.

"Will my dad be different?" she says. "I mean, will he be better?" Her voice sounds the smallest bit shaky and it makes me snap my head toward her. Sadie is so rarely uncertain of anything that it's jarring.

"I don't know," I say. "But *you* won't know unless you go."

She smiles. "Good point."

We're near the edge of the park, and I look up at the buildings lining Central Park West. Julia's surgeon had an office near here, and I remember going with her to her first follow-up appointment after her surgery, the one we thought would fix everything. She was still using a wheelchair then, just as a precaution, and I had helped her get into it from the town car. While she was with the doctor, I read outdated copies of *Better Homes and Gardens* in the waiting room because I'd forgotten a book. When she was ready to go, I maneuvered her out the doorway and into the hallway slowly, her leg in its plastic cast safe against the chair's footrest.

"Eight weeks until I can dance," she said, tipping her head back to look at me. "And I can start to walk in three." She looked back down and touched her knee gently. "In the meantime, get me out of here, Sylvie."

Julia's purse was open in her lap, so as I pushed her down the hall I could see what was inside. A purple hairbrush, a blackberry-flavored egg-shaped lip balm, a hardcover copy of a biography of Isadora Duncan that my mother had bought for her before she went into surgery. And there, touching the open zipper, a brown pill bottle with a white top.

I'd like to say that I felt something when I saw it. A dark-sky sense of foreboding, a little jolt of electricity up my spine.

But I didn't. Because it wasn't a clue, and nothing was wrong. It was just medicine, I thought, something a doctor had given her, and I had no idea what was going to happen next.

Rejected Romance Novels

AN HOUR LATER, THE SKY yawns above us, charcoal-colored and empty of stars. I know because I keep looking, waiting for secret constellations to appear in the gray. Sadie and I are drinking lemon soda mixed with a little vodka. Our friend Clara has the vodka, a water bottle full she swiped from her parents' bar cart. They have so many parties they don't notice, apparently, and anyway their house-keeper is the one who orders the liquor.

Mine just tastes like lemony carbonated sugar, with the light tang of liquor underneath the bubbles. I feel bubbly too, my bones a little loose, as if my whole skeleton might come apart. The sky spins gently above me.

The High Line is an old elevated rail track on Manhattan's west side that's been turned into a long, narrow park, winding its way next to apartment buildings and offices. It's planted with tall grasses and clumps of flowers that might as well be wild, like some- one dropped tiny meadows from the sky. It's a bit of a tourist trap, I know, but I still love it up there.

Sadie settles down next to Tennis Dude (blond, tall, tan, still not very memorable—I swear I couldn't pick him out of a lineup unless he was carrying his racket) and his friends. I hover at the edges of the group for a few minutes, listening to them talk about world soccer (Italy! France! Brazil!), and then I wander over to another bench in the middle of some black-eyed Susans. I can hear cicadas humming from inside of the vegetation, and I close my eyes for a second, pretend I'm somewhere else. Where? I'm not even sure where I'd go if I could choose.

When I open them, I see a boy I don't know leaning against the rail across from me, talking to Clara and some of the guys. He's tall, with messy black hair and dark eyes. He's wearing a Pinegrove T-shirt, so of course I notice him. I catch his eye accidentally, but when I do it's like flint striking a rock. I feel the spark.

He smiles, and I think: *maybe I could just spend an hour kissing some cute boy.* That would be a decent use of my time.

"Hi," he mouths.

I smile.

He comes over and sits down on the bench, leaving enough space between us that he can sit half-sideways, his arm along the back.

"Hey," he says.

"Hi," I answer.

My brain spirals off in the direction of a romance novel—*Love on the High Line, Elevated Train Track of Passion*—but then he ruins it, stops my insta-love before it even gets started.

"I'm Sean," he says. "You're the ballerina, right?"

The air shifts around me then, the High Line tilts. I nod, but my mouth pulls tight. I wanted to be no one right now. Or at least I wanted to be me but have no one know it.

"Sorry," he says. "That was probably creepy." He smiles. "It's just that I know who you are. My brother was friends with Thatcher."

He shrugs like this is no big deal, but it makes my heart thump out of rhythm. Thatcher from the list. My sister's stoner boyfriend, the one who got her the pills after her prescription ran out. Which means this boy thinks he knows something about me. Or, rather, he does know *some*thing about me, but he doesn't know everything.

He doesn't know what it's like to have your favorite person transform before your eyes. He doesn't know the world has gone all wonky inside my skull. He doesn't know how very, very little I want to talk about Julia right now.

"Lucky brother," I say. I keep every bit of sarcasm out of my voice. "Nice talking to you."

I stand up and walk away, over to the edge of the walkway, then off it and straight into the garden edging it. I stand with the mini meadow at my feet, black-eyed Susans still blooming gold, long grasses spiking next to them. I can hear the cicadas again, their deep hum rattling in the grass. When I look up between the buildings, I still can't see any stars.

I lean forward, on tiptoe, my hips pressed against the guardrail.

I look over the side. Just two or three stories down to the street, cars trailing red taillights pass twenty feet below and to my left. When I turn back around, Thatcher's Friend's Brother is gone. I'm alone for this moment, at least, half-hidden by vegetation.

I brace my arms against the guardrail's metal top and lift myself up, then neatly lift one leg and then the other over the side. I've never been a gymnast but it feels like I'm on a pommel horse. And then I'm sitting, easy as that, on the railing at the edge of the High Line.

This is different from last time, on Sadie's roof. Safer, maybe, because I'm not as high as I was then, or because I'm sitting. However:

1. I'd still end up dead—or at least terribly maimed—if I fell off the side.
2. What I'm doing—the dangling here—still makes me feel undeniably calm.

I sit there and revel in the calmness for a moment. I close my eyes and listen to the traffic noises below, the cicada hum. This is when I see a flutter of wings in my peripheral vision. I turn my head toward it just as it grips the handrail with its tiny, wiry feet. It has a reddish breast and blue feathers so bright it looks like it can't possibly be real. A bluebird. I sit up straighter.

"Come on," I say. "No more. I'm tired."

The bird tilts its head and looks at me. It has beady black bird eyes.

"Fine," I say. "What? What do you want?"

The bird doesn't answer. (Am I expecting it to? Maybe.) It just keeps staring at me and I keep staring at it, until I hear my phone ding in my purse. The bird looks at my purse like maybe there's a strange mechanical bird in there. I swear it does. Then it takes off in a blur of blue feathers.

I pull my phone out carefully. There's a text from Rose.

I haven't seen her, it says. She's gone, Sylvie, and I think we have to let her go.

My heart sinks like a stone in a lake, falls so fast I wonder if it might keep going straight down off the side of the High Line. Would a heart bounce when it hit the pavement? Or maybe make a *splat* sound? I look down. My feet dangle over the street, two stories below. I start thinking about other things I could drop, like this book my sister sent me, which is messing up my life. My ability to forget. What would happen if I dropped it, on purpose, all the way to the blacktop and left it there for someone else to find? Would the weirdness transfer to someone else? Or has it already broken the universe, as far as I'm concerned?

I'm about to give it a try. My heart is beating hard—in my chest, in my ears—and my fingers rest on the cover of the book. But then I feel a hand on my shoulder and all these thoughts fly out of my head.

Theories of Gravity

I FEEL THE HAND ON one shoulder, then the other. I gasp a little, but almost immediately I feel better. *Tommy*. My heart rate starts to slow. Tommy will fix this. He'll help me figure this out.

"I'm not going to jump," I say, but my voice sounds shakier than I want it to. My heart rises up toward my throat. "You might as well start believing me."

"It's not about jumping." The voice is right by my ear, but it's not Tommy's. It takes me a second to place it. "I'm afraid you're going to fall."

It's Sadie's brother, Jack.

Fantastic.

"I'm not going to fall," I say, but he's still holding on, squeezing my shoulders.

"You're right," he says. "Because I'm not going to let you." He slides one arm across my collarbone and slips the other underneath my knees, then sweeps me right off the railing. He backs away from the edge, and then he doesn't seem to know what to do next. He holds me, frowning, and in spite of myself I smile.

This isn't awkward at all.

"I think you can put me down now," I say, and he does.

"My hero," I say. I keep my tone breezy but I can feel my cheeks pinking. I always feel stupid around Jack, and that's even when I'm not putting myself in dangerous places.

"Do you have a death wish?" he asks. He doesn't sound angry or accusatory. Just curious.

"Not that I know of," I say. "What are you doing here, any-way?"

"Sadie invited me." His tone switches to defense.

"And you actually came. You don't ever come."

"Yeah, well, I'm here now," he says. "And my sister would be mad if I let you fall off the High Line. My mother too."

Sadie catches sight of us at this exact moment and bounds over like a border collie.

"I wasn't going to fall," I say to Jack, but quietly enough that she won't hear. He just looks at me, still frowning.

"What's going on?" Sadie says.

Jack shakes his head. He actually looks upset. "I just pulled Sylvie off the guardrail."

"Tattletale," I say. I turn to Sadie. "I was fine." I sound sure of myself this time, or at least I think I do, but Sadie's face still clouds over.

"What is happening to you, Sylvie?" she says, grabbing both

my hands. "I don't understand."

She must know about yesterday. Shit. I shake my head. "Tommy told you. Of course he did."

Sadie narrows her eyes. "Tommy said you went too close to the edge of the roof. He said you were just standing there."

"What the heck, Sylvie?" Jack says. "At our building? It's fourteen floors up."

"I'm fine." I try to make this sound as final as possible. Then I switch the subject. "So, Jack, what are your plans for next year?"

Smooth. Real smooth.

"What kind of question is that? Who *are* you?" Sadie asks, her brow furrowed.

"Just an interested citizen," I say. "Plus, he just saved my life. Right?"

Jack blushes a little and I almost feel bad about it, but then I remember how dumb I always feel around him. I wait for him to answer, but Sadie does it for him.

"He's going to design bridges," she says. "He's going to UVA and he's going to learn how to build bridges." This sounds like a mini speech, like something she's rehearsed.

"Really?" I ask.

"No," Jack says.

Sadie shakes her head so hard her hair falls in her face. "Don't listen to him. He's pretending he's modest."

"I like bridges," I say. I look at Jack. His green eyes look dark.

"So do I," he says. "But I'm not going to UVA."

Sadie puts her hands up. "No one needs to decide today," she says.

"Most likely I'm going to take a year off," Jack says, talking to me, not Sadie. "I'll figure things out. I'll probably work construction or something." He shifts his gaze to a lit-up building to his left. "I skipped third grade anyway. I have time." He sticks his chin out a little as he says this, like he's challenging Sadie to disagree. She doesn't take the bait.

"Anyway," she says to me. "*You* need to stay away from everything higher than you."

"Gravity is a cruel bitch," I say. This is something one of my teachers at the Academy used to say. We were nine and giggled at his curse word every time he said it. Actually, for the longest time I misheard it as "cool bitch," which would mean something else entirely, I guess.

"Gravity is science," says Jack, Official Killjoy of Our Evening. "And if it was revoked, we would float off into space where there is no air and no sound. We'd just drift apart, in opposite directions, slowly turning in the airless space until we looked like pinpoints to one another. And then we'd disappear forever. I mean, we'd be dead already. But, you know, if you don't consider that part."

We look at him. He blinks.

"Well, that was uplifting," Sadie says. She pats him on the shoulder. He's blushing now.

"You're right, brother," Sadie says, nodding. "Gravity kills."

Jack shakes his head. "Gravity saves."

Look Up

WE STAY A WHILE LONGER, Sadie and I sitting on a bench together, watching the parade of High Line walkers go by. Across the way, Jack and Amal, Sadie's friend from her pottery class, are sitting next to a clump of grass. Amal keeps touching Jack's elbow. I don't know why it bugs me so much. Maybe because he lets her?

Because he sort of hates me?

Sadie's Tennis Dude comes over to sit on the arm of our bench. They commence flirting, so I just take out the book again and flip through its feathery pages. I read the first line of "Little Red Riding Hood."

Once upon a time there was a girl who was so beautiful and kind that she was loved by everyone.

Seems sort of hard to take, honestly, that she could be loved by everyone. She never pissed anyone off? She never screwed up?

Well, at least until we get to the day when the story takes place, where she's supposed to take the safe way to her grandmother's house and instead lets a wolf trick her into going through the deep woods. We all know what happens: *What big eyes you have, Grand-mother. What big teeth.* It's pretty much the same no matter what version you have.

Now I'm reading so intently that my lips are actually moving. I look up and of course—of course—Jack is still sitting on the bench across from me with Amal, and he totally sees me doing that. He raises his eyebrows at me, a slight smile on his lips. Because yes, it's great for him to see me being weird. Again.

Sigh.

I angle my body away from him and reconsider the flower drawing. *Sylvie Grace Rose Thatcher Daniela.* It's a list, sure, but maybe it's also a map, a compass. A call for help.

My pulse kicks up. Maybe Julia's telling me where to find her. Maybe all I have to do is go.

This is when Sadie pokes me in the shoulder. I startle.

"Jumpy, much?" she says.

I take a deep breath, let it out. "Just thinking," I say. I glance to the side and see that Tennis Dude is gone. He must have wandered off to Wimbledon or wherever.

"Men," Sadie says, flopping down on the bench. She pulls her knees up to her chest.

"Yes," I say. "They comprise slightly less than half of the population."

"Don't I know it," she says. "Those inferior life spans of theirs. I can't wait until I'm an old lady. All the men will be gone, and it'll just be us left." She looks at me. "Will you be my roommate in the nursing home?"

"Yes," I say, smiling. "I'd be happy to." This is not untrue: Old Lady Sadie is bound to be a doozy.

"Good," she says. "That's settled." She leans her head back on the bench and closes her eyes. My pulse is still all wonky, so this is when I tell her. I need to say it out loud.

"Sadie," I say. "Strange things have been happening."

She opens her eyes. "What kind of things?"

"Fairy-tale things, I think." I wait. I take a breath and let it out. "I saw this girl in a red shawl with a wolf-dog, and then Rapunzel was in the subway."

Sadie's just staring at me, blinking once in a while. I realize how this must sound. At least Jack is too far away to hear it.

"You saw some of them too. The fox, and the girl with the lost shoe earlier," I say. "Like Cinderella."

"Cinderella," Sadie repeats. She's still staring at me. She blinks her long lashes.

"And there was this particularly aggressive bluebird," I say.

Sadie's eyes widen. "It attacked you?"

"No!" I laugh a little, in spite of myself. "It didn't attack me. But it landed right next to me and then just kept staring at me."

"Bluebird." Sadie's looking at me like she's trying to understand. Or maybe she's looking at me like I've finally lost it.

"Yeah."

"There's a bluebird in *Sleeping Beauty*," she says. "But he's actually a guy. He dances with Princess What's-Her-Name."

"Florine," I say, and I can't help but smile. Sadie doesn't really *get* ballet, but she pays attention because of me.

"Maybe it's a sign." Sadie tilts her head. "From the universe. Maybe you should try to find Julia."

This is why Sadie's my best friend. She makes all the right connections.

"Actually," I say. "There's something else."

Sadie waits. I open the back cover and hand the book to her.

"I didn't notice this at first," I say, "but she drew a picture in the book. This wasn't here before."

She holds the book close to her face for a moment, examining the flower, then looks back at me. "What does this mean?"

"I don't know," I say. "I have to go see Grace, I guess. I sent a text to Rose. She says she hasn't seen Julia, and that I need to let her go." My molecules start vibrating again. My blood whirls in my veins.

"Do you think she's telling the truth?"

Rose wouldn't lie to me unless she was trying to protect me. And given what I was asking—

"I don't know," I say.

Sadie is frowning, thinking. She fusses with the strap on her sandal. "Rose is at Princeton?"

I nod.

"Thatcher?"

"I have no idea." Honestly, I haven't wanted to know. I was glad when he left town. I didn't care where he went.

Sadie takes out her phone and begins tapping furiously on the screen.

"Philadelphia," she says, a few moments later. "Being a burn-out on Daddy's dime, I assume." She turns her phone my way and there's Thatcher's face, on the staff page of his father's consulting firm.

I look at it. He looks mostly the same as he did the last time I saw him, in the hospital after the worst day. Same brown eyes and dumb smile and dark brown hair. "I didn't know they had offices in Philly."

"Maybe they didn't before." Sadie tosses her phone into her bag. "Daddy Price probably started a brand-new office just to get Thatcher out of town." She shakes her head. "Who's Daniela?"

"I have no idea."

I can almost see the gears in Sadie's head turning.

"You could email Thatcher," she says.

The idea of this makes me feel sick. What would I say? *Remember my sister? The one whose life you helped ruin? I think maybe you know where she is.* Either he wouldn't answer, or he would, and his answer would be something like Rose's. There's no way he'd tell me anything useful through email.

But Julia sent me a fairy tale book, and here's what I know about fairy tales: when you have to, you go into the woods. You trust that you'll find your way out.

"What if I went to see them in person?" I ask. "That way I'd know if they were telling the truth."

Sadie lights up. She loves this idea.

"Start with Rose," she says, leaning forward. "Get right in her face so you can see if she's lying. Shake her down."

I smile. "She's my cousin. Not a perp on a crime show."

"Sure," Sadie says. "But if she's lying, you'll have to use perp tactics on her."

I give her a raised eyebrow.

"Not handcuffs. Just proximity." Sadie's eyes are bright. "Go next week!"

I frown. "But I'm supposed to be at Fancy Dance Camp." It's a reflexive reaction, I know—I'm a Good Girl—thus I can't quite imagine skipping.

Sadie makes a face. "Do you really need to go drink smoothies and get massages with a bunch of ballerinas? I'm going to lose you to them soon anyway." Her tone is about three steps short of sad, and it makes me lean toward her.

"Hey," I say. "You're not going to lose me."

"Sure," she says. She moves her head in a *shake it off* kind of way. "Anyway, this is the right answer. I know it."

I think I know it too, and I feel a fizzy sort of excitement rise in my chest. "So, do I just take a bus?"

"Don't worry about it. I think I have an idea."

Sadie always has a capital-I Idea.

"Let me figure it out," she says, "and then I'll meet you at the bottom of the stairs."

"Okay," I say. Sadie unfolds her legs and stands up, then heads over to the cluster of guys off to our left. I keep sitting. I feel a little dizzy, actually.

Near the end, Julia meant chaos. She meant lies and sickness, a too-tight feeling in my chest. She turned my body into a galaxy, molecules always swirling and spinning apart. Being near her was like standing next to the sun. She blotted everything else out.

I hear a low rumble, and when I turn in the direction of the river I can see that someone's setting off fireworks way downtown. A crimson burst of light explodes across the sky, then rains glitter over the water. Or what I assume must be the water, because from this angle it's hard to tell. Artificial stars in gleaming white streak across the sky, and after that a pinwheel in shades of blue.

The sky goes black for a full ten seconds. Then there's a flash even higher in the sky, and I crane my neck to see it.

My heart knows the shape before my brain does. It's Julia's flower, the one she wrote our names on, lit up purple above me. That same shape repeats again and again across the sky like some giant is block-printing it up there in sparks and chemicals. I look for Sadie—to point to it, to show her—but I don't see her right now.

So I watch it sparkle and fade by myself.

Signs and Signals

IT'S LATE NOW AND I'M leaning against the railing at the bottom of the stairs, waiting for Sadie. I don't know if she's up giving a prolonged, kissy goodbye to Tennis Dude or what, but I feel confused and spinny and I want to go home. In general, and definitely before I have to see Jack again, lest he glare at me with that *you are a weirdo, aren't you?* look in his green eyes. Or asks me to sign over my firstborn child to him, Rumpelstiltskin-style, since he thinks he saved my life. Anything's possible at this point. I hear footsteps on the stairs behind me and turn around. Sadie's bare legs appear at the top of the flight, then the shorts-wearing rest of her.

"Success," she says. She's grinning.

I smile too. Because we're solving something. We're figuring something out. "The plan?" I ask.

Sadie nods. "Jack," she says.

"'Jack' is not a plan."

"Um, he kind of is." Sadie is smiling, cat-that-ate-the-canary-style. "You know my dad gave Jack his old Volvo, right?"

"Yeah," I say. I have a vague memory of Jack blah-blah-blahing about a car of some sort.

"He loves to drive that stupid car," Sadie says. "He'll take you. He'll deliver you to all the people on your list."

My stomach goes into a free fall. "Your brother would never want to do that," I say. "He doesn't even like me. He thinks I'm a bad influence."

"He doesn't." Sadie waves off the idea. "And anyway, he doesn't have to *like* you. He just has to drive you. I *may* have already asked him."

"Sadie!"

She puts up a stop-sign hand. "He'll do it. Listen. It's perfect. I had already convinced him to come see my dad for one night. Drive down, drive back. This just means that it'll take a little longer, and he'll get to drive more. With excellent company." She gestures toward me like she's trying to sell a boat with a hole in it. *Sure, it doesn't hold water as well as it used to,* she'd say, *but it's a fabulous deal!*

"And you," she says, "can make sure he actually does that."

Sadie is actually beaming, she's so satisfied with herself. I'm frowning so hard I'm sure my eyebrows are meeting in the middle.

Driving down the Eastern Seaboard with Sadie's cranky brother is not on my top-ten list of Great Ideas for the Summer, but I don't have a whole lot of choices. If I stay in town, it's becoming increasingly likely that something terrible, or ridiculous, or terribly ridiculous will happen. (I'll be imprisoned in a gingerbread house! Kidnapped by a wicked stepmother! Eaten by a wolf!)

Right? That's obviously where this is heading.

Plus, leaving town to find Julia feels like dangling out on a ledge, but with my heart instead of my body. And that feeling is a feeling I like.

"Okay," I say.

"Okay?" Sadie sounds delighted. "Yay!" She throws her arms around me and I let myself be hugged.

When she releases me, we walk out to the street. I feel a little dizzy, like gravity has been revoked and I'm about to float off in the atmosphere. Which, of course, would spell my doom as Jack has explained. This is what I'm imagining—the weightlessness, the floating feeling, the approaching star-studded sky—when I hear something behind me. Hoofbeats—actual hoofbeats—on pavement. A horse. I look at Sadie, who's glancing behind us. Her eyes are wide.

When I turn around, I see a carriage heading our way. The horse—a sleek chestnut, no blinders on, with a blue sash wound around his halter—clip-clops the remaining thirty feet, and then his driver stops him right in front of us. The horse stomps his hooves a few times and snorts.

"Well, hello," says Sadie. The horse swings his huge head toward her and sniffs her ear.

The driver hops out and steps to the door of the carriage, which is so close to me I could reach out and touch its glossy black side.

"My lady," he says, extending his hand toward me.

I open my mouth and then close it again. Because what the hell do you say to that? I look at Sadie, and I expect her to be amazed. But she's just her normal fierce self.

"Dude," she says. "We don't know you. There's no way we're getting into your carriage."

He smiles and tips his hat—his actual HAT—to us. Then he and his horse go clip-clopping off into the dark, the lights on the back of the carriage blinking gold until they reach the end of the street and wink out.

Looking for Trouble

THE NEXT AFTERNOON, I'M STANDING on Grace's hallway doormat with my dog at my feet, waiting for her to answer. Pavlova's panting. I can feel my heart butterflying behind my rib cage, even though I shouldn't be nervous. It's just Grace, my second sister. Grace, who's been around since she started taking ballet classes with Julia before I was even born. And she knows I'm coming.

Pavlova hops up to put her front feet on the door and looks up at me. "She's on her way," I say. She already buzzed us in from outside.

The hallway here is dark, and Grace's door is painted the deep green of a woodland cottage. In the middle is a small square grate with frosted glass behind it. I can't see past the glass except for the pearly light coming through it, and then the shadow as Grace approaches. I take a breath and hold it. I let it out as she turns the lock.

When Grace opens the door, she looks beautiful, as usual. She's wearing a long, loose-fitting tunic with leggings. Her feet are bare. She's not wearing makeup but her dark brown skin is still flawless, dewy and smooth. Her eyes look sad.

"Sylvie," she says. She opens the door a little wider. "Come in." She folds me right into a hug and I feel a catch in my breath. I haven't seen her much this year—we passed in the NBT hallways a few times, and every time she'd touch my shoulder or squeeze my hand, but that was it. She'd keep walking without saying much. I might as well have lost two sisters when Julia left.

When Grace lets me go, I look at the living room behind her. It's large, with big windows through which I can see the brick building across the way. The walls are white. None of that matters as much, though, as the fact that there are plants everywhere. Palm trees in terra-cotta pots on the floor, baskets hanging from every window frame, tiny succulents in ceramic mugs on the coffee table. It wasn't this way before. Honestly, it's a little out of control.

Julia lived here with Grace for a while, nearly two years ago. Before her first surgery and all the trouble that followed. They moved in together when they became members of the corps. Julia packed her things into my mother's fancy luggage, and Everett and I helped her and Grace carry stuff up the stairs. I think the only plant they had then was a peace lily my mother sent as a house-warming gift. It's gained a lot of friends in the meantime.

I step farther into the room, Pavlova at my heels. It's humid in here, like a jungle, but the air smells so clean. It's verdant and lush and leafy. Bookshelves edged with trailing vines line the wall next to the blue sofa I watched the movers bring in two years ago. It's cat-scratched now. Pavlova trots right over to it and hops up.

"Just make yourself at home," I say to her. Then I turn to Grace. "Sorry my dog is rude."

She shrugs. "It's okay with me. She might have to apologize to the cat, though."

"Noted," I say. "So what's up with the plants?"

Grace smiles. "I don't know," she says. "I guess I have a green thumb." She reaches out and touches the fringed leaf of a fern. "It seemed empty here after Jules moved out. I bought a few, and then a few more." She gestures toward the room. "It became a thing."

"I can see that," I say. "I think it's pretty." True, but also *pretty overwhelming*. "You never got a new roommate?"

"No," Grace says. "It's rent-stabilized, so I've been able to cover it. I think in the beginning I thought Jules would come back and she'd move in like we planned." She shakes her head. "Now I just like living alone. Plus, your dad paid Julia's half for six months after she left." She looks a little embarrassed. "I told him it wasn't necessary, but he insisted."

"Really?" I don't know why this surprises me. It's sounds like something my father would do: throw money at a problem. I never considered what Jules moving out would have meant for Grace. It's not like corps members are bringing in the big bucks.

Grace nods. A teakettle whistles in the kitchen.

"Do you want tea?" Grace asks.

"Sure," I say, and she goes into the kitchen. I sit down on the far corner of the sofa since Pavlova's stretched out over much of the rest. For a tiny dog, she can really take up space. Vines fall over the bookcase next to me, covered in heart-shaped leaves. I reach out to touch one.

It moves.

I swear it does. It moves before my fingers reach it, drifting to the side a little and catching on another vine, winding itself further into a tangle of leaves. It leaves an open space, and in the middle of that is a photograph in a frame.

It's of Julia and Grace in gleaming pale pink costumes, their arms thrown around each other. The light from the flash reflects off the beading on their bodices. Their smiles are wide.

I remember this performance. I was there in the dressing room, the first time Julia took me along with her. I was fourteen and she was twenty-one. I sat in a folding chair next to her at the vanity, watching her apply her lipstick in the big square mirror on the wall. She didn't seem nervous at all. She was as calm as a quiet pond— no ripples, just smooth blue water. Her eyes were already done by the makeup artist: black winged liner, shimmery silver shadow, and false eyelashes so thick I wondered if they made it hard to blink. The lights lining the mirror shone like small suns, but Jules looked straight into the glass. And then she looked at me.

"What do you think, Sylvie?"

"Perfect," I said.

She smiled. "You can't trust a looking glass," she said, quoting Miss Inez.

"That's why I'm here," I said. "You look beautiful."

I watched in the mirror as the other apprentices glided behind us. Irina, Pia, and Marisol, who ruffled my hair with her long fingers. They weren't dancing *Swan Lake*, but they still reminded me of birds. Herons, maybe, balancing on long legs, trailing glittering feathers. They were the most beautiful things I'd ever seen, made more beautiful by the fact that they were in a dressing room, not onstage. It felt like I was seeing a spectacular accident.

Grace appeared next to me then and squeezed my shoulder. Her tulle skirt was a cloud around her waist. Her lips were painted a dark shade of berry.

Julia stood up and lifted her leg in front of her, toes in a hard point. She winced, then took a deep breath and forced her face into a smile.

"Are you okay?" I asked.

"Yep," she said. I wanted to believe her, but I knew she wasn't telling the truth. I didn't know what was happening to her yet and she didn't either. She still thought she was safe after her first surgery. Already, though, I understood that ballet was supposed to hurt, and that we were supposed to pretend it didn't.

Grace faced the mirror and rose up on her toes, balancing for a moment like she was hoping to lift off and hover straight over the ground. Then she smiled and turned toward me.

"This will be you someday," she said.

Julia pulled me up to stand next to her in front of the glass, hip to hip, shoulder to shoulder. We looked at each other in the mirror, my face bare and hers with its sweeping, shimmering makeup. She touched my cheekbone gently with her pointer finger, still looking at my reflection instead of my real face.

"If you want it to be," she said.

Back then, I couldn't imagine wanting anything else. I don't know when that changed.

Now I can hear Grace pulling mugs out of the cabinets. Pavlova lets out a grumbly sound from the couch, turning over onto her back. I rest my hand on her belly.

Grace comes back and sets two steaming cups on the coffee table. She curls up on the couch and tucks her legs below her.

"All right," she says. "Spill it, Syl. What's up?"

I'm ready. I look her right in the eyes. "Where's Julia?"

Grace frowns. "I don't know." She looks back at me for a few seconds, and then down at her mug. I sit silently, watching her. What would Sadie do? She'd go big or go home.

"I don't believe you," I say.

"What? Why?" Grace's brow is furrowed. "Sylvie, she's supposed to be here. She's not. I don't know where she is." She takes one hand off the mug to gesture in the air, staccato movements meant to punctuate her words. Meant to make me believe.

"Then why is your name in here?" I pull the book out of my bag and open it to the last page. I hand it to Grace. She takes it with her free hand and looks at the page.

"Probably because she came here that first night, after she left your parents' place. She left the next day, though." Grace sighs. "This wasn't her apartment then anyway. She'd already been gone for months."

"So where did she go after that?"

"I don't know. She left when I was at the studio," Grace says. "I came back home and she and her bag were both gone."

I press my thumb into my opposite palm, hard. "You haven't heard from her at all?"

Grace looks at me for a second, considering. Then she nods.

"Once. She sent me an email." She blows on her mug, and I lean forward in my seat, waiting.

"What did she say?"

Grace takes a sip of her tea, swallows. She looks up. "She said she was all right, and that I shouldn't worry."

"She didn't say where she went?"

"No." She sets her cup down. "And I didn't ask. I figure she'll tell me when she wants to. If she ever wants to."

There's a sheen of bitterness at the edge of Grace's voice, and it makes my stomach ache. I don't know what I thought—that Grace would be able to tell me exactly where Julia was, that she's sober, that she's coming home soon. That the first person I went to see would give me all the answers and I wouldn't have to look any further. Wouldn't even have to leave town.

Of course it couldn't be that easy.

I pick up my mug and wrap my hands around it. It's too hot still, but I don't mind the mild burn of the porcelain. The tea is golden brown and steaming. I keep my eyes on it.

Grace takes a deep breath and lets it out. "Jules stole from me, you know."

I snap my gaze up to look at her. "What?"

"Yeah." Grace presses her lips together. "It was after her surgery. When she ran out of pills." She looks off toward the kitchen while she tells me the story, as if she's watching it happen in her memory. "We used to keep cash in the silverware drawer for take-out or whatever. I kept doing it after she left. She stayed here one night after she was cleared to go back to dancing, because she was planning on moving back in." Grace looks at me. "There was maybe a hundred dollars in the drawer. She left ten."

"Grace." I exhale her name like a breath. I don't know what I mean by it, why I'm just saying her name. I don't know what else to say.

"I asked her about it, but she denied it." Grace's voice is even, steady. "I thought maybe I made a mistake, that I'd spent it somehow, but when she got hurt again and we found out about the pills, I knew." She bites her lip. I want to lean forward and touch her shoulder or her hand, but I don't.

"It wasn't just you," I say. Julia had stolen from my parents too, money from my father's wallet and my mother's purse. They didn't notice at first, but I heard them whispering about it later, after everything came out. Still, it feels different, somehow, that she'd steal from Grace.

"Yeah, I figured," Grace says. "She was buying pills for maybe three months, right? That had to get expensive." Her voice sounds hard. "They told her when they prescribed the meds in the first place, you know? How careful she had to be, dancing while taking them. Because she might not feel the pain anymore, and the pain is the thing that tells you to stop." Grace's voice wavers. "She didn't want to stop."

Tears well up in my eyes so fast the world goes blurry. I try to blink gently in that way you do when you're trying not to let someone see you cry, but it's a flawed method because it's not like the tears are going to absorb back into your eyes.

"Syl." Grace's voice is soft.

I try to look at her. She might as well be underwater. I squeeze my eyes shut and tears spill down my cheeks. I wipe them with the back of my hand.

"It's fine," I say. I look up. "It's okay if you're mad at her."

Grace sinks back a little further into the cushions. "Sure, I'm mad. We were supposed to do this together. We've been dancing together since we were four years old." Her voice sounds tired. "And let's be serious. She had it easier than I did in plenty of ways. She worked so hard, I know. But I had to work harder. I didn't think I resented her for that but"—Grace tosses up her hands—"turns out I do."

Grace picks up her tea again and looks into the cup. I don't know what to say. I know it's true, what she's saying, both about Julia and about it being harder for Grace. The Academy and the company are both more diverse than they've ever been, but it isn't enough. The leads still often go to white dancers.

"I'm sorry," I say. And I am, but saying it still feels useless.

Grace shrugs. "Look," she says, "Julia had a shot and she threw it away in the end. I'm mad about that. But I also understand why she was desperate to keep dancing. She had a chance to be one of the greatest. She was willing to do anything to keep it." She leans forward and looks at me then, right in the eyes. "Sometimes the people we love disappoint us. Sometimes they absolutely break our hearts."

I look away and Grace leans back on the sofa. Pavlova puts her hard little paw on my knee and I swear for a moment she knows what I'm feeling.

"I don't want to be mad at her anymore. It's exhausting."

Grace is staring at me again; I can tell even though I'm looking at the dog. "I'm sorry too, by the way."

"For what?"

"For not being there for you this last year. I had a really hard time with everything." She reaches out and touches my ankle, her fingertips light on my skin. "I didn't know how to help anyone else."

I look up, finally. "It's okay."

"It's not, really." Grace smiles in her mouth and not her eyes. "But I can't change it now. I can't change any of it. I can't even get your brother to talk about it with me."

"Everett?" I ask, stupidly, as if I have another brother. Grace nods.

"He sent me that drawing about a month ago," she says. She points to a black frame on the bookshelf next to the photograph of her with Jules. "But when I sent him a text to thank him he didn't respond."

I pick up the frame. It's a quick sketch of Grace onstage, colored in the kind of cheap pastels Everett likes to use sometimes. He has everything right: the shape of her eyes, the way she positions her hands, the way her thin shoulders look strong enough to hold up a whole building.

"It's beautiful," I say. I don't know what this means, the fact that Everett would send Grace a drawing he'd done of her. I never really considered that they'd be more than friends, but suddenly that seems stupid. Everett is two years younger than Jules and Grace, but Grace was always around as they were growing up. She's beautiful and talented and kind. It's not hard to believe that my brother would fall for her.

"You know," Grace says, "you lose one person and it starts to feel like you're going to lose every person. One by one."

We sit without saying anything for a minute. I can hear her neighbor's television murmur through the wall, and the soft sound of Pavlova's snores. I watch the vines to my right, but nothing happens. They don't move, not even in the slight breeze coming in the window.

"What are you going to do?" Grace's voice is quiet.

I look at her. "I'm going to go talk to Rose."

"Why can't you just call her?"

"Because I already texted her and she told me she doesn't know where Jules is. But I don't think she's telling me the truth."

"So you're going there." It's not a question.

Pavlova rolls over again, exposing her belly. I put my hand on her rib cage. I can feel her heart beating.

"Yes," I say.

"Okay." Grace nods. "Promise you'll call me if you get into trouble?"

For some reason, this makes me wonder what would have happened if Jules had just told someone what was going on. If *she* had called someone when she got into trouble. I wouldn't be searching; Everett wouldn't have packed up and moved to Nashville; Grace wouldn't have turned into the Princess of the Plants. We could have helped Julia. At least I think so.

I turn to Grace. "Yeah, I'll call you," I say. But I doubt I will. And anyway, I've read enough fairy tales to know how it works. Whether you're looking for trouble or not, it knows how to find you.

Sleeping Lessons

WHEN I LEAVE GRACE'S BUILDING, the streets are quieter. The heat has eased since earlier, and sunlight shines golden on the sidewalk.

There's a little café across the street from Grace's building. If Julia still lived with Grace, this is where she would stop for coffee and toast in the morning. In some other universe, one where things never got so bad with my sister, that's what she's doing. She's sitting in one of these vinyl booths, spreading strawberry jam on bread. She's living her normal old life.

Pavlova sniffs the lamppost in front of me and I let her. I'm not in a hurry to go anywhere. There's really nowhere to go but home. This—my standing still—is why I hear the music, I think. My brain is empty and the song enters it like it's entering a room.

It's too quiet to hear well at first, but then it gets louder, falls like rain out of some apartment window above me. I recognize it:

it's a Shins song on a record Everett listened to constantly after Julia's accident. I heard it mostly through his closed door, but sometimes he'd let me do my homework at his desk while he did his own on his bed—and he'd pull the needle back to start the album again and again.

I stand here and I listen to the music swell around me in the street. It fills all the space from asphalt to sky, and I let it. I don't move.

This is when I see the next girl.

This one is wearing a gauzy lavender dress, her hair hanging in black curls over her shoulders. She's almost shimmering in the gold light of early evening, but when she turns for a moment to face me, I can see the dark circles under her eyes. She looks exhausted, like she's one step from sleepwalking. I can barely bring myself to look away from her, but I drag my gaze up to the sign on the building she just left. *Sarita Patel*, it says. *Sleep Therapist.*

It's still possible that none of this is real, and my brain's just falling apart, but Julia was Sleeping Beauty onstage—before she got hurt. I stand still for one beat, two, and watch this girl glide down the sidewalk. Away from me. And then I take off after her.

Sadie has made me watch about a hundred detective films from the forties, and I would like to take this chance to call bullshit on the whole genre. Those movies make it seem as if all you have to do is leisurely follow your subject in a nice trench coat, your deerstalker cap pulled down low over your forehead. Maybe duck behind a lamppost once in a while. It turns out it would be better to be a track star than a gumshoe because this girl is fast. She's maybe fifty feet from the corner and moving so quickly I'm practically running to keep up, and Pavlova is full-out sprinting. The girl turns the corner and I follow ten seconds later.

Then she's in the street, hand up, hailing a taxi. In a way that proves she must be magic, a yellow cab turns off the side street and slides to a stop in front of her. No one gets a taxi that quickly in New York City. I stop when I see it; I watch her open the door, slide in, and pull the door shut. The taxi drives away and I'm left standing there.

The real magic waits to happen until I turn around. Above me is a wide metal sign. *Butterfly and Bee*, it says, letters spelled out in winding, burnished steel. There's a fat bumblebee at one end and a butterfly at the other, wings outstretched and glimmering in the evening sun.

I've been here before.

And I have the unshakable feeling that I've been led here now.

The Tale of the Tattoo

ONCE UPON A TIME, JULIA brought me to a tattoo shop called Butterfly and Bee. She practically dragged me there from the subway, her arm linked through mine. The streets were lined with slush, the sky pearl gray over the tops of buildings. She was walking the way she always did. She never *looked* like she was in a hurry but somehow she'd get there fast anyway. Julia stopped in front of Butterfly and Bee and I stood under that sign for the first time. Then she opened the door and swept me inside. The guy at the front desk smiled when he saw her. He was handsome, with dark square glasses and full-sleeve tattoos on both of his arms.

"Hey, ballerina," he said.

Jules smiled her megawatt stage smile. "Hi, Toby." She walked farther into the room, head held as high as it would have been if she were stepping out on a stage floor. Her long scarf fluttered behind her.

"Today's the day," she said.

"I've been waiting," he answered.

I liked Toby right away, both his easy smile and the way he squinted when he concentrated on something. He told me his sister danced with Julia in the corps. They had met at a party, he and Jules, and she must have told him she was thinking of getting a tattoo. He knew it wasn't something most ballerinas did, at least not in places where the tattoo would be visible in a leotard or a costume. I was afraid she'd get in trouble. There was talk of letting her dance a principal part for a couple of performances each week, which was a huge deal for someone in her position. When I told Julia that, she shook her head.

"Don't be so worried, little sister," she said. "Concealer exists for a reason."

I sat on a stool next to her and held a book of designs open in my lap. Not that I needed them; I just wanted something to do with my hands. Julia sat perfectly still, her lake-blue eyes looking right at me.

"Are you going to pick out a tramp stamp?" she said to me, smiling her crooked smile. "Mom would love that." Her shoulders were straight, her posture ballerina-perfect, even in that chair. I watched as Toby positioned the stencil on her smooth, clean skin. His own arms were etched with blossoms and bumblebees, and when he lowered the needle, I could almost believe the buzz came from them. I looked at Julia's arm on the table, palm facing up, drops of blood rising in constellations. I tried not to faint. There was nothing I wanted more than for Julia to think I was brave and worthy of being taken on an adventure like this one.

I leaned toward her.

"Does it hurt?" I whispered.

"Mm-hmm," she said. Her eyes were closed by then.

"So what does *twenty-six bones* mean, anyway?" Toby asked. He didn't take his gaze off the needle as he spoke.

My sister opened her eyes, but she didn't answer. She smiled a Mona Lisa smile.

"All right," Toby said. "I'll guess. You're a secret pirate and this is the name of your ship."

"No," said Julia.

"You're writing a mystery novel and this is the title."

She laughed softly, staying totally still.

"Then what?" He pulled the needle away from her skin for a moment.

Julia lifted her right hand and stretched it across her body to touch his cheek. "It's a just a good-luck charm, Toby."

She looked at me then, half a smile playing on her lips. She knew I wasn't going to tell. Julia knew if she had a secret, I was going to keep it. Even if it ended up hurting us both.

Good-Luck Charm

I STARE AT THE GHOST of my own reflection in the window: dark hair pinned up in a neat bun, blue sundress. Silver sandals.

Just past Ghost Me, I can make out the fiberglass curve of the bench in the waiting area, the reception desk off to one side. Above it, a string of fairy lights glowing like a tidy line of stars. I squint and lean closer to the glass, but the actual tattooing happens farther back, too far to see from here. Right now, I bet there's a girl back there gritting her teeth against the whir of the needle, getting her lover's name inked on her hip. She hopes she'll stay with him forever, or maybe she already knows that she'll leave him next week. Either way, that tattoo is going to become part of her. Like a sealed-over crack in a broken bone or a scar zigzagging over the skin of her knee, it'll settle in and stay.

I remember everything about my sister, because that's how

memories work. They're layered into our bodies like tattoo ink, hopscotching across neurons to find their own safe place. They hang around, even if you don't want them. They lead you to places you don't expect to go.

Like this shop, today.

The door is open to the sidewalk, air-conditioning leaking out into the street. As if you might be walking by, feel the cold air and say, *It's hot today. Perhaps I'll duck inside to get cool and, hey, while I'm here, might as well get an illustration that can never be erased from my body.* In the front window, a man-sized shape approaches, and when he gets close enough to the glass I can see him. It's Toby.

I was last here eighteen months ago, so I'm sure he doesn't remember me. I'm just some strange girl standing out on the sidewalk, looking at her reflection in the window. But I lift my hand anyway, not a wave exactly but something close to one. The puzzled look on his face shifts into a smile, though I can still see a question in his eyes. He waves back.

This is when I know what I have to do.

When I walk in it's so dim I'm blind for a moment. It's quiet except for the Clash playing on the speakers above me, all jangle and drums. When the room sharpens into existence, my eyes adjusting, Toby's there.

"Hey," he says.

I echo him. "Hey."

"You have a dog." We both look down at Pavlova, panting near my feet.

"I do," I say. "Is that okay?"

He smiles a little. "Probably," he says. "I'm Toby. What can I do for you today?"

"I'm Sylvie," I say. "Actually, we've met before." I put my hand out and he shakes it. "My sister is Julia Blake."

"Oh," he says. "Right." His cheeks flush. I don't know why I didn't notice before, but I see it now: Toby had a crush on my sister. I imagine an alternate universe where she dumped Thatcher before things fell apart and dated sweet, well-inked Toby (Nancy Drew #62: *The Secret of the Tattooed Beau*). She'd have a couple more tattoos in hidden places and I would have gotten to see the look on my father's face when she first brought him home. I bet Toby wouldn't have given her drugs.

"It's okay," I say. "People always remember her first."

He watches my face. "You look like her." Even though I can tell how he felt about her, somehow this doesn't sound creepy.

"Thanks," I say. "She left."

"Yeah, I heard about that," he says. "My sister told me she got hurt."

I nod. "Did she tell you about . . . ?" I don't even know how to put it into words, everything that happened. Especially here in this place where my sister was once okay.

"Yeah," Toby says, his voice quiet too. "I was really sorry to hear that. How is she now?"

I shake my head a little. "I don't know."

Toby looks surprised. "You haven't talked to her?"

"Not since she left New York," I say. "A year ago."

"Wow." He leans back against the desk behind him. I stand up straighter.

"I'm going to find her."

"Good," he says, but he doesn't sound certain. He runs a hand through his hair and I see a tattoo of a tiny pointe shoe near his elbow. For his sister, I'm sure. It only makes me like him more.

"I need a favor," I tell him.

He looks at me. I'm almost afraid to ask, but I can see it in his eyes. I've got him. He'll say yes.

"I want to get the same tattoo you gave Julia."

His brow furrows. "Sylvie, you're what? Sixteen?"

"Eighteen," I say. I hold his gaze and pull my fake ID from my wallet. Sadie and I got them from a kid who works with her at the coffeehouse, when we wanted to go to eighteen-and-over shows and not get hassled at the door. It's my picture here, with lots of makeup and what I thought would be a believable grown-up person's frown. It worked well enough.

Toby takes it from me and squints at it.

"Please." I know my voice sounds desperate, and I let it. I know I'm asking for something I shouldn't, and I don't care.

"I need a good-luck charm," I say. All the things I want to say: how magic needs a place to land and I'm giving it my body. How the only way I'll be able to move on is if I can see my sister again. How I need this to find her.

"Sit down," Toby says.

He walks over to pull down his binder, flips through until he finds Julia's tattoo. He holds it up for me to see.

"Yes," I say.

He sits down on the stool next to me. I put my arm on the table between us, palm facing up. I think about Julia doing this a year and a half ago, with me sitting next to her. I almost believe that if I were to close my eyes, I could be back there when I open them.

"Are you sure about this?" Toby asks. He's looking right at me. "It's a choice that can't really be undone."

I nod. "You could say that about most choices," I say. "Right?" I press my fingers to the inside of my clean, empty wrist one last time. My pulse is steady. "I'm sure."

Toby sighs and starts to fuss with the needle. In spite of how certain I am, I feel nervousness bubble through me. I start to chatter.

"Where did the name of the shop come from?" I ask.

"Muhammad Ali." Toby looks at me. "You know, 'float like a butterfly, sting like a bee'?"

I nod, and at that exact moment I see one: a yellow butterfly, fluttering up near the ceiling. I'm about to ask Toby if this is normal, if he sees it too, when he asks me a question instead.

"Are you going to tell me what *twenty-six bones* means this time?"

I watch the butterfly land on the chair across from me, just above my bag. The white corner of the fairy tale book pokes out next to the zipper. The butterfly opens its wings gently, then folds them again.

I look at Toby. It seems only fair to tell him. I open my mouth to answer, but that's when the needle first touches my skin. A ribbon of pain streaks through my body.

"Oh, shit," I hear myself say.

How I'll Die

A FEW HOURS LATER, TOMMY and I are eating mint chocolate chip ice cream and watching the ballet movie *Center Stage* for the eleventy billionth time.

"Why don't *we* ever have soap fights while washing the mirrors in the studio?" Tommy asks, pointing his spoon at the screen. Our heroine and her friends are tossing handfuls of bubbles at each other, whipping their squeegees around, basically just making a huge mess.

"Because no one lets us wash the mirrors in the studio," I say. "Honestly I don't know if anyone washes them. I've never seen it happen."

Tommy nods, chewing. I've already told him that I'm not going to Fancy Dance Camp. He's coming to terms with my decision, going through the stages of grief. So far, we've covered:

1. Denial
2. Anger
3. Bargaining
4. Frozen dessert

I think acceptance is nearing, if only because he knows me well enough to know I need to do this.

Tommy takes a gigantic spoonful out of his bowl. Anyone who thinks ballet dancers don't eat has never met us and our runaway metabolisms.

"Are you going to call?" he asks.

"Yeah," I say. "I guess I'd better."

I look up the email from Fancy Dance Camp and dial the number on the bottom. A woman answers.

"Hello!" Her voice is friendly and brittle, like if glass could be cheerful.

"Oh, hello," I say. "This is Elizabeth Blake." I draw out our last name the way my mother does. "I'm afraid my daughter Sylvie won't be joining you this week. She's pulled a tendon in her foot and we feel it's best that she stays home before the intensives."

Tommy claps softly at my performance. I wave him away and try not to laugh.

"I'm so sorry to hear that, Ms. Blake," says the cheerful glass-voice lady. "We wish her the speediest of recoveries. It's too late for a refund on the deposit, unfortunately."

"That's no problem," I say magnanimously.

"All the best to Sylvie," she says.

"Thanks," I say. "Um, I'll tell her." I hang up.

Tommy lifts his palm and I give him a high five.

Could it be that easy? Maybe. I lean my head against Tommy's shoulder.

"Is this dumb?" I ask. Pavlova is dozing in my lap, and she lifts her head at that word. She looks at me.

"Is what dumb?" Tommy asks.

"Going on this trip," I say. "I'm getting in a car and driving around for days with someone who does not enjoy my company."

"Who cares?" Tommy says. "He's just transport. At least he's nice to look at." He taps me on the head. "Don't tell me you haven't noticed."

I make a face. "He's Sadie's brother."

"And? Brothers can be cute. *Your* brother is cute."

"Ew," I say. "Please don't say that." I cross my arms. "You understand that Jack doesn't speak when I'm around."

Tommy shakes his head. "I think he's just the strong silent type."

"He's not a cowboy in some old movie, Tommy," I say. "You weren't there the other night. It was so awkward."

"Yeah, well, Jack wasn't the one perched dangerously on a narrow ledge." Tommy points at me. "So who's the awkward one?"

I smile and take a spoonful of ice cream from my bowl. I hold it out toward him. "Uh-oh. Are we back to anger? Do you need more ice cream?"

"All I'm saying—"

I give him a stop-sign hand. "I know what you're saying."

"Just let Cute Jack drive you around and deal with it."

"Crabby Jack."

Tommy shrugs. "Tomato, tomahto."

I'm shaking my head but I can't keep from smiling. "I honestly have no idea what we're talking about anymore."

We're quiet for a moment, until Tommy looks up at me. "What if she doesn't want you to come?"

"Why would she send the book, then?"

"I don't know," he says. "It just doesn't sound like Julia. You know, communicating in secret messages."

"Well, things are different now. And besides, she's not who we thought she was, is she? All she did for a year straight was lie—to everyone."

"Now who needs more ice cream?" Tommy mutters.

The fairy tale book is on the coffee table, and I put my palm flat on the cover. I think about the girls in trouble, all the heroines who need saving. My tattoo feels hot, like someone pressed fiery metal straight into my skin like a brand.

I look at Tommy. "What if she's in trouble?"

"What do you mean?"

"I don't know. I mean, what if—sending this—she's calling for help?"

Tommy nods, slow and steady. "Then you are going to go and find her and help her. You, my friend, are the sister cavalry."

I should have known he'd say something like that. In the end, he's always on my side.

"I'm not sending Pavlova to the kennel," I say. "I'm taking her with me."

"Damn straight you are," Tommy says.

On-screen, the dancers are still frolicking in soap bubbles, sloshing water all over the studio's wood floor. I'm thinking about how slippery that wood must have been, and how no dancer I know would be willing to risk getting hurt just to run around in some soap. Not to mention what it would do to the floors.

Tommy looks at me.

"I can't believe you got a tattoo," he says. "Totally badass."

I smile. It hurts, my *twenty-six bones,* but it's a comfortable kind of pain, twinging in a regular rhythm. It's a secret etched right into my skin.

"Also," Tommy says, "your mom is going to kill you."

On a Mission

WHEN THE SUN RISES ABOVE the rim of the building across the street and slips between the slats of my blinds, I've already been awake for hours, staring at the mountain-range crack in my ceiling. My tattoo burns on my wrist. Tommy's asleep on a pile of pillows on my rug, his face turned toward my dresser. Pavlova's curled up against his back.

When Julia first left, Tommy slept over for three nights in a row. My parents barely noticed, and Everett was crackling with anger, so he never let me get close enough to him to actually talk. Tommy made sure that I wasn't alone, that I ate my meals, even if they were only cereal and the takeout my parents had delivered. He watched marathons of 1960s TV shows like *Bewitched* and *I Dream of Jeannie* with me. He skipped ballet class too.

Julia had left her bedroom door open that last night, but my mother closed it the next day, pulled it shut so hard the doorframe shook. I saw her do it, and she saw me see—or rather, she turned around to find me watching. "Dust," my mother said. I guessed she was talking about keeping it clean, but I wasn't sure. We never talked about it again, and I never opened the door myself, as ridiculous as that sounds. I never really wanted to. Until now.

I slide to the foot of my bed and step around Tommy's long legs, then walk as softly as I can across the floor. I push my door open carefully, stopping just before the spot where the hinges squeak. Then I squeeze through the opening, first one leg, followed by the rest of me. I'm barefoot on the hardwood, still wearing the clothes I slept in: my brother's old Sleater-Kinney T-shirt and leggings with a tear in the knee. Totally rock-and-roll, except for the Band-Aids on my feet. Or maybe that makes it even better.

Light pours from the window at the end of the hall, falls in a golden square on the floor. I walk past Everett's room and my parents' to Julia's.

I put my hand on the doorknob. It's smooth and cool, clear glass in an octagon shape. I'm ready to turn it, when I hear footsteps in the hallway behind me. I whirl around, heart pounding.

It's Tommy, of course. I don't know who else I could expect. He stretches slowly, arms raised over his head.

"Do you always creep around the apartment like a burglar in the morning?" he asks.

"Only sometimes," I say.

"Well, it's a really charming habit." He smiles. "What are you doing?"

"Going in," I say, but I might as well say *time traveling*. I put my hand out and he takes it. I squeeze. "Come on."

We Go In

TOMMY AND I STEP INTO the room carefully, like we're entering a museum. Which I guess we are. This is a place made of past-Julia, the Julia who's been gone for a year. Who was gone before that, really, ever since she stopped being able to dance.

I think some part of me half expects to find Julia in bed like a comatose princess, wax-figure beautiful and completely still. But all I see is her lavender quilt pulled tight around the mattress. Her empty desk. Three pairs of old pointe shoes, trailing ribbons, hanging from a hook on the wall. When I was little I couldn't wait to have my own pairs of busted toe shoes to hang like a trophy, and I hung my first three pairs too. Now I'd have dozens more if I kept them, but I throw all the rest away. Just like Julia used to do.

I kneel down in front of her low dresser and open the bottom drawer. I sift through her tank tops, then pick up ones in dark red and sapphire blue. I lift out one covered in gunmetal-gray sequins.

"That's going to be itchy," Tommy says.

"Thanks, Mom." I drop it into my pile. Pavlova pads over and sniffs it. I wonder if she can still smell Julia. I can't.

"Just saying." Tommy's smiling.

"I don't care if it's itchy. I like it," I say. "I've always liked it."

"If you're going to bring Julia home," Tommy says, "I guess you might as well wear all her clothes now." He pulls out a shimmery camisole the color of honey. "You're not going to wear her underwear, though, are you?"

I smile. "Probably not. But hers *are* nicer than mine."

Tommy steps closer and boops me on the nose with his finger.

"Des Moines," he says. This is our joke, our special code. If we don't make it into the studio company we say we'll end up together in some second- or third-tier company across the country: Albuquerque or Pittsburgh, if we're lucky. Maybe Fargo, North Dakota. Fairbanks, Alaska. I haven't looked into the possibilities, but Tommy always has a somewhat-obscure American city at the tip of his tongue. There aren't even ballet companies in most of them, at least I don't think so. Maybe we'll move somewhere and we won't even be dancers. We'll just be normal people.

"Des Moines," I say. "Where's that again?"

"Iowa." Tommy raises his eyebrows. "Cornfields and pigs."

I smile. "I can't wait."

It's almost true. Give me a home where the buffalo roam, or something.

"Are you sure you have everything?" Tommy says. He's

holding one of Julia's old black leotards. "Are you ready for any situation that comes your way?"

"I don't need a leotard," I say. "That's for sure."

"Are you certain you're not going to have to break into spontaneous dance? Maybe your half of that pas de deux from *Giselle*? You can pretend I'm there with you."

"I hate that pas de deux from *Giselle*," I say.

"I know," says Tommy. "Hang on." He disappears down the hallway to my room.

"Where are you going?" I call, but he doesn't answer. And then I'm alone in Julia's room, like I haven't been in years. I stand over her dresser and pick up a jar of seashells, the tiny ones that look like butterfly wings when they're still attached in pairs. There's a photograph here of Julia and Everett when they were maybe five and seven, sitting on the dock at my aunt's lake house in the Catskills. They have the same dark wavy hair, the same wide smiles. I didn't even exist when that picture was taken. At the dresser top's edge, there's a small enameled pillbox with Van Gogh's almond branches on it, delicate, white-flowered branches crisscrossing over peacock-blue sky. I know this box, because once, I brought my sister trouble in it.

That was when Julia was about to dance her third performance as Aurora in *Sleeping Beauty*. I was in the performance too, as one of the Lilac Fairy's attendants. I sat next to her in the dressing room and watched in the mirror as she streaked blush across her cheeks.

"Can you get Thatcher for me?" she asked. "He's in the lobby." Her skin was pale under the makeup. She glowed silver in the mirror.

"I don't think I'm supposed to be walking around like this, Jules." I swept my arms as wide as my tutu.

"Sylvie, it's fine. He has something for me." She took out her phone and tapped the screen with both thumbs, spelling out a message.

Grace appeared in the doorway. A wreath of pale blue flowers crowned her head.

"Jules," she said. "I'm going down there."

My sister nodded, but she didn't look toward Grace. "I'll be there in a few minutes," she said.

I saw Grace frown then, just for a second or so, before she smoothed out her face and smiled at me.

"Looking good, kid," she said. "Lilac's lucky to have you."

"Thanks," I said.

In the hallway, Grace headed one way and I went the other.

Out in the lobby, I was a small fairy in the midst of mortals. White-haired grandmothers smiled at me, and a little girl reached out to touch the edge of my skirt. I was afraid that seeing me would break the magic spell of ballet for them, but they didn't seem to mind. I wasn't a fairy; I was just a girl. They could plainly see that.

I saw Thatcher standing at the edge of the crowd, his back against the wall. I called his name, and somehow, he heard me. He smiled and strode over, weaving around the people coming in.

"Here," he said, handing me a small, smooth metal box. His fingers were warm as they brushed my own. "Tell her I said good luck. Thanks, Sylvie."

On my way back through the hallways, I examined the box. I recognized it. Julia had bought it when we were in Amsterdam four years ago, the only vacation she'd taken with us in recent history. In the hallway, I didn't open the box. But I didn't have to. I had an idea of what was inside.

Back in the dressing room, Jules was alone. Everyone else must have been warming up.

"Thanks, kiddo." She crushed me into a hug. "Go find the rest of your fairy girls."

She smiled at me and sat still until I left. She didn't open the box.

Now I catch my reflection in Julia's mirror, and I reach out and touch the glass. When I pull my fingers away again I see my fingerprints over my own face. And this is when I hear her voice—I know it's her—say my name.

Sylvie.

The door creaks behind me, opening wider. For a split second, I almost believe it could be her.

But when I turn, it's just Tommy, of course, carrying my most recent pair of toe shoes.

"What's wrong?" he asks.

"Nothing," I say.

"Okay." He holds out the shoes, which are near the end of their life cycle, gray with dirt.

"Take these," he says, "for good luck." He pinches his nose, smiling. "Though they're a little stinky and pretty much trashed."

I shake my head, but he doesn't pay attention. I can still feel my tattoo hot on my skin, and I watch as he tucks them into my bag, deep down under the clothes, where I'll put Julia's book later, before I leave. For some reason, I let him.

PART TWO

There Once Was a Girl

(WITH SONGS BY
FLEETWOOD MAC)

TRACK 1:

Don't Stop

IT'S ONLY WHEN I COME up from 181st Street station that I start to feel like I'm on the run. Like I've done something illegal and I have to flee the scene of the crime. Things I could have done:

1. Stolen the world's largest diamond in a late-night heist.
2. Freed all the penguins at the Central Park Zoo.
3. Shot a man in Reno just to watch him die.

But really all I've done so far is skipped out on Fancy Dance Camp, and that's not a capital offense. At least as far as I know.

I am off to find my sister, though, and that feels dangerous enough.

The sun is shimmery white and high in the sky and the sidewalks here are alpine steep. I'm at the top—or the middle, maybe—of Washington Heights' hill, and a breeze pushes me gently down the slope in the direction of Sadie and Jack's place. I set

Pavlova's bag down on the sidewalk and unzip it. She comes tumbling out, licks my fingers and puts her paws on my knees. I snap on her leash.

It's warm out, but I'm still wearing the cardigan I took from Julia's drawer last night. It's soft and loose enough in the sleeves that it doesn't bother my wrist, but it also hides both the tattoo and the irritated skin around it. I don't feel like explaining anything to Jack. At least not right away.

A few minutes later, I'm standing on the concrete in front of their building on Cabrini Boulevard, looking way up to the top, to the rim of the roof where I stood a few days ago. I can see the café table and matching chairs on the patio below and I wonder, if I had fallen, is that where I would have landed? Or is there a chance I could have dove straight down to the ground?

"Hey." A voice calls from behind me. I jump in a supremely undignified way and spin around to see Jack leaning against the side of his car.

"Hi." I'm standing awkwardly, my arms at my sides. Pavlova trots right over to Jack and starts sniffing his shoe so intently that it might as well be the last clue in a mystery she's been trying to solve for months. He looks down at her for a long moment. I hold my breath.

"Soooo," Jack says, drawing out the word. "You brought your dog."

I smile. "Oh." I look down at Pavlova, her nose still glued to his sneaker laces. "You noticed."

The look on Jack's face isn't exactly a smile, but it might be approaching that general vicinity. "I'm observant like that," he says.

"She'll be good," I say. "I swear." This is more a wild hope than something I have any actual reason to believe. Pavlova has spent barely any time in a car in her entire five-year-long life, and she is an intense canine companion even under the best of circumstances.

"I brought a blanket," I say. I crouch down on the sidewalk and dig around in my bag to pull it out. "See?"

Jack nods, somewhat suspiciously.

"Don't you like dogs?"

"I like dogs," he says. "I'm just not sure I like them in the Volvo." He crouches down to pet Pavlova, who rises up on her hind legs and dances a little. She's trembling with happiness.

"That's what we call it?" I ask. "The Volvo?"

Jack stands up. "That's what it is. It's Latin for *I roll*."

Latin. Hmmm. "Okay," I say, "but normally people just call their cars 'car.'"

"Normally," Jack says, "people don't drive Volvos."

I wait a moment, looking at him. I blink. "Um," I say, "I'm pretty sure lots of people drive Volvos."

"Not this one," Jack says, shaking his head.

What a weirdo.

This is going *so* well.

"Okay," I say. I look at the Volvo. It's a car, that's for sure. Black and boxy. Old-looking, with tan leather seats. Says Volvo on the back, to the left of the license plate. Nothing special about it as far as I can see.

"Do you want to put your bag in the trunk?" Jack asks. "Or just in the back seat?"

I think for a moment. "Back seat," I say. "It might help keep Pavlova, um, contained."

Jack grimaces, but tries to hide it. He opens the door and I toss my bag in.

"Thanks for doing this," I say.

"Sure," he says. "So, Princeton first?" He leans his hip against the car. Sadie must have filled him in on some specifics.

"Yeah. My cousin Rose lives there. She's in grad school." I feel like I'm bragging. But I should be allowed to brag about my smart cousin if I want.

"Okay," he says.

"I know it seems weird that I have to go all the way to New Jersey to talk to her when, you know, cell phones are a thing." I pull mine from my pocket and give it a shake.

"Sadie explained."

"Oh," I say. "Okay." What I want to know is *how* Sadie explained, because even though I decided to do it myself, I don't think *I* totally understand why. But then Jack answers.

"She said she told you that you have to go right to them, or you'll never be sure they're telling you the truth." He smiles. "She said you have to look them dead in the eye."

"Right. She convinced me."

"Yeah," he says. "My sister is intense."

Jack opens the door, then, and gets into the car. I walk around to the other side and do that too.

"Anyway," he says, "I'm heading south either way, so it doesn't matter if I have a passenger." He pauses. "*Two* passengers."

"Ha," I say, not a laugh but the actual word. Because I'm not awkward at all.

Jack adjusts the mirror a tiny bit, then adjusts it again. Presumably he's the only one driving the car, since Sadie doesn't drive and their mom is away cooking for some family in the Hamptons, so yeah, it's clear he's a bit of a perfectionist about this car.

He puts it in gear and pulls away from the curb. "Honestly," he says, "I don't even want to go to my dad's. I'm doing it for Sadie."

I already know this, but I pretend I don't. "That's nice of you," I say.

"Yeah." Jack slows to let a woman with a stroller cross in the middle of the block. "Unless my dad breaks her heart again."

I don't know what to say to that, so I just settle back in my seat and look out the window. Nervousness fills my lungs like a mist, making it hard to breathe. I've never spent much time with Jack, and definitely not in such a small enclosed space. Even without the heavy dad talk, this would be strange enough.

It's not that I don't think Jack is cute. He is, objectively, cute. The green eyes, the floppy brown hair. I get it. But I don't necessarily want any of it. He was never interested in being my friend, not even from the first summer his mom brought him and Sadie out to my aunt's house in Montauk for the summer.

My aunt had hired Mrs. Allister as a personal chef, and I was thrilled that my best friend could come on vacation with us. Sadie and I were nine. We toasted marshmallows over bonfires in the yard and spied on Jack, who was usually reading books or riding his bike along the road by the bluffs. Sometimes Everett was there, but by that point, Julia was never with us on summer vacations. She was always dancing at intensives or at Fancy Dance Camp herself.

"You've never driven a car?" Jack asks.

"I'm only sixteen, as of a few days ago, so it's not really that surprising." I say this and then I regret it immediately. Am I trying to argue that I'm immature? I regroup.

"Plus," I say, "I live in New York, where you don't have to have a car." Message: I'm not immature, I'm a New Yorker. Therefore, I'm sophisticated.

He nods. "I know. My mom is not thrilled that my dad gave me this one. But I like it. Even if I don't like him."

I run my fingers along the bottom of the window frame. "So what's so special about it?"

"Well, for one thing," Jack says, his voice spreading out into that taking-his-time drawl of his, "I have paperbacks in the door pockets."

"You do?" I turn toward mine and pull out a copy of Kurt Vonnegut's *Slaughterhouse-Five*. And then, deeper, *God Bless You, Mr. Rosewater*. Also Vonnegut.

"What's in your door?" I ask.

He keeps his right hand on the wheel and slips the left into the door pocket. He pulls out two small paperbacks, *Cat's Cradle* and *Breakfast of Champions*. Three guesses who wrote those.

"Was there a sale on Vonnegut?" I say. "Like, fifty percent off if you buy everything from one shelf?"

Jack smiles his slow smile. "Something like that."

"Well, you're lucky I like him."

"Yes," Jack says. "*That* was a close one." He's smiling with half his mouth. He's making fun of me.

Pavlova hops down off the seat, then puts her paws up on the armrest between Jack and me. She's panting, and every so often she lets out a small whine.

"It's okay," I say to her. I twist around and pick her up. She settles in my lap.

"She hasn't spent a lot of time in a car," I explain. "Much like me."

Jack laughs. "Are you also going to start panting nervously?"

"Possibly." I smile then, a real smile that's dangerously close to a grin. "But I'll try to keep it under control."

If we can keep up the light banter, like a couple of sitcom characters or some actors in a 1930s screwball comedy, we can get through this trip.

There's a postal truck double-parked on the street in front of us and a tiny traffic jam beginning behind it. I shift in my seat.

"So, there's just one thing," Jack says.

I look at him. He's looking back. His face is serious.

"I'm only listening to Fleetwood Mac this month," he says.

"What?"

"Fleetwood Mac," he says again, as if that's an answer.

I tilt my head. "I've heard of them, yes."

He smiles. Someone ahead of us honks three times.

"I'm listening to one band per month this year," Jack says. "It's called the Artist of the Month Project."

I'm still looking at him. "You titled your project?"

"I mean, yeah. How else would I refer to it?" He flushes and looks ahead. The guy in front of us lays on the horn. There's no sign of the mailman who's holding us all hostage.

"Anyway, June is Fleetwood Mac." He takes one hand off the wheel and flutters it around a little. "The rule applies to the interior of this car, solely. I can't really control what happens outside of it." When he says this last part, he's basically talking to himself.

I wait. He glances over at me.

"Are you *kidding* me?" I say this so loudly that Pavlova lifts her head and lets out one sharp bark. "This car ride is going to be one giant multi-day Fleetwood Mac festival?"

"Hey, I'm doing *you* a favor here, remember?" Jack is smiling. Satisfied, maybe, that I'm flipping out.

Jerk.

We sit in silence for a moment. I watch the mailman come out of the building next to his truck. The guy in the car ahead of us actually shakes his fist at him. The mailman waves cheerfully.

"So why Fleetwood Mac?" I ask. "Why not, like, David Bowie or something?"

Jack's face is dead serious.

"Bowie was April."

"You're kidding."

"I'm not," he says. The car in front of us begins to move, and we do too. "Besides, what's wrong with Fleetwood Mac?"

"I don't know," I say. "Aren't they a little . . . cheesy?"

"No!" This is more than an exclamation. It's a sharp utterance of outrage. I look down at Pavlova, but she doesn't move.

"Whoa. Okay," I say, raising one palm in a gesture of surrender. "Yeesh."

"I just mean . . ." He thinks for a moment. "That's what people think about them. But I've listened to a lot of Fleetwood Mac this month—"

"Obviously," I say.

"—and they have really great songs." He signals and switches lanes. "Artist of the Month Project is the best way to really get to know a group's catalog."

"Exhaustively," I grumble.

He paves over this. "It's like time travel." Then his voice turns serious. "Though I should tell you, I'm exclusively listening to the post-1975 version of the band, the Buckingham/Nicks version, not the original band with Peter Green."

I look at him. "Now you're just saying words," I say. "Names."

"I want you to have the full understanding."

I sigh, but I'm smiling too. "All right. I do know that Stevie Nicks is fierce."

"She totally is," Jack says.

"Fine." I look at him. "I submit to your tyrannical control of the soundtrack."

"Thanks," Jack says. "There are only ten days left in June."

"And lucky me," I say. "I get to spend several of them with you."

Jack shrugs. He's smiling.

"What's July?" I ask.

"Prince," he says.

"August?"

"Aretha Franklin."

"I have terrible timing," I gripe.

Jack smiles with half his mouth and points quickly to his phone in the cup holder. "Let's start with 'Don't Stop,'" he says.

I scroll through the playlist and find the song. We're coming up on the bridge now and I see it stretching out in front of us, eight lanes under a beautiful gray latticed arch.

I press Play.

TRACK 2:

Save Me a Place

JUST BEFORE WE GET TO Princeton, my stomach growls. We got caught in traffic past the bridge, so we've been driving for nearly two hours. Suddenly, I'm starving, and I don't think I can make it to Rose's apartment without eating something. This *might* have something to do with my nervousness about confronting Rose, but it's manifesting as hunger and I'm going to go with it. Jack, on the other hand, seems to be nourished solely by the mellifluous melodies of Stevie and Lindsey.

My stomach growls again.

"So," I say.

Jack glances over. "So," he echoes.

"What if we stopped for something to eat?"

He raises his eyebrows. "Before we get there?"

"Yeah," I say. "If that doesn't break any of your rules. Are you eating only one kind of food this month?"

He smiles, just a little. "Luckily, I'm not. And anyway, we already broke the no-dogs-in-the-Volvo rule, so who knows what comes next?"

Just ahead of us, there's a small restaurant by the side of the road, a take-out place, it looks like, with picnic tables scattered over the patchy grass out front. Most of the tables are full of people eating, which seems like a good sign. Jack slows when he sees it.

"What do you think?" he asks.

"Sure," I say. "Let us take our repast at this charming shack!"

Jack gives me a Look, but he puts his turn signal on and pulls into the parking lot.

When I open the door, Pavlova hops out and starts peeing right away.

"Yikes," I say. "Thanks for waiting." She looks up at me, pant-grinning, still peeing.

Jack walks around the car to me. Pavlova stops peeing and gets super happy. He seems semi-charmed by it.

"You save the picnic table," Jack says. "I'll get the food."

I salute him. "Aye, aye, Captain."

He ignores me, but there's a tiny smile on his lips. "What do you want?"

"Somehow I doubt they have a veggie burger," I say. "Maybe just french fries? And also some kind of non-potato vegetable if they have one?"

Jack nods. "I'll do my best."

The table is weathered and gray. I sit down on one bench,

facing out, and pull Pavlova up next to me. My tattoo itches, and when I look at it it's a little red but it looks good. The blue-inked words are steady and true.

A seagull sails by now, screaming softly. It lands near my feet. It takes a few steps forward, and then a few hops back.

Another lands behind it. Then another. No one's told them that there's no sea for miles. They glide in, wings outstretched, hopping to a stop. Half a dozen, then a dozen more. Pavlova barks at them from the bench next to me, just one sharp bark, but they don't seem to care. They keep coming, keep hopping, keep looking at me. Every once in a while, one lets out a stifled cry.

"What is with you, birds?" I say through gritted teeth. "Not every fairy tale has an animal sidekick. And I'm not auditioning. Shoo!"

Just before the whole scene turns into something out of a Hitchcock movie, I see Jack heading across the lawn from the restaurant. As he gets closer, the seagulls back away. This makes Pavlova brave, and she hops off the bench and runs toward them, barking, until they scatter.

"Quite the fan club," he says when he gets to the table.

"Yeah," I say. "It's a thing lately."

"What is?"

"Birds," I say, and then I finish in my own head: *and wolf-dogs and maybe-princesses.* "They like me."

"Maybe you should see a doctor about that." He hands me a drink cup. "Dr Pepper."

I smile. "Dr. Dre."

"Dr. Who." Jack drops the bag of food on the table between us.

"Doctor Zhivago."

"Anyway," Jack says, sitting down, "they *did* have a veggie burger. Not so bad for a shack. And sweet potato fries, so I got you those. I hope they count as vegetables."

"They do," I say. "Thanks."

We eat in silence for a few minutes. Mercifully, the seagulls stay away, begging for food at other tables, and no other animals (squirrels) (chipmunks) (wide-winged albatrosses) come to replace them.

A little girl from the closest table starts to shadow Pavlova, who's walking circles on her long leash, sniffing for scraps. The girl turns her face toward me. She has a purple barrette in her dark hair and round nearly black eyes.

"You can pet her," I say, smiling, "but she might lick you."

The girl says nothing, but she crouches down by Pav and runs her hand gently from my dog's head to tail. Pav wiggles with happiness.

"She's a hit," Jack says. He takes a sip of his soda.

"She always is," I say. "I mean, almost. Except with people who are overly fussy about their cars."

Jack shakes his head, smiling.

"So," he says. "Ballet."

I laugh without meaning to. I don't know why—whether it's because my ballet life already seems so far away, or because the word sounds strange coming out of Jack's mouth. "What about it?"

He shrugs. "What's it like?"

"It's like flying," I say, "but it hurts. It's like making something really, really hard look completely effortless." I point my toes without meaning to. "Have you ever heard what it sounds like? Dancing in pointe shoes?"

Jack shakes his head.

"It's loud. Sounds like a herd of horses, clomping all over the stage. Pointe shoes aren't soft." I tap my sandal against the ground as if to demonstrate. "The music mostly covers it up. We're supposed to look like we're weightless." I think of how free it feels, leaving the earth for seconds at a time. It's like magic, or an illusion anyway. I wonder now if those two things are the same.

He picks up a french fry. "Sadie said that you'll only be going to school half days next year."

"Yeah. It's a pain to figure it all out. Maria Mitchell School is flexible enough, but they're not really used to this." Pavlova begs for a fry at my feet, and I drop one down to her. "They haven't had any other pre-professional dancers." Julia had gone to Maria Mitchell too, but she quit when she went into Level Seven, just started working with a tutor right away. I just can't imagine leaving school completely right now. If I did, I'd be admitting that it's ballet and nothing but ballet for me, for now and forever.

Pavlova puts her head on Jack's knee and sighs. He rubs her ears a little, and she closes her eyes and sneezes.

"Where did you get this creature?" he asks. "She's like a cartoon."

I laugh. "She totally is. She came from a rescue group that brings dogs up from the south. I think she's from Mississippi."

"She must have the dog version of a Southern accent."

"I'm sure she has a drawl," I say. "Or at least a decent recipe for corn bread. She was already about three years old when we adopted her. I have no idea what her life was like before then."

Jack's eyes fall on my wrist.

"New ink?" he says.

"It's my only ink," I say.

"Well, yeah, I figured." He touches my arm then, gently, just below my wrist. His touch is so unexpected that I breathe in sharply. "What's the story?" he asks.

What *is* the story, Sylvie?

Well, I was lured in by a song my brother used to listen to, and then I saw Sleeping Beauty, and I followed her for blocks and . . .

"It's just something I had to do," I say.

He nods. "I get it."

We finish our food. He stands up then, crumpling the cardboard box from his fries. "You ready?"

"Yep," I say. I watch him head toward the garbage can.

I gather my trash and toss it. Then I walk toward the car, giving the seagulls the side-eye until I'm inside and I shut the door.

TRACK 3:

I Don't Want to Know

A HALF HOUR LATER WE pull up in front of Rose's house, which is tall and blue and boxy, with huge red rosebushes out front. Jack turns off the car.

"This is it?" he asks.

I look down at my phone, like I'm checking, but I already know this is the right house from the GPS. And, you know, because of the big silver *523* hung over the door.

"Yep," I say. I don't move. I just keep looking at the house out the window. The sun illuminates a white awning over the porch, making it look like half the house is glowing.

"Now what?" Jack says, his voice low.

I slip my hand into my bag and feel the cover of the fairy tale book. Still there. I look at Jack.

I take a deep breath and let it out slowly. "We go in," I say.

When I knock, it takes Rose about thirty seconds to appear. She opens the door wide and steps out onto the stoop. She looks at me and I look at her: the same beautiful Rose, her hair red and wild, freckles sprinkled in constellations over her ivory skin.

"Sylvie," she says. "What the hell are you doing here?" She pulls me into a hard hug before I can answer, so I just press my face into her bony shoulder and hug her back. When she lets me go it's with the same kind of force. She flings me backward, then looks right into my face.

"What's wrong?" she says.

"Nothing," I say, though of course that isn't true. A hundred things are wrong. A million. "I need to ask you something."

"So you drove all the way here?"

I nod. "Well, Jack did."

She turns toward Jack and squints a little. She's suspicious. Then she looks back to me.

"You *do* have a telephone, right?"

"Yeah." I look down at my purse. It's in there, obviously. I don't take it out.

Rose is tapping her bare foot like an old woman in a movie, impatient and wary. I shift my weight on her doorstep.

"Can we just come in?"

"Fine," Rose says. "Who's this?"

"This is Jack." I gesture toward him. "Like I said."

"Hi," he says. He steps forward to shake her hand.

"You said his name," she says. "I mean who *is* he?"

"Oh. Do you remember my best friend, Sadie?" I say. "This is her brother. Their mom is Renata, who cooks for us sometimes."

At this, Rose finally smiles. "She made tart cherry pie for us the last time I was there."

"Exactly," I say. I know Rose has a major sweet tooth. Cherry pie for the win.

"So why is he here with you?" She's squinting again.

"He's my ride," I say.

Rose lets out a frustrated sigh. She reaches out and ruffles my hair as if I'm six years old again, still following her and Julia around.

"All right," she says. "Come in." She steps aside and we follow.

Edge of Seventeen

ROSE'S APARTMENT IS ON THE first floor, all warm golden wood and wide windows. An orange striped cat walks over to us, tail held high as a flag. She bops my leg with her head. Pavlova is struggling to get out of my arms but I don't let her.

"That's Ruth Bader Ginsburg," Rose says to me. "RBG, this is Sylvie and Jack."

"Supremely pleased to meet you, Justice," Jack says to the cat. He ignores my groan, bending down to run a hand across her back. "I'm a big fan."

Rose looks at me over the top of Jack's head. She's frowning just a bit, still suspicious, but I think she's softening. He may win her over with his love of liberal Supreme Court justices.

"Will she mind it if I let Pavlova down? She loves all animals. Maybe too much."

"Ruth can handle it."

I set Pav down on the floor. Her nails skitter across the wood as she dashes over to the cat. Who can certainly handle it, if *handle it* means leaping to the top of the closest bookcase, then looking down, hissing. Pavlova barks in frustration.

Rose is unfazed.

"Do you want something to drink?" she asks. "I have lemonade." She pulls a glass pitcher from the refrigerator, and I can see lemon slices floating inside it.

"Actual homemade lemonade?" I ask.

Rose nods. "It's part of my procrastination process. I have research I'm trying hard to avoid today." She smiles. "Might as well squeeze a dozen lemons. And I didn't even know I was going to have company."

She pours three glasses, and then motions over to her green velvet couch.

"Sorry about the cat hair," she says.

I sit down. Pavlova hops up next to me. "It's okay. Soon there will be dog hair too."

"Right," Rose says. "Now tell me why the hell you're here."

I look at Jack. There's a hint of a smile on his face.

"Um." I take a deep breath. "I think you lied when I asked you about Julia." I watch her face as I say this, but her expression doesn't change. "I think—I know—she was here for a while."

I'm bluffing—I don't really *know* that, exactly—but apparently I should be a poker player or a police detective, because Rose tells the truth immediately.

"For a week and a half," she says, nodding a little. "Last

summer." She pushes a lock of hair behind her ear. "Then she left in the goddamn middle of the night."

"I'm finding out that's kind of what she does," I say. "She didn't say goodbye?"

"No," Rose says. "She was in rough shape when she was here."

"Using?" I ask this even though I'm afraid of the answer.

"No." Rose sounds sure when she says this, but then she frowns. "I don't think so. I think I would have known." She sounds less certain by the end.

"I want to find her," I say.

"Why?" Rose's voice is even-toned, a little flat.

I look at Rose. "She's my sister. I want to know she's okay." *And, while I'm at it, I want to know why she sent me this book and I'm suddenly chasing Sleeping Beauty down West 14th Street.*

Rose's mouth draws into a hard line. "Sylvie. Chances are she's not okay. Have you considered that?"

"Yes," I say. (*No. Not really.*)

"So be careful what you wish for." She squints at me. "Does Aunt Elizabeth know where you are?"

I look down at my bare feet and then back at Rose. "She's in Paris with my dad."

"So she thinks you're where?"

"Um," I say. "Dance camp in New Jersey? But I called and canceled. I—"

Rose holds up a stop-sign hand. "You know what? I don't want to know. The fewer details I have the better. Plausible deniability."

She sighs. "Do you have somewhere to stay?"

I smile. I've got her. "The car?"

"Jesus, kid." She's shaking her head. "The couch pulls out. Jack sleeps on the floor, and as far as your mom goes, I never saw you, okay? The last thing I need is to hear it from *my* mother."

"Thank you, Rose. I'll make sure Aunt Katie doesn't find out."

"You better," she says.

Later, Rose orders pizza and we eat it out on her patio, a small square of concrete with a picnic table and blue striped umbrella. Farther back is a yard full of shrubs and flowers. Next to us is a fence wound with fairy lights, glowing gold like a field of stars against the chain link.

My tattoo is so itchy I can barely keep from scratching the hell out of it. I press my fingers to it, hoping the pressure will help. Then I let go.

When I do, I realize that Rose is looking at my wrist.

"Oh my god," she says. "Is that real?"

Instead of looking at my cousin, I look at the tattoo. It looks like Julia's tattoo. My wrist looks like Julia's wrist.

"Yeah," I say.

"You're sixteen, Syl!" Rose says. "What are you even doing?" She looks right into my eyes, then, and I don't look away. My stomach feels hollow.

"I don't really know," I say.

Between her fingers, Rose holds my wrist, the one without a

tattoo on it. She squeezes so hard it hurts.

"Well, stop it," she says. "Okay? Just stop it. I know you, okay? And you . . . you're not her."

My heart sinks at the words.

I've never heard anything so true in my life.

TRACK 5:

Say You Love Me

WHEN WE FINISH EATING, ROSE gets up and walks toward the back fence to examine a trellis.

"Come here," she calls. I get up and Jack does too. When we get to Rose, we stop and look.

"See that?" she asks. She's pointing to a long narrow bud, mostly green but white at its end.

"Yeah," I say.

Rose steps back. "Now watch it."

I look at her instead, because why the hell is she asking me to watch a plant? She widens her eyes, points toward the bud again in her bossy-pants way. I turn back.

The three of us are crowded together in front of the trellis, looking at I don't know what. Minutes pass. I'm standing so close to

Jack I can feel the warmth of his shoulder through his T-shirt, and just as I'm about to pull away the bud starts to tremble.

It twists itself open, unraveling and flattening out like a small white parachute. It's ruffled at the edges, pinwheel-shaped. So purely white it seems to glow. My heart drops out like an elevator in free fall—it's happening again, this fox-and-bird/flora-and-fauna weirdness—and I turn to look at Jack.

"Are you . . . seeing this?"

He nods. He's smiling, amazed.

So I'm *not* losing my hold on reality, at least not at this moment.

"They're moonflowers," Rose says. "Aren't they amazing?"

"Wait. Moonflowers?" I ask.

"Little werewolf flora. They come out with the moon."

"So they just *do* this?" I ask.

Rose nods. "Magic," she says.

"Science," says Jack, nearly under his breath. His standard line. He wanders farther down the fence, inspecting the other buds wound tightly and waiting to open. When he gets far enough away, Rose leans toward me, puts her lips right up to my ear.

"I didn't bring you out here because it's romantic," she says, pulling me back over to the table. "Remember: Jack sleeps on the *floor*." She sounds so fierce that I look at her, concerned, but she's trying to hold back a smile. She's messing with me.

"You don't have to worry about that," I say. "He doesn't even like me."

Rose shrugs. "That doesn't always matter," she says. She settles into her chair and picks up her glass. "Anyway, I'm pretty sure you're wrong."

My phone rings then, a long ring like an old-fashioned rotary phone. The one I picked for my mother.

"It's my mom," I say.

Rose sets her glass on the table with a clink. "Well, answer."

"I can't," I say. "Not while you're watching me." The phone is still ringing, patiently, long trills that say, *You can't ignore me forever.*

Rose lets out a dramatic sigh. "Come on, Jack. Let's give Sylvie the patio so she can continue her subterfuge."

He stands up and follows her. Just before she opens the door, she looks back in my direction.

"I have ice cream," she says. "Keep it short and sweet."

"Hi, Sylvie," my mother says when I answer. Her voice on the phone sounds far away and echoey, like she's speaking to me from down a corridor.

"Hi, Mom."

"Did you get in all right?" she asks. "I feel bad that I couldn't take you. I always liked that drive to New Jersey."

"It was fine," I say. "I'm all settled in."

"I'm glad," she says. It's amazing the way she believes me, no matter what, even after Julia spent the better part of two years lying. I guess she came to expect it from my sister, but never from me.

"It's so late there," I say. "Why are you still awake?"

"Oh, I couldn't sleep. I'm outside. There's a small terrace off our hotel room." I try to picture it: wrought iron, shadowy cobblestone street, gold lamplight. "It's a little chilly, but lovely anyway."

I picture her wrapped in her favorite ash-gray cardigan.

"Is Dad sleeping?"

"Like a log. As usual." She laughs.

"What can you see from there?"

"Oh," she says. Her voice sounds happy. She loves this game. We used to play it whenever she and my father were away. She'd describe the snowy peaks of the Alps, the narrow side streets of Berlin, the beach in Capri. "I can see the building across the way. It's gray stone, with these beautiful windows. And below"—she's leaning over the edge, I can tell—"a stone street and a tiny red Italian car."

I close my eyes for a moment. I can see it too: the stone, the street, the car. I wish I were there on the terrace with my mother. Maybe I'd tell her that I've been sitting too close to the edge of things, lately. That I can't seem to stay away from places where I could fall.

"What do you see?" she asks.

"Moonflowers." I say this without thinking about it, and then I panic. There are no moonflowers at Fancy Dance Camp, at least not that I remember. Though my mother can't know that, can she?

Anyway, she just repeats the word. "Moonflowers," she says dreamily.

"There's a trellis," I say. "Outside my cabin."

Right in front of me, another moonflower bud trembles, then shudders open, stretching its petals outward. I don't care what Jack says. This *is* magic.

"Have you ever seen a moonflower open?" I ask.

"I haven't."

"It happens all at once," I say. "Like, *pop*! It's incredible."

"That must be lovely." My mother's voice sounds sleepy. "Actually, it's getting late for you too, honey. I should have waited until tomorrow to call. I just wanted to make sure you got in all right. I missed you."

"I miss you too, Mom."

There's an ache in my heart like a creaky door, and I think about all the things I should have told my mother and never did, about how I knew what was going on. About what it was like when Julia hurt herself. I consider telling her now.

Instead, this is what I say: ( ).

I let the quiet hiss on the call fill the space in our conversation until my mother speaks again.

"Good night, Sylvie," she says.

I wait a moment. The moonflower glows. "Good night," I say.

I listen for the click of her hanging up but I don't hear it. My mother's there—on the other end of the satellite—and then she's gone.

TRACK 6:

I Know I'm Not Wrong

THE MOON HAS RISEN OVER Rose's house, a round white pearl in the near-black sky. I'm still sitting out here on a bench with the moon-flowers, several of them splayed open against their heart-shaped leaves. The air is full of cricket-song.

I hear flip-flop footsteps behind me that I know are Rose's, but I don't turn around. She stands next to me for a moment. I can hear her breathing, and my own heart in my ears.

"Sylvie." She lays her fingertips lightly on my shoulder. "What are you really doing here?"

"I already told you."

"I know what you told me." Rose sighs. "Listen—"

Rose is one of the most capable people I've ever met. She's always known what she wants to do: become an urban planner so she can help make cities a better place to live, and help make life easier for the people with the least power and money. She literally wants to keep people safe. So it's no surprise: here comes a lecture about leaving this Julia thing alone, or why I shouldn't have run out on Fancy Dance Camp in the first place. But honestly, I don't want to hear it.

"Rose," I say. "Please. Just let me sit here." I look up at her. "Or sit here with me."

I expect her to say no, or to sigh theatrically, but she doesn't. She just sits down next to me, so close our shoulders are touching.

"Okay," she says.

Rose was in New York visiting us the day Julia tore her hip flexor, what we call "the accident." She'd had surgery on her knee before, of course, but that was a wear-and-tear injury, not one terrible day.

Rose wasn't at the studio, though. I was, in technique class, sweaty and dirty from floor stretches. Julia's friend Henry appeared in the doorway, his mouth drawn into a line. Miss Charlotte stopped the class, and we all stood there at the bar, staring at Henry. He said my name.

"Sylvie," he said. "Come with me."

His voice was like an ice cube pressed against my temple. I blinked, and the studio lights turned into flashbulbs, flashing dizzyingly.

When I got to the doorway, Henry took my hand. That's how I knew it was bad. When we got closer to Julia I could hear her crying, her voice a thin wail. We were nearly running by then, Henry and I, and I was crying too, but silently. I couldn't make myself peek at Henry to see how his face looked. What I'd seen in the studio was enough.

When we burst through the doorway I stopped. Miss Diana was kneeling next to Julia stroking her hair. Her face was completely drained of color.

"We called an ambulance," she said, and I walked toward them without even trying to move my legs. It just happened, like they were magnetic north and I was a compass needle. Miss Diana had answered a question I didn't know I was asking. I saw it in her eyes: the certainty. She knew Julia wouldn't dance again. Not like before, anyway. It was over.

I wobbled and knelt down next to my sister. I thought I might throw up on the worn wood floor.

"Sylvie," Julia wailed. Then she switched to a whisper. "Sylvie, Sylvie, Sylvie."

All she could say was my name and I couldn't say anything at all.

I put my hand in hers and she squeezed it so hard I thought my fingers would break, but I let her. I didn't know that the painkillers had kept her body from knowing when it had had enough. They had let her push herself past breaking. Still, my heart was busy crystalizing, cracking into hard little pieces. Getting ready for what was going to come next.

In the garden, Rose shifts next to me, then kicks off her flip-flops. She leans closer to me, so I can feel a real pressure from her shoulder against mine.

I wonder if Rose knows what I'm thinking about. I wonder if

she's thinking about it too: the way she met us at the hospital with my parents, standing between them with her face stained with tears. The way she pulled me away from my sister and left the three of them with the doctor. The way I cried until I fell asleep in the waiting room, my head in Rose's lap. I wished then that she'd tell me that it was going to be okay, but I didn't ask her to, and I don't think she was ready to lie.

"I'm sorry," Rose says.

I lean into her one millimeter more. "I know," I say.

TRACK 7:

That's Enough for Me

ROSE GOES TO BED AT eleven after setting Jack and me up with sheets and pillows. I've decided not to pull the couch out, as it seems weird to sleep up there in a double bed while Jack sleeps on the floor, and it would be weirder still to offer to share the bed. Plus, in that scenario I would face the wrath of Rose. So I'm tucked in on the couch with a pink flowered sheet, Pavlova curled against my side. When Jack comes back from the bathroom with his toothbrush in his hand, he lies down on top of Rose's old camp sleeping bag, then shakes a flowered sheet of his own out across his body.

I hear a car drive down the street playing a samba beat. Its headlights trace across the wall.

"Are you okay down there?" I ask.

"I'm fine," he says.

"I'm sure it's not very comfortable." I prop myself up on my elbow and look down at him. "Maybe we should switch spots."

He shakes his head. "No, stay there. My only worry is that Ruth Bader Ginsburg here is going to end up sleeping on my head." He's smiling.

"You're talking about the cat, right?" I tease.

"The cat, yeah."

"Because if the real RBG shows up be sure to wake me." I flop back on the mattress. "I want to be a part of it."

"Noted," Jack says.

The ceiling fan spins above us. I feel like we're waiting for something, but I'm not sure what.

"Thanks again for doing this," I say. "Driving me, I mean."

"You're welcome," he says. "Like I said, it's not a big deal. It's on the way, basically."

"Yeah, but . . ." I wait, and the silence says, *Why not?* "I know you don't really like me." I don't know what makes me say this. Maybe because I can feel it, same as I always have, and I know he'd just as soon drive to his dad's on his own. I'm a stowaway, a ride-along. And I can be braver here in the half dark.

"Sylvie, I like you fine."

"No, you don't. You never have." It's easy, somehow, to say this to Jack now, when I can look at the ceiling fan instead of him. When we've been together all day.

"So why is it?" I ask. "Am I not good enough for Sadie? I'm honestly just curious."

"That's ridiculous," he says.

"It's not." I shake my head, though he can't see it.

"Do you really want to know?"

My stomach contracts a little. "Yes."

He pauses. "I have a problem with the dynamics of our families."

"I don't even know what that means," I say. I turn to my side again and look at him. "Our mothers are friends!"

"Do you really believe that?" Jack raises himself up onto his elbows. "Our family is completely beholden to yours. Your mother gets all these jobs for my mom, cooking for other rich ladies, making appetizers for their parties. She got Sadie a scholarship to your school. She would have done the same for me if I'd let her."

I almost say, *But it's a girls' school*. But I know he doesn't mean that my mother would have gotten him into Maria Mitchell. He means she would have gotten him in somewhere else, somewhere comparable.

"You didn't need help," I say. "You got into a great high school."

"Right." Jack lowers himself back down. "That's the point."

I don't know what to say, so I don't say anything for a minute. I can hear Rose's refrigerator humming in the kitchen. Then I take a breath.

"What's wrong with wanting to help someone?" I say.

"Nothing. But it's not always easy for the one who needs the help." He shakes his head a little. "Listen. Your mom's nice. But there's no way she understands what it's like for my mom. For our family. Your mom grew up rich, and she stayed that way." He looks at me. "My mom raised Sadie and me mostly alone."

He says this like I don't already know it. Like Sadie's not my best friend.

"Yeah, well, it's not like my mother's life is perfect," I say. I think of how lost she seems sometimes, underneath her impeccable veneer. The kind of lost you get when something huge is missing from your life.

"No one's life is perfect," Jack says. "But some people get a hell of a lot closer to it than others."

I don't know what to say to this. He's not wrong, but it doesn't feel right, exactly, either. Suddenly, I think I might cry. I breathe in and out as evenly as I can until the feeling is gone. Or if not gone, totally, pushed far enough away that I can't feel it hovering anymore.

"I'm going to sleep," I say.

"Okay," Jack says.

I turn my head to my left, toward the picture window that looks out over the yard. It's wide open, just a screen between us and the night. The purple flowers of the rhododendron bush are lit up in the moonlight, neon-bright against the deep green leaves. I'm watching a silver moth fly in a spiral in front of them when something huge and feathery swings into view, landing on the branches without making a sound. An owl.

It's enormous, easily the biggest bird I've ever seen. It folds up its wings and sits there, its round gold eyes looking right at me. I squeeze my own eyes shut and when I open them, it's still there. I can't make it disappear.

It's real, or at least I think it is, and I'm not going to ask Jack. I lift one hand to wave and it shakes out its wings like that's an answer. Then it lifts off toward the sky.

Pavlova twitches in her sleep, runs a few steps in a dream, her legs moving over the sheet. I hear Jack's voice again.

"Sylvie," he says. His voice is barely more than a whisper.

I take a breath as quietly as I can. I don't know what he's going to say, and I don't really want to. I let him think I'm already asleep.

TRACK 8:

That's All for Everyone

IN THE MORNING, ROSE STANDS next to me on the sidewalk in sandals and a dark blue sleeveless dress. The breeze blows her curls around her shoulders and her skirt around her knees. Somewhere behind me, Jack is loading our bags back into the Volvo.

I managed to get through our toast-and-jam breakfast without making eye contact with him. (This required lavishing much extra attention on Pavlova and the feline RBG, which is fine.) Right now, I'm not sure how I'm going to get through the rest of this day, much less the rest of this trip. Rose is onto me.

"Go easy," she says, her voice low.

"On what?" I ask.

"On the boy." She tilts her head. "He's growing on me."

I feel my cheeks flush. "Yeah, well, he's doing the opposite to me. He's . . . shrinking on me."

Rose smiles a lopsided smile. "He told me about that."

I feel a rush of heat through my body. My tattoo blooms with pain. "What? When?"

"You were in the shower."

"Really? So you're best friends now?" I sound like a brat and I know it, but I can't seem to stop myself.

"No. I could tell something was bothering him, so I asked. I'm nosy. You know that."

She smiles. I don't.

"You sure are," I say.

"Think about it, Syl." She runs her hand over the branches of the bush closest to her. "He has a point. And I think he feels bad about saying it, under the circumstances."

"He should," I say. I don't even think that's true, but I'm just trying to find my footing lately. I don't need people making it harder for me to do that.

"Okay," says Rose. Her voice is so calm, so *kind*, even, that I think I might cry. Again. But before I can decide one way or another, Jack walks over.

"Thanks, Rose," he says. He puts out his hand for her to shake it, but instead she pulls him in for a hug. He looks happily surprised.

"Take care of my Sylvie," she says when she lets him go.

He flushes a little, glances at me. "I'll do my best."

"I'm right here," I say, waving my hand. "I can take care of myself."

"Obviously," says Rose. "But it's not a bad thing to have some help."

The ice in my heart melts a little. I uncross my arms. My tattoo twinges again.

"I'll be in the car," Jack says. I don't watch him walk away, but I hear the door open and shut again. He'll probably start reading Vonnegut while he's waiting. There isn't much else to do in there, besides listen to freaking Fleetwood Mac.

Sigh.

"Thanks," I say to Rose. I turn to face her. "For everything."

"I didn't do much," she says. Her freckles make a Milky Way across her cheeks. I smile without trying.

"You didn't turn me in," I say. "That's something."

She smiles and leans forward, taking my chin in her right hand. "I'll never turn you in, cowgirl."

I make a face. "Cowgirl?"

"Imagine an Old West–type setting," Rose says, letting go of my chin and sweeping her arm toward the lawn. "The sheriff is approaching. That sort of thing."

"Okay."

She furrows her brow. "I need to know you're going to be careful," she says. "Because otherwise I'm going to have to come with you, and then I'll lose my summer position and fail out of grad school, and it'll be all your fault."

"No pressure," I say.

Rose smiles. "None at all."

The wind blows my hair over my shoulders. I can hear a bird somewhere, singing, its voice repeating *too-wheet, too-wheet.* (Thought: I'm glad he's speaking birdsong and not English. When I start understanding what the birds are saying, that's when I'll know I really have a problem.) I look at Rose.

Here's what I want to say: *I'm tired of people telling me to be careful.*

Here's what I say: "Of course, I'll be careful."

Rose nods. "Because can you imagine?" My cousin's eyes are wide. "If something happens to you and Aunt Elizabeth finds out I knew? Between your mom and mine, I would be completely and utterly dead."

"You totally would be," I say.

She puts her palms on either side of my face and squeezes a little. "Don't let anything happen to you."

"Okay," I say. Rose lets go of my cheeks.

"I think I know why she left," I say, too quickly, my words tripping over themselves. "She didn't want to let us down."

"Maybe," Rose says. "But she did. She did let us all down." She doesn't sound angry, or even sad. Just certain.

I pull the fairy tale book out of my bag. Rose needs to know the whole story.

"She sent this," I say. "For my birthday, I think. Look." I flip to the endpapers first, and show Rose her name among the others.

"Who's Daniela?" she asks.

"I don't know. I thought maybe you would."

She shakes her head. I take the book back from her and then flip to the front, show her the *Girls in Trouble* on the title page. Rose squints a little, like the sun is hurting her eyes. Then she looks up at me and hands the book back.

"Sylvie, I meant what I said in the text a couple of days ago.

It might be easier for you if you find a way to let Jules go. Maybe she'll come back and maybe she won't, but what is the point of all of us torturing ourselves about it?" The breeze blows Rose's curls into her face, and she stops to push them out. "She's an addict, Syl. You have to remember that."

My molecules start their swirling, every electron doing a pas de deux with its closest neighbor. "She wasn't always."

"No." Rose sighs. "But she is now. That's the Julia we have from now on, even if she's sober. Always."

She's right, I know: there's no going back in time for Julia, or for any of us. But I don't think life is unchangeable. Or at the very least, I'm determined to find a way to change it.

I open my mouth to reply to Rose—I don't even know what I'm going to say—but I can't because she crushes me into one of her violent hugs. While she's crushing me, I let out all the breath I've been holding, finally. Maybe Rose squeezes it out. Either way, when she lets me go, I feel like I can keep going.

Rose looks right at my face, her eyes intense.

"You're going to Thatcher next?" she asks.

I nod.

She sets her mouth in a straight line. "Give him a kick in the crotch for me."

I laugh then, one sharp sound that's as much out of relief as anything else. This is Rose's blessing on my journey, basically, telling me to maim Julia's ex-boyfriend.

"Will do," I say.

"As for the boy," she says, her voice a loud whisper, "same advice. Be safe."

I glance at the car. Jack is looking at us, but he turns his head away when he sees me see him.

"Rose, we're not dating," I say.

She smiles. "Yeah," she says, giving me a gentle shove toward the Volvo. "Whatever you say."

I get in the car.

"Hi," I say to Jack.

"Hi," he echoes.

Great start, team! Pavlova's in his lap (traitor), though she hops over the armrest to me after I put my seat belt on.

When we pull away from the curb I wave to Rose out the window, and she waves back. She stands there on the sidewalk, still waving, ready to watch us drive away until she can't see us anymore.

TRACK 9:

Over My Head

IN THE CAR, WE DON'T talk. Jack asks me to start the Fleetwood Mac bonanza for the day, and I press Play on his phone, but that's it. I spend the time watching trees out the window. Pavlova spends the time sleeping in my lap.

Before we get too far past the suburbs of Trenton, I've convinced myself that I've made a huge mistake coming on this trip with Jack. I should have just taken a bus. I feel lonely and lost, traveling just under sixty-five miles an hour (no speeding!) down a highway with a boy who resents me.

This is when my phone chimes a text. Tommy.

Bored, it says. **And full of smoothies.**

Then below it, in its own little bubble: **Miss you.**

"Oh my god." An idea announces itself in my head and refuses to leave. I look at Jack. He glances over at me for just a second. He looks relieved, I think, that words are actually coming out of my mouth.

"We're basically driving straight past Fancy Dance Camp." I hold up my phone with the map, but of course Safe Driver Jack won't look. "It's like a half hour out of the way. Can we stop and see Tommy?"

"Sure," Jack says, glancing sideways at me. "But isn't that a little risky? Considering that's where you're actually supposed to be?"

"Probably," I say. I don't know why I don't care.

A couple of hours later we're parked in a hikers' lot at the edge of a state park. There's a clearing before a thick line of trees ahead. I stand by the Volvo and stare at the forest while Jack leans against the car's back bumper, reading *Breakfast of Champions*. I watch the woods for five minutes before I see any kind of movement, and even then, all I see are shadows cast by the trees. The shapes might as well be wolves—or bears. My skin prickles for a moment.

Then, in the afternoon sunlight, I can see it's Tommy.

He's with a boy. A red-haired boy with long limbs and freckles. Pavlova goes nuts at the end of her leash as soon as she sees Tommy, and when he's twenty feet away I set her free. She gallops over to him and jumps straight up into his arms.

"Pavlova!" he says. "My surrogate daughter." He rubs her ears the way she likes and she grumbles happily.

When he sets her back down, I throw my arms around him. He lifts me right off the ground. Warmth bubbles up in my chest.

Tommy glances behind him. "I feel like I'm on the lam," he says.

"No, silly," I say. "That's me. I'm the one who ran away."

"Oh, right," he says, grinning. "With a dashing consort."

"Um, not really. But you, you're emerging from the woods like an actual Boy Scout," I say. "I'm impressed."

"Yes," Tommy says. "I have earned several badges since you've seen me last."

"Right," I say. "In smoothie drinking, in getting a massage . . ." I roll my eyes. "What particular amenity are you escaping from right now?"

"Oh," Tommy says. "It's free time now. I could be napping. I chose you." He turns to the boy with him. "This is Rusty," he says.

"Of course it is," I say. "Hi, Rusty."

"Hey," says Rusty. He reaches for my hand. His handshake is firm and his smile is kind.

"I almost forgot," Tommy says. "I brought you a muffin." He pulls one from his pocket, wrapped in wax paper. "There's way more food in this place than they need for a bunch of ballet dancers."

"Hey," I say. "I eat. You eat." I look at Rusty. "Rusty eats. Right?"

"Yep," Rusty says.

"I know," says Tommy. "I can't say the same for the rest of them. Anyway, I think it's bran. But it has blueberries!"

I put it in my purse. "It's much appreciated," I say. "I'm running low on snacks."

"How's the search?" Tommy asks.

"Okay so far. We've seen Rose."

He looks at me expectantly.

"Julia was there for a while, but Rose doesn't know where she went after that. We're heading to Philly now to see Thatcher."

"Kick him in the balls for me," Tommy says. He kicks out his own leg as he says this, but it's a ballet dancer's kick and thus higher than you'd need for balls kicking. I smile.

"Jeez," I say. "That's exactly what Rose said."

Tommy shakes his head. "That guy just brings it out in people."

Rusty clears his throat then, probably wondering what he's gotten himself into with these weirdos in the middle of the woods.

"What year is this Volvo?" he asks Jack. "My dad used to have one."

"It's a 2000," Jack says. He's obviously pleased that he's been asked about his precious car. Rusty is pleased too, to have something to talk about in general. So Tommy and I let them. I hear Jack saying something about the Volvo symbol and the ancient chemistry sign for iron. Truly fascinating stuff. Tommy links his arm into mine and pulls me over to sit in the grass.

"Rusty?" I whisper to Tommy. "That's his real name? Has he recently arrived from a 1950s sitcom?" I try to keep from smiling. "Did he originally show up in black and white?"

Tommy laughs. "Possibly. But he's cute."

"Affirmative," I say.

Tommy gives me a look. "Affirmative? We're not communicating via walkie-talkie here."

"True," I say. I hold an imaginary CB radio up to my mouth. "But I've missed you. Over."

"Roger that," he says, holding his own fake radio. He puts his hand down. "How's Jack?"

"Fine," I say. Then I sigh. "I think we're in a fight."

Tommy puts his hand on my knee and pats it like an auntie. "Well, get out of it," he says. "You're stuck with him."

"Yeah, I know." I pull my hair into a knot at the top of my head, secure it with the hair tie I've been wearing on my wrist. "Have you made friends?" I raise my eyebrows. "Besides Rusty, I mean."

"I guess. There's a girl named Lauren. I like her."

I feel a twinge of jealousy then, somewhere deep in my belly, and Tommy sees it on my face.

"Stop it. I'll always love you best," he says, putting his arm around my shoulders. "Even more than Rusty."

"What?" says Rusty. He must have heard his name. He's leaning against the back bumper of the Volvo, next to Jack. In his white T-shirt and jeans, he looks like a page from a cute-boy calendar, circa 1958.

"Nothing," Tommy says. He stands up and walks back toward Jack and Rusty, so I follow. Sunlight throws dappled shadows on the grass.

"Jack," Tommy says. "Sylvie says you're mad at her."

I gasp. "I did not say that!"

Tommy shrugs. "Well, you said something like it."

"I'm not," Jack offers. "Mad at you, I mean."

"I said we had a misunderstanding," I say.

Tommy shakes his head. "Um, no, I don't think you used that word."

"*Tommy,*" I say. "Shut up."

Tommy makes the zipper gesture over his lips. I look at Jack.

"Let's just start over," I say.

He smiles. "Okay," he says.

I turn toward Tommy. "You should know that he's making me listen to nothing but Fleetwood Mac." Tommy squints at Jack, sizing him up.

"What's your game here, Jack?" he asks. "Is this some kind of interrogation method? Do you want to know all her secrets? Because I'm pretty sure she'll just tell you if you ask nicely."

Jack blushes. "It's something I've been doing," he says. "Every month."

"Interesting." Tommy raises his eyebrows. "Every month you subject a captive girl to a Mac Attack?"

To his credit, Jack laughs. "No," he says. "Every month I choose a band and listen only to that one."

"Why?"

"Well, it time-stamps the music, for one. Soaks it in memory." He shakes his head. "That sounds stupid."

"It doesn't," I say. Which is true. It doesn't sound stupid at all. It makes sense. No matter what happens, I already know that for the rest of my life when I hear Fleetwood Mac I'll be brought straight back to this summer, for better or worse, depending on how all this turns out.

When I turn back toward him, Tommy is looking at me. Hard.

"What?" I say.

"Nothing," he says, but his tone says the opposite.

"Anyway," I say, drawing out the word, "we're allowed selected solo material from the band's members. We've mostly used that on Stevie and Lindsey."

"This doesn't mean much to me," Tommy says. "I barely know who they are. Remember that I was raised on New Age music and classical from ballets. If you want to talk about Enya or the score from *Coppélia*, I'm your guy." Pavlova is rubbing her head against Tommy's leg like a cat.

"I'll keep that in mind," says Jack.

"I won't," I say.

"I've never even seen a ballet," Jack says.

"You're kidding me!" Tommy says. "Well, I made her pack pointe shoes, so you should request a show." He pokes me in the ribs.

I turn away from him, shaking my head. "Yeah, that wouldn't be awkward at all."

"You live for awkwardness, Syl," Tommy says.

I stand on my tiptoes so I can look straight into his face. "Tell me again why I stopped to see you?"

Tommy flips his hands up like it's obvious. "Because you love me."

"Yeah, but besides that."

Jack and Rusty look mildly amused, at least, watching this episode of the Sylvie and Tommy Show.

"Well, I hate to cut this short," Tommy says, "but we have yoga in ten minutes and we have to, like, head back through the freaking woods to get there."

"Be careful," I say. I mean it.

"Oh yeah," Tommy says. "I'll watch out for wolves and poison ivy. And speaking of poison," he says, smiling, "I'll say hi to Emma for you."

"Or don't," I say. "I would be fine never seeing her again."

"We won't," Tommy says. "Once we move to Duluth."

"Duluth?" Jack asks.

"Did I say Duluth?" Tommy says. "I meant Des Moines."

"Albuquerque," I say. "Charleston."

Tommy smiles. "Louisville."

"Now you're just naming cities," Rusty says.

Tommy shrugs. "It's what we do." He picks up my wrist and angles my tattoo toward Rusty.

"Here it is," he says.

I drop my mouth open in mock-shock. "You told him?"

"Your legend precedes you," Tommy says. Rusty comes close to study the ink.

"Cool," he says.

"Cool until her mom sees," Tommy says. I give him a gentle shove. He leans toward me. "Before you go, let's show Rusty the lift."

"What?" I look around. "Here?"

"Why not?" Tommy grins. "I always catch you. And we're on grass so even if I don't, you'll be fine."

"Yeah, I don't think that's true," I say. Tommy ignores me.

"This one," he says to Rusty, "she's special. She has perfect form. Once you see this, you won't be able to get it out of your head."

"Oh, come on," I say.

"Please?" Tommy begs.

I look at Jack, who is looking at me too, and smiling. The sky is too blue behind his head.

Fine.

It's ridiculous, really, doing this out in a field at the edge of a forest like an overenthusiastic wood sprite, but I do it. I take a running start, flying over the grass barefoot. It's totally different from running in the studio; the ground raises me even before I jump. I'm airborne for a few seconds but it feels like longer, and then I land in Tommy's arms. He catches me at exactly the right moment, his hands around my rib cage, then follows my momentum forward, holding on. Then he lifts me straight into the sky.

TRACK 10:

Silver Springs

THINGS ARE A LITTLE BETTER in the Volvo after our visit to Tommy. Less awkward, less *I'm going to hijack this car and personally go murder Lindsey Buckingham if I have to hear one more feathery 1970s love song.* We're not talking a whole lot, but we'd had some pleasant conversation about the lack of traffic on Route 30 and a cloud in the sky that looked like a duck.

Progress!

I've come to terms with our soundtrack, actually. I'm very Zen about it. Here's a Lindsey, here's a Stevie, here's one sung by Christine. Maybe it's Stockholm syndrome, but I might even be beginning to like Fleetwood Mac. I'm not going to go out and buy their entire catalog in the original, still-sealed vinyl, but if I'm honest, I've enjoyed many of the songs. Particularly the one we're listening to now, which is called "Silver Springs." As a peace offering, I say this to Jack.

He nods. "It's a great song," he says. "About loving someone who doesn't want her to."

"I got that," I say, smiling. "I mean, Stevie pretty much just said it in the lyrics."

"Right." Jack glances at me, then back to the road. He's smiling too. "Okay, here's something. Supposedly Stevie was driving with Lindsey when she saw a freeway sign for a town called Silver Spring. She thought it sounded beautiful, like someplace she'd want to go. So she wrote the song." He runs his hand down the steering wheel and holds on to its bottom. "You can't read about the Mac without coming across stuff about Lindsey and Stevie's relationship. It was legendary."

The Mac. That's the first time he's called them that. I don't have time to tease Jack about it, though. He's still going.

"I mean, imagine being in a band with a great love after your relationship fell apart completely." He puts his signal on and carefully switches lanes. "Spending all that time together in a tour bus, onstage, in the recording studio. They fought a battle through the songs they wrote. They cast each other as villains and themselves as heroes."

"So Stevie was like a rock-and-roll princess," I say, "and Lindsey was her prince."

"And it was a big terrible mess."

I nod. "But kind of a beautiful one."

Jack grins. "Exactly."

"Silver Springs" has ended, but I pick up Jack's phone and start it again. The trees keep whipping by outside the window.

"So what did Lindsey think?"

"Of 'Silver Springs'?" Jack asks. "He was mad. Stevie wanted it to be on *Rumours*, but there wasn't enough space. Or at least that's what the band said. I think Lindsey just didn't want a song on the record where she tells him that he'll never be able to forget her. That her voice will literally haunt him for the rest of his life."

If you're going to be haunted by a voice, I guess Stevie Nicks's is a pretty good choice. But I don't understand why the song didn't end up on the record. "He was the one who got to decide?"

Jack shrugs. "I guess."

"That's bullshit."

"Hey, I'm on Stevie's side." He lifts his hand off the steering wheel. "It's like my mom and dad. He made all the decisions, and now he's the one with the fancy restaurant and she's working as a personal chef." Jack's voice is hard. "He got to have this whole other life."

I hear the heartbreak in Jack's voice, all bricked up with anger and resentment. I get it, I really do, but I think about what Sadie said to me, that she'd rather have a dad than not, even if he wasn't perfect. I think maybe Jack feels that way too, deep down.

"Sometimes you talk about your dad like he's an actual villain," I say. I try to keep my voice gentle. "I'm pretty sure he's just a guy."

He opens his mouth to answer, but then something distracts us both. There's a hitchhiker on the side of the road in front of us, standing with her thumb out. I didn't know people actually did that outside of the movies. And it would be fine—not weird; really, not a problem at all—except for one thing.

She's wearing a yellow ball gown.

TRACK 11:

Rhiannon

JACK PULLS OVER BEFORE I can stop him. Not that I would stop him. I mean, should I? I have no idea. Picking up a hitchhiker is probably not the best choice, but I bet there aren't many ball-gown-wearing serial killers in the world, at least not since women stopped wearing ball gowns on the regular. (Too bad, because there's so much potential for great names: the Chiffon Shooter, the Taffeta Terrorist, the Sequined Slayer.)

She's not an illusion. Jack sees her too. I know because he says half under his breath, "Pretty fancy for a hitchhiker."

When Jack slows to a stop next to her, of course I'm closest in the passenger seat. Close up I see that she's about Julia's age. Her skin is light brown and her thick black hair is wound elaborately around her head. Her dress is low-cut and lace-edged, with bell sleeves and a skirt that spreads in a wide circle around her on the asphalt. We look at each other for a moment. She's grinning, and I don't know what I'm doing. Maybe I'm smiling. All I know is that my molecules have started up again, swirling.

"Hi," I say. A brilliant greeting.

"Hey," the girl says. "Are you heading toward Ocean City? I have to be at a wedding in an hour and a half."

Okay. That explains something. "Are you getting married?" I ask. This can be our good deed of the day. Of the week! Get the girl to her wedding, and show the universe we're worthy. Just like in a fairy tale.

The girl laughs then, loudly. "God, no," she says. "I'm just the maid of honor."

Okay. Still a good deed, a necessary service. Still proof of our goodness.

"Ocean City is on the ocean, right?" Jack asks.

She peers around me and gives him a Look. "Um, yeah."

Jack blushes. "I mean . . . I figured. It's just that it's in the opposite direction." He points across the highway. "You're pointed the wrong way."

The girl's eyes widen.

"You. Are. Kidding. Me." She's leaning on the doorframe now, her elaborate hairdo framed by my open window. "I swear, my phone GPS is out to get me. And my car, which is dead in that parking lot over there." She points. "Or maybe my subconscious is leading me astray. Because"—she lowers her voice to a whisper—"I don't really want to go to this wedding. I mean, not dressed like this." She sighs. "But I have to. The bride's my best friend."

The choice is clear, as far as I'm concerned. If the universe drops a girl in a princess dress on the side of the road for us, we have to do what she needs.

"We'll take you," I say. I look at Jack. "Okay?"

He looks a little surprised, but he nods. "Okay."

"Oh my goodness," the girl says. "Thank you so much. You are absolute angels."

Jack and I get out. While he puts her bag in the trunk, the girl sort of pitches herself into the back seat. I push her skirts in and slam the door. It won't close at first and I push harder, gather up the silky fabric and shove it further into the car. Pav barks. To her credit, the girl is laughing.

As for me, I'm sweating by the time I get back in the front seat. I turn around while I'm clicking my seat belt.

"How were you even driving in that dress?" I ask.

"I had my skirt bunched up in a ridiculous way," she says. "It was not the safest way to drive. Seriously, thank y'all for stopping."

"You're welcome," I say. "I'm Sylvie. And this is Jack."

"Rhiannon," she says.

The world goes all wonky. I see stars circling my head like a cartoon character might. "What?" I say. Jack looks at me. His eyes are wide.

"Oh, I know," she says. "It's a weird name. Even worse when you consider my last name is Rodriguez. Killer alliteration."

"It's a Fleetwood Mac song," I say.

"My mom was obsessed." She notices the music then. I can tell because a light goes on in her face. She frowns. The stereo's not playing "Rhiannon" (thank goodness), but "Blue Letter." She looks worried, like maybe we're obsessed with Fleetwood Mac too (or one of us is, hmmm, I wonder who) and this is an elaborate kidnapping.

Jack is cheerful, oblivious, because he doesn't know what it's like to be a girl and always in danger. "We're on a Fleetwood Mac kick, actually," he says. "Hope you don't mind."

Something in his Model Human demeanor must reassure Rhiannon. She smiles.

"Oh, it'll be just like my entire childhood," she says.

Turns out Rhiannon can pretty much carry a conversation on her own. After we take off toward Ocean City, she starts talking and barely stops. I can't say I mind. It's nice to have a new infusion of personality into the Volvo.

"I know I look ridiculous," she's saying. "Casey wanted a Marie Antoinette–inspired wedding. I was like, 'Do you know how Marie Antoinette ended up?'" She draws her hand across her neck and sticks her tongue out. "And she was like, 'Well, obviously, I mean before the decapitation.'" Rhiannon rolls her eyes. "Can you believe it? On the bridal shower invitation I put: *We're going to party like we're going to the guillotine tomorrow.*" She sweeps her hand through the air as if she can see the words there. "It's amazing what you'll do for your best friend."

She's right. I mean, I would totally dress as one of Marie Antoinette's groupies if Sadie asked me to.

But I kind of hope she doesn't.

About forty minutes later and Rhiannon's whole life story later, we arrive in front of a gray stone church. I can smell the ocean from the parking lot—it smells like salt and seaweed and wind over sand. This is New Jersey, so there's a little whiff of algae/sewage/

chemical waste, but I try to ignore that.

There are four other women in saffron-colored ball gowns standing out in front of the church, their hair in various states of eighteenth-century French fashion. The bride's dress is white and ruffled and resembles a wedding cake as much as it does an article of clothing. She shades her eyes and peers toward us. Rhiannon is looking out the back window.

"Casey doesn't look too angry that I'm late," she says. "I mean, I dressed like a high-class eighteenth-century whore for her, so she better forgive me." I hear a rustling sound and then Rhiannon laughs.

"I can't find the door handle," she says.

"Coming!" I say. I get out of the car and open the door for her. She tries to get out but there's too much skirt. She can't get her legs to a place where they can make their way to the ground. She's laughing, still, when I grab her hand and pull.

Once on the asphalt, she throws her arms around me and then Jack.

"You two have saved the day," she says. "And you're obviously coming to the wedding."

"It's just that—we have someplace we're supposed to be," I say.

Rhiannon tilts her head. A curl that's come loose from her updo slides across her cheek.

"Can it wait a bit?" she asks.

I look at Jack. He smiles.

"It can," I say.

TRACK 12:

Where We Belong

THE RECEPTION IS IN A restaurant right on the water, a glass-enclosed dining room and a terrace right next to the sand. Pavlova sleeps in the bride's dressing room while Jack and I eat a semi-awkward-but-actually-kind-of-fun dinner with three cousins of the bride, plus their dates and a great-aunt named Ruth. I like the great-aunt best. She has silver hair set in perfectly arranged waves and is wearing a grass-green shift dress she said she first wore in 1967. When I tell her that I'm a dancer, she gets excited.

"I love ballet," she says. "You know, I saw NBT's *Sleeping Beauty* thirty years ago."

My heart seizes. "Did you like it?"

"I loved it. It was beautiful." She's smiling but her gaze is far off, as if she's remembering, watching a film reel of memory in her mind. Then she turns her eyes back to me. "I must say that I never totally understood Sleeping Beauty's behavior, though. It seems like she caused all her own problems. It shouldn't be that hard to avoid a spindle, should it?"

"No!" I say, too loudly. "She didn't know. No one told her. They just burned all the spindles they could find."

Great-Aunt Ruth looks surprised at first, but then she nods. "I see," she says.

Jack is watching me. He looks the tiniest bit worried. I'm not sure what I'm talking about anymore, but it's not Sleeping Beauty. Or not *just* Sleeping Beauty.

It's not just Julia either, though. She had to have known that those pills were dark magic, that they might help for a while but would find a way to hurt her in the end.

She chose them anyway.

After dinner, Jack and I stand at the terrace railing, looking out over the dark sparkling water.

"I haven't seen you two dance once," Rhiannon says, coming up behind us. "It's required, you know. If I have to wear this getup *all night,* you have to dance." She leans back against the railing and crosses her arms in a *case closed* fashion.

So we dance, even though we haven't been this close since he pulled me off the railing on the High Line. We stand facing each other and move a little closer, until we're stiff-armed and swaying off beat. Rhiannon gives me a little shove when she passes and I get a little closer to him. Somehow, this helps.

I can't look at him, though. I look past his shoulder to the water, intermittent whitecaps glowing in the moonlight. I half expect to see a mermaid tail out there, disappearing beneath the water. At first glance, I'm happy to report, the water is mermaid-free.

"So what's the plan, boss?" Jack's mouth is close to my ear.

"Boss?"

"Well, I'm clearly not the boss," he says. "You're sailing this ship."

"And you're driving the car."

"Right," he says. "Where are we going to sleep?"

"That is such a good question," I say. We could get a hotel room somewhere, I'm sure, even here in Ocean City. I have my emergency credit card, and we might as well go for broke. But I think that would feel too strange, being alone with Jack in a room with miniature toiletries and a Gideon Bible in a drawer. It's too much, somehow.

This is when an idea occurs to me. A plan, you might say. I don't know if it's a good one, but plans don't always have to be good to work.

"I've got it covered," I say.

TRACK 13:

Walk a Thin Line

IT'S PAST TEN O'CLOCK WHEN we pull into the parking lot of the Wegmans supermarket in Cherry Hill, New Jersey.

Really. This is my plan. I mean, I never said it was great.

"What's this?" Jack asks.

I point to the sign on the building, its letters lit up in red. "It's Wegmans."

He rolls his eyes, smiling. "I can see that."

"It's a grocery store," I say. "My mother's, like, weirdly obsessed with it. We always stop when we're on road trips. Why don't you park over there?" I point through the windshield toward the last row of cars, bordering the left side of the parking lot. Just past the asphalt is a narrow strip of grass and then some bushes dotted with red geraniums. Even farther is a line of trees, planted as a windbreak or a border, maybe, or perhaps there's a whole forest out there. That makes me reconsider my decision here for about ten seconds. But I don't have another choice at this point.

When he pulls into a parking spot, I turn around to kneel on the seat and dig through my bag. Pavlova wags her tail. It's less than seventy degrees right now, in the silvery light of the parking lot, so Pavlova should be okay in the car for a half hour as long as the windows are cracked.

"You're going to have to hang out in the car for a bit after you get out to pee," I tell her. "But I'll bring you a treat."

I look at Jack.

"You might want to bring your toothbrush," I say.

The first thing I remember about Wegmans is how big it is. Like, you could park a few airplanes in here if you wanted to, and still have space to sell carrots and cake mix. Jack and I wander around the prepared food section—big as a cafeteria—for a while and then climb the stairs to the "café seating" upstairs to eat our late night snack. For me: avocado sushi rolls. For Jack: a yogurt parfait.

"So what's the plan, here?" Jack says. "We sleep in the cereal aisle?"

I laugh. "I thought we'd sleep in the car, actually. But at least there's a bathroom in case we have to pee at night. And we probably won't get murdered in a supermarket parking lot."

He nods. He's smiling at me.

It still feels a little weird.

I look over the edge of the balcony. Below me: loaves of bread, donuts in a glass case, the elaborate fruit tarts I admired earlier. I reach out to touch the railing. I feel my molecules swing dancing and in the next moment I wonder: what would it be like to sit up here? For a moment, I want to swing my legs over the side and balance on the edge over the bakery section. Then I hear Jack's voice.

"Sylvie," he says. "Are you okay?"

I shake myself out of the weird reverie, quiet my quivering atomic parts. Or rather, Jack's voice does.

"I'm fine," I say. "I better get back to Pavlova. If she starts barking in the car, we're screwed."

We throw away our trash and go back down to the bottom floor. The bathrooms are next to one another, just before the wide exit.

"See you in a minute," I say.

After I pee, I come out of the stall and wash my hands. My phone chimes a text in my bag: Sadie.

How's it going? Did you find her?

I answer right away. Not yet. She stayed with Rose for a while. Thatcher tomorrow.

Why not today?

We got delayed. We . . . ended up at a wedding. Long story.

Sadie sends an open-mouth emoji face. You can tell me WHEN YOU GET TO RICHMOND. How's Jack?

How is Jack? I don't know. He's fine, I type.

He's going to try to get out of seeing my dad. But I'll be here for five more days so remind him there's no excuse.

Short of wolves or witches, I guess.

Of course, I text.

There's an older woman standing at the mirror next to me. She has a cloud of silver hair and a black uniform with a name tag that says *Francesca*. She's watching me in the mirror, as I put toothpaste on my toothbrush.

"Did you find everything you need?" she asks.

"Like, groceries?" I say. "Yes, I'm fine. Thank you."

She shakes her head. "I mean, do you need anything? Any help?"

For a second, I wonder if this is her. My fairy godmother. Because if I'm honest, since the book arrived, that's all I've been waiting for. Some benevolent lady who can wave her wand and fix everything and tell me what the hell I should do. I can almost see the glitter, feel the magic. But then I see the way she's looking at me and I know she must just think I'm in trouble, homeless, maybe, brushing my teeth here in a grocery store bathroom.

I'm not in trouble, I want to say. *At least not that kind.*

"Oh, thanks," I say, "but no. I just have really good dental hygiene."

She looks at my reflection in the mirror. I look at hers. She's magic or she's ordinary. I can't tell.

"Okay," she says. And then she goes.

TRACK 14:

Dreams

IT'S NEARLY MIDNIGHT BY THE time we leave. Jack's waiting for me just past the automatic doors. Together we walk to the Volvo on the far side of the lot, bathed in the glowing light of the tall lamps overhead. Moths circle in tiny snowstorms.

When we get to the car we each go to our sides, then look at each other over the top.

"How are we going to do this?" he asks.

"I don't know," I say. "Just lean the seats back? Do they lean?"

Jack smiles. "Of course they lean. This is a very luxurious car we're dealing with here."

"Right," I say. "It's a Volvo." I walk to the passenger side door.

"Damn straight." Jack looks at me over the roof of the car. "So we'll just see who Pavlova chooses to snuggle with?"

I open the door and my dog jumps out. "I guess we will," I say.

When I shut the door I almost reach up to put on my seat belt before I remember that we're not going anywhere. We're staying right here this time, right in front of this supermarket in Nowhere, New Jersey. All night long.

Pavlova settles next to my hip (she chose me, obviously), and Jack's already reclined in his seat, leaning straight back and looking at the sky (I think) out the back-seat driver's side window. It's warm in the car but not hot, thankfully, and the air smells like the geraniums planted at the edge of the lot.

I don't know if it makes more sense to face toward Jack or away from him, so basically I just wiggle around in my seat a little and then end up in the middle, facing the ceiling. I'm about to say good night when Jack speaks.

"I'm sorry about what I said last night," he says.

As soon as he says it, I'm back in Rose's living room on her lumpy sofa bed, ceiling fan spinning overhead. I can't believe that was only one day ago. It feels like a week.

"It's okay," I say. "We started over, remember?"

"Yeah," he says. I tip my face toward him.

"But still," he says. "It wasn't completely fair."

"Maybe it was," I say. "I do think my mom wants to help—"

"I know," Jack says.

"But yeah." I wait. "She has it easier. *We* have it easier." I think about what Rose said, and I echo it. "You have a point."

"Thanks." Jack pushes his hair back off his forehead. "I don't know why I said it right then, though. I think I was feeling a little anxious, totally on your turf, there."

"Rose's turf."

"Right. Rose's turf *is* your turf, though. And I could tell she was suspicious of my intentions." His cheeks redden. "I mean, not that I have intentions." His words are tripping over each other. "Besides, um, driving you where you need to go."

"Of course you don't." I say this quickly.

"Okay," he says.

"Okay." The silence that follows is filled by the buzz of a parking lot light above us. "Yikes," I say. "We might have to find a new spot. That thing is loud."

Jack smiles. "Are you like Sadie?" he asks.

"Like Sadie how?"

"Are you one of those people who likes to talk until she falls asleep?"

I smile. "Not really. I mean, with Sadie I just end up listening, mostly. Anyway, you should know that. We slept in the same room last night too."

"Yeah," Jack says, "but I pissed you off right before we went to sleep."

"True." I'm watching through the windshield as small black creatures—bats, probably—swoop above the trees.

"Tell me something," he says. "Tell me a story. Like Sadie would."

"About what?"

"Tell me about Julia."

When I hear him say her name I realize I haven't thought of my sister in hours. All day, maybe, at least not since this morning with Rose, and that feels so long ago. But as soon as Jack asks me to talk about her, she's here, sailing back into my mind.

"Okay," I say. I take a breath. "She almost quit dancing when she was five."

"When did she start?"

"Oh," I say. "She was three."

"Geez."

"It's pretty normal," I say. "I mean, for people who end up as professionals. Misty didn't start until she was a teenager, but that's really unusual. Misty Copeland, I mean. She's—"

Jack puts his hand up to stop me. "Even *I* know who Misty Copeland is."

"Good job," I say. "You're practically a ballet expert."

He laughs. "So why did Julia almost quit?"

This is a story we tell in my family all the time. My mother loves to tell it most. "She came home from her recital so angry, just, like, stomping all over the room, and my mother asked her why. 'Everyone thinks we're funny and cute,' she said. 'But I'm trying to be beautiful.'" I never saw this happen, of course. I wasn't even born. But still, I can practically see it in my mind. "Jules always wanted to be taken seriously. Even when she was five."

A moth lands on the windshield then, and I watch it slowly move its wings. Jack is watching it too.

"When did you start dancing?" he asks.

"Three," I say. "I think I can remember my first class, but sometimes I think I'm just remembering the picture my mother took of me." It's framed on our living room wall: me in a tiny black leotard, pale pink tights with a dark smudge on my knee. I had fallen on the pavement outside the studio, but my mom said I didn't cry at all. I just wanted to get in to my dance class. I just wanted to be like Julia, even when I was three years old.

"I always thought of us as stars," I say, "but she's so much bigger than I was. Like, she's a red giant and I'm a white dwarf." I can't believe I'm saying this out loud to him, but I am.

Jack shakes his head. "White dwarfs are hotter."

"Hotter?" I'm smiling without meaning to—*hotter?*—and Jack blushes.

"Um, warmer, I mean. Brighter."

As he says it, I realize that I knew that. Deep back in my memory, where I keep all the facts I learned at astronomy day camp when I was nine, is that fact. White dwarfs are the brightest star.

"I forgot about that."

"So maybe you're both spectacular in your own way. Julia is supermassive, and you're small but burning furiously."

"I am pretty furious," I say.

Jack smile-sighs. "Tell me about it."

I can see the moon past Jack through the driver's side window, a waxing pearl in a black square of sky. It doesn't feel like it could possibly have been only one day since I sat outside and saw the moon above Rose and the moonflowers. I look back at Jack. He reaches out and touches Pavlova's head gently. She sighs.

"Good night," he says.

"Good night," I echo. My tattoo doesn't itch anymore. It just feels mildly warm in a pleasant way. It's almost comforting. I can hear crickets chirping, and that parking lot lamp still buzzing, and somewhere, the faint sound of a siren. I close my eyes. I sleep.

TRACK 15:

Monday Morning

THE THING ABOUT SLEEPING IN a car is that you can't help but wake up early. I'm awake with the first hints of a sunrise, just as the sky turns silver past the trees. Jack is still asleep next to me, his face tipped toward me, one arm thrown over his head.

I raise my seat to a normal position as gently as I can, then roll down the window and lean out to lower Pavlova, on her long leash, to the ground. She trots over to the grass and pees on it, then sniffs all the places she hasn't yet peed. I loop the leash around the mirror and sit back.

Jack's still sleeping. His fingers flutter against the headrest, and he sighs. I never noticed how long and dark his eyelashes are, but with his eyes closed, I can tell.

Pavlova barks then and it startles me. This is when it occurs to me: I'm literally watching Jack sleep.

What. Is. Even. Happening.

The obvious answers are:

1. I'm under a magical spell.

That's the best I can come up with.

I manage to sit up and lean back out the window before he wakes up. Pav is barking at a flock of small brown birds, sparrows, probably, who've landed in the trees past the lot.

"Shhhh," I tell her, and I pull her back toward me. When I turn toward Jack, he's awake.

"Hey," he says.

"Hey." Pavlova barks again. "Um, hang on." I open my door and Pav jumps in. She starts sniffing wildly for her kibble, which I find and put in her dish. She eats it on the car floor.

"Okay," I say. "Let's make our escape while she's busy."

I hop out of the car and Jack follows. He stops to stretch. The sky is streaked with pink and gold, and I can hear the birds Pavlova was barking at chattering in the distance.

"The accommodations here are really fantastic," Jack says, grinning.

"Five-star," I say.

In the bathroom, I change my clothes and brush my teeth. It's empty in there, no almost–fairy godmother this time, but when I leave the bathroom Jack is waiting in the hallway.

"Fancy meeting you here," he says.

We wander the aisles for a little while, then leave with coffee and a bag of pastries. Outside, the sun is higher in the sky, hotter already than it was yesterday. There's a cat on the concrete, just at the edge of the lot. It's black and white and making a beeline for me.

When it gets there, it starts threading figure eights around my ankles, meowing.

"What is up with this cat?" Jack says.

"Um." I look down at the cat. "I don't know." I take a step farther and the cat moves too. I trip over it and nearly fall on my face.

Jack's brow is furrowed, but he's smiling. He steps toward me and slips one arm around my back. Then he picks me straight up. I can't help but think of being in his arms on the High Line. This is slightly less awkward, but still not quite comfortable. Not like being lifted by Tommy, who can make me feel half-weightless and free.

The cat stops moving and looks at us. She lets out a mournful howl.

"Sorry, kitty," Jack says. "We have someplace to be."

The cat doesn't follow. She sits on the asphalt, staring at me, as we pass.

"I don't know what you want from me," I say. She opens her mouth and I expect to hear her meow again, to make that terrible sound, but instead she just yawns.

I can hear Pavlova barking as Jack carries me to the car. When we get there, he opens the door, still holding me, and sets me down gently in the front seat.

"That wasn't weird at all," he says.

"Nope," I say. "Not at all."

TRACK 16:

Go Your Own Way

THATCHER'S OFFICE IS IN AN old stone building on a wide street. We find a parking garage a few blocks away and show up dogless. I didn't know how seriously Thatcher (or anyone) could take me with a tiny white fluffy dog in my arms, so on the way here I found a doggy day care for Pavlova. I guess it makes sense in a city like this, full of people who feel guilty leaving their dogs alone for long hours during the day and have the money to blow. I was worried that she'd freak when we left, but in seconds she was halfway across the room sniffing around with her tiny doggy friends, so she barely noticed. And anyway, it's just for a few hours.

We walk through the revolving door, first me, then Jack, and then stand on the slick marble floor together. I can hear some wood-windy music that I'm pretty sure is supposed to be calming, but it's not helping me. My heart is beating hard. It's been more than a year

205

since I've seen Thatcher. Actually, I think my brother was the last member of the Blake family besides Julia to see him, and that didn't go well.

"You okay?" Jack asks. He puts his hand on the small of my back. I can feel the warmth of his fingers through my shirt and my heartbeat kicks up, though I don't know if it's because he's touching me (why is he touching me?) or because I'm about to see Thatcher. I take a deep, shaky breath. There's a glossy wood desk in the center of the room, a bank of windows to my left, and at the desk a receptionist with blond hair so perfect I'm pretty sure it wouldn't move if a tornado blew through here. Which is a real possibility, the way my life is going lately.

"I'll sit down," Jack says.

"Okay," I say. I just sort of stand there in the doorway. He stands there too.

"Don't worry," he says. "I'll go back there with you if you want me to."

"I do," I say.

He smiles. "Okay."

I feel a little better, at least enough to walk up to the receptionist's desk. "Hi," I say to her. "I'm looking for Thatcher Price."

She smiles without showing her teeth. "Do you have an appointment?" She glances at her computer screen.

"I don't," I say. "But I'm sure he'll want to see me. My name is Sylvie Blake."

"Let me call up," she says. "You can sit down over there."

I sink into the chair next to Jack's. I try to hear what the receptionist is saying (to Thatcher? his secretary?), but the ethereal waiting room music is too loud. She hangs up the phone and motions me over with an efficient flick of her fingers.

"He's out of the office," she says, "at a meeting. But he'll be back at three o'clock, and he'll see you then."

She says this in such a businesslike way I'm taken aback. As if I'm just some client, waiting to talk about a contract or something. As if anything with Thatcher could be just business.

How could he not be here?

When I turn around, Jack stands up. He smiles, and somehow the smile settles me.

"I hear they have a good zoo," he says.

Hold Me

I HAVEN'T BEEN TO A ZOO since I was a kid. Officially they make me a little sad: the neurotic leopards pacing in front of their cage's glass wall, the elephants that are meant to walk across half a country in enclosures half the size of a football field. But this zoo is pretty nice, actually, even if it makes me nervous in my present circumstances to be in a place with so many animals.

After we pay our entrance fee, we stand still just past the gate. "What do you want to see?" Jack says. "We have two hours."

I think about it, but I don't have to think hard. "Bears," I say.

We find a bear—an Asiatic black bear—on the foldout map, and walk a while to find it. And then we stand by the enclosure's border and look at it: a black bear with a spiky ruff of fur around its neck and round Mickey Mouse ears.

I think about Ursa Major, those bear stars I saw over Sadie's roof last week. Callisto didn't do anything wrong, but she ended up twice changed, first into a bear and then into stars. So what's the lesson, here? That you can get transformed into an animal if you're not careful? That you won't be safe until you're made into a constellation?

I can honestly say I've never wanted to be stars. I've always wanted to be real, even when it hurts.

The bear stands on its haunches and sniffs the air. It turns in my direction.

"Um, let's go," I tell Jack. Better safe than sorry.

When we leave the bears we walk for a while, and then Jack sits down on a bench by the giraffe enclosure.

I sit down next to him, but I misjudge the distance between us and end up with my shoulder pressed against his. He doesn't move away and I don't either, though my cheeks warm.

"I like giraffes," Jack says. "They sleep about four hours a day, five minutes at a time."

"Really?" The only one I can see from this spot is walking slowly, elegant and otherworldly. "And they don't even have to sleep in a Volvo."

He laughs. "True," he says. "They're so unusual and they don't even know it." He looks at me. "I don't know if that's a bad thing or a good thing."

"I don't either."

"Are you nervous?" he asks.

I startle. My molecules do their same old spin. *About what?* I think. But then I realize he's talking about seeing Thatcher, which is just minutes away.

"No," I say. "Yes. Maybe." I watch a giraffe walk slowly, ethereally over the grass. "You know, the last time Everett saw Thatcher, he punched him."

"Really?" Jack sounds surprised. "Your brother doesn't seem like the punching type."

"He's not," I say. "But things got so weird."

Everett had a run-in with Thatcher at a show downtown, a show he got thrown out of later, when Thatcher's friends told the bouncer that Everett had been the one who started the fight. My brother, who before this had never punched anyone in his life, as far as I know.

I tried to picture it then: the two of them in the dark club, lit by the dim glow of the stage's spotlights. The way the crowd would back away from them or maybe turn toward them, watching and pressing forward. The way it would hurt Everett's hand to hit him, maybe as much as it hurt Thatcher.

None of it made any sense. Except for the way pain seemed to ricochet around my family back then, catching on all our sharp edges.

Jack elbows me gently. "*You're* not going to punch him, are you?"

I shrug. "Maybe. Now that you've reminded me."

Jack smiles. "Oh, shit," he says. "Sorry, Thatcher." He glances at me past his shoulder.

This is when the weird thing happens. Jack grabs my hand

and holds it. Just my fingers, really. I'm surprised at first, so I don't do anything, but then I close my fingers around his.

He looks down at the ground and smiles the tiniest bit. Then he lets my hand go.

"We better head back," he says.

TRACK 18:

Second Hand News

IT'S TWO MINUTES TO THREE when we get back to Thatcher's building. The lobby is still all gleaming marble, but the music is gone. This time, I notice a photograph of Thatcher's father on the wall by the firm's sign. He used to be a friend of my own father's, but I know they don't speak anymore. That happened for good after Everett's fight, when Thatcher's father called mine. I listened to my father's half of the conversation, my back pressed to the hallway wall outside his home office. I could hear Mr. Price's voice as an angry hum through long stretches of my father's silence.

"Listen," my father finally said. His voice was cold enough to flash-freeze hot soup. "It would take a lot more than that to make us even. As I'm sure you understand. I would advise that you let it go." He hung up his phone then, and must have just dropped it on his desk because I heard it hit the wood. I went back to my room and shut the door before my father came out.

Now I look up to see the receptionist staring at me. "Sylvie?" she says. "Mr. Price is ready for you."

Part of me wants to run in the other direction, to keep not knowing whatever Thatcher knows. But I stand there for a moment, drawing all my energy straight up in a silver line down my spine the way Miss Inez taught me when I was ten years old. Jack is next to me, waiting for me to go. So I do. Before I can stop myself, I walk straight toward the open door.

The office is small and bare, with expensive-looking cabinets built into one side. There's no art on the walls. Thatcher is sitting behind a big desk, both hands on the polished wood surface. He's frowning, and there's a deep furrow between his eyebrows, but he's as good-looking as ever. He looks like he's posing for the Uncomfortable Male Catalog, Office Edition.

"Syl," he says, standing. He starts walking around the desk and I fight the urge to back up, to turn around and run straight out the door.

"Sylvie," I say. The tone of my voice stops him midstep.

He breathes in slowly, half a sigh. "Sylvie," he repeats. My name is his exhale. "Are you going to hit me?"

Behind me, Jack lets out a small chuckle.

I shake my head a little. "Why does everyone keep asking me that?"

Thatcher looks down at my hand, so I do too. It's curled into a fist.

"No," I say. I unclench my fingers. "Maybe I was thinking

about it. Subconsciously."

"I wouldn't blame you," he says. "But since your brother already did, maybe we can avoid that."

"Okay," I say. "You deserved it, though."

He leans against his desk. "I know."

I take a step closer to his desk, but I don't touch it. "I don't even really want to talk to you, like, ever again, but I'm looking for Julia." I cross my arms. "Do you know where she is?"

He looks straight at me. "*You* don't know?"

"Do you really think I'd be here otherwise?" I'm channeling Sadie-Pretending-She's-a-Detective-in-a-Cop-Show. He's the perp, and I'm using perp tactics, just like she would. It makes me feel better, like Sadie's here with me.

Thatcher rubs the back of his neck. "I didn't know she wasn't in touch with you. When was the last time you heard from her?"

I wait a moment before I answer. "When she left New York."

His eyes widen a little, and then he catches himself. "Well, it's not like she did a lot of talking while she was here. She was only here for one night. She slept on the couch." He says this last part like he's trying to reassure me.

I'm not reassured.

I picture it—the tacky, expensive leather couch Thatcher probably has, Julia stretched out in the darkness, trying to fall asleep. Did he even give her a blanket? The thought of it makes me want to cry. I bite my lip hard instead.

"Did she tell you where she was going?" I ask.

"No." He shakes his head. "How did you know she was ever with me in the first place?"

"She put you on a list," I say. I don't explain any further. "Who's Daniela? She's on the list too."

"I don't know." He's looking down at the floor. "Look, Sylvie, I know I messed up."

"That's the understatement of the century." I realize that I'm shaking, and I don't know if it just started or if I've been vibrating (with rage? sadness?) the whole time I've been talking to him.

"I was trying to help her," he says, looking up at me. "She was terrified she'd have to stop dancing."

"Yeah, and if you'd asked anybody—*anybody*—they would have told you how dangerous it was for her to dance while she was taking so many pills." My fists are clenched again, my nails digging into my palms. "You could have freaking googled it. Julia knew. She just knew you were dumb enough not to check it out."

I feel a hand on my right shoulder. Jack, who is still here, still standing behind me. I had almost forgotten. I don't know if the hand means I should stop or keep going, but I choose the latter.

"Do you know what it was like?" I ask, and I don't let Thatcher answer. "No, you don't know, because you weren't there. Well, I was."

Here's what it was like: Everett had taken me to a movie. An art theater downtown was playing the Beatles' *Help!*, and we'd eaten Junior Mints and popcorn in the warm dark theater, our scarves and sweaters piled on the seats next to us. We took the train uptown and then walked back to our apartment through the slushy streets. Everett was the one who unlocked the door, but I stepped through the doorway first. I'm the one who first saw her: Julia stretched out on the couch, her head tipped toward us. She was asleep.

She wasn't asleep.

"Jules," Everett said. His voice was loud and seemed to echo in the apartment, but she didn't move. He crossed the room in maybe two steps and knelt on the floor next to her. He shook her shoulders. She didn't wake up.

It's ridiculous, but I thought of Sleeping Beauty then. How many times had Julia practiced that scene? How many times had she sunk down to the stage floor and played at being unconscious?

Everett turned around. "Sylvie," he said, his voice calm. "Call 911."

I stared back at him, frozen.

"*Now*, Syl."

I fumbled in my bag for my phone, and dialed with shaking fingers. When the dispatcher answered, Everett took the phone from me. I sank to the floor next to my sister.

Wake up, I told her, or maybe I just thought it. Every time my heart beat I said it, so the words matched the rhythm of my blood pumping through my body. *Wake up wake up wake up.*

She didn't. The dispatcher told Everett to get her down to the lobby, that the ambulance would be there soon, so he slipped his arms underneath Julia and picked her up. She looked so small then, my sister who took up so much space when she danced. Who could leap from stage left to stage right while barely trying.

My sister, who defied gravity.

Everett carried her to the elevator. I ran ahead and pressed the button and we waited, waited, waited while the numbers ticked up to six. I pressed the lobby button when we got inside. Actually, I threw all my weight against that button, like if I hit it hard enough it would get us there faster. It didn't.

Our doorman Rafael was there, and his face turned gray when he saw us. He ran over to us and tried to take Julia from Everett—I don't even know why, to try to help, out of habit—but Everett wouldn't let her go. He just sank down to the floor, and I knelt down next to him, cradling Julia's head in my hands.

I could hear the sirens by then, but they never seemed to get any closer. I think I already knew I'd be hearing those sirens for the rest of my life.

"She could have *died*," I say to Thatcher now, my voice rising on the last word.

Thatcher is shaking his head. "Don't you think I know that? I think about it *every day*." His voice breaks. "Why do you think I didn't get her any more pills after she tore up her knee?"

A chill runs through my blood like ice. "What? No. You got her the pills. All of them. It was you."

Thatcher slumps backward, leaning on his desk. "Sylvie, in the end, whatever she did, she did on her own," he says. "She told me she stopped using. That she didn't need the pills anymore. I had no idea."

I feel so suddenly unsteady that I take a step back from him.

"Are you okay?" Jack says, his voice low. I can't make myself answer. I don't know if this makes it better or worse, knowing that Julia had to find some other way to get the drugs. Knowing that she could have stopped and didn't, even after she knew she wasn't going to dance again, at least the same way she had before.

Suddenly, it all comes at me in a rush: she wasn't trying to stop the pain, that last time. She was trying to stop the world, or at least stop living in it. I whirl around then and head toward the door.

"Sylvie." Thatcher's voice is sharp.

I stop. I don't turn around.

"If you see her?" He takes a breath. "Tell her I've been thinking about her. Tell her I'm always thinking about her."

I stand there, feet flat on the floor, my arms at my side. I could let him off the hook here, just nod my head or something. But this isn't really about him anymore. When it comes down to it, it wasn't really about him at all. So I just start walking: through the door, down the hallway. Away.

TRACK 19:

The Ledge

OUT ON THE STREET, THE sun is too bright, too golden. The world looks like a postcard and I don't know how to fit both myself and my despair into it. I'm moving down the street so fast I'm practically running.

"Sylvie." Jack sounds breathless, but he catches up to me. I stop.

"What?" I know my voice doesn't sound friendly. I don't really care.

"Are you okay?"

I focus on the lamppost behind him, on the black sticker on its middle that says *Stop War*.

Stop everything, I think.

"No," I say to Jack. "I'm not." I feel like I might cry, and not the quiet kind.

Jack walks next to me for half a block without saying anything. I'm still walking really, really fast, and he keeps up. Somehow this calms me a little. I slow down.

"Okay, listen. This whole situation sucks," he says. "And I think that guy's a douchebag."

I laugh then, one loud *ha*, and Jack seems surprised. To be honest, I am too.

"Douchebag?" I say. "Really?"

Jack flips up his hands. "What's wrong with that description?"

"I've just never heard you use that word."

He looks embarrassed. "Well, I don't usually use it. But it seemed to fit. As does *wanker*."

"*Wanker* works really well," I say.

"I mean, if you want a British insult. He's named after Margaret Thatcher, right? So he would have to be an idiot."

"I think it's a family name," I say.

"Well, I just don't see what your sister saw in him."

"He never told her no." I stop walking. "At least, until the end, apparently. But you know what? I didn't tell her no either."

Jack doesn't ask what I mean. He just cocks his head toward a bench near the end of the street, and goes to sit down. I stand on the sidewalk for a beat, two, then I follow.

This time, I make sure to leave a few inches between us. I even set my purse down between his hip and mine. Then I sit there with my hands folded in my lap, watching the streetlights turn from green to amber to red and back again.

"Can I ask you something?" Jack says.

"Yeah." I keep my eyes on the streetlights. They go amber, then switch to red.

"Why did you keep dancing if you wanted to forget Julia?" he says. I look at him. He looks straight back at me.

"I'm not saying you should have stopped," he says, "but I guess I'm wondering if you ever considered it."

It's a good question. I say I want to forget about her—or at least stop thinking about her all the time—but how can I do that when I spend so much time at the studio? Julia was the one who taught me how to pull out the nail in the shoe, how to soften the shank by closing it in a door. She was the one who held my hands the first time I put on pointe shoes at eleven so I could balance on my toes. She helped me sew the ribbons, slowing down her stitches so I could see the angle of the needle going through the satin. It's all so wrapped up in her.

"I think I was trying to keep her with me," I say. "I never wanted to forget her. It just seemed like . . . like *she* wanted to forget *me*." I rub my left thumb into the palm of my right hand. "Do you remember when I said that ballet is supposed to look effortless? I mean, I always knew it wasn't, but I didn't know it could be so ugly. That Julia could be. It's like seeing behind the curtain. Now the whole thing feels tainted."

Jack is nodding slowly. "It's not like I can judge." His voice is soft. "I say I want to forget my dad, but if that were really true, I wouldn't be driving his car." He leans his head back. "I mean, it's not even like it's a cool car. It's a freaking *Volvo*. I mean, nothing against Volvos." He says this quietly like the car might hear, even though it's parked in a garage blocks away. I smile.

"Obviously," I say.

"I drive it because I like it, and I like it because he gave it to me." The way he says this sounds like it pisses him off.

"I get it," I say, and I wonder: Did I like ballet because Julia gave it to me? Or did I like it for its own sake? I couldn't be sure anymore.

"You know, the thing you have to remember is that Julia didn't just break your heart. She broke your parents' hearts, and your brother's. Her friends'. Even that asshole Thatcher's."

I look at Jack. "Is that supposed to help?"

He laughs. "Maybe. What I'm saying is that you're not alone. In all sorts of ways." He's looking at me and I'm looking at him and then we both look away.

"I guess," I say. I look down at the worn wood on the edge of the bench. "You know, recently, I have thought about quitting." When I say it, I realize that it's true. I've doubted what I do in the studio. I've questioned its purpose. I've wondered if I want to do this all the time. Forever.

Jack is looking at me, and I'm looking at him. A warm feeling bubbles up in my chest, and I look away. I point my toes in my sandals a little, stretching, as if even talking about ballet makes me want to go on pointe. "If I go into Level Seven, I have to give up high school. I'll have tutors instead. I don't know if I want that." I look back at Jack. "But I'm not sure. Maybe that's why I need to see Julia."

He nods.

"Of course," I say, "if I quit Tommy's going to kill me."

"Probably," Jack says. "At least at first."

"Right," I say. "He'll kill me and then bring me back from the dead."

Jack smiles. "Sounds about right." He leans forward and puts his hands on his knees. "So what's the plan?"

"I don't know," I say. "I don't know who Daniela is. We've hit a dead end." I look up over the buildings to the cloud-streaked blue sky above. "I think it's time to give up."

"Really?" Jack says.

"I guess." I shrug. "We might as well drive to Richmond so you can visit your dad."

"I don't think so," Jack says. "We've had enough drama today." We both sit there, silent, watching the traffic light *green-amber-red* itself again. Then he takes out his phone and starts texting.

"I have an idea," he says, still typing. "It's not a supermarket."

"That's good," I say. "I think I may have had enough of sleeping in the Volvo."

A reply dings back almost immediately. Jack smiles at the screen.

"Who are you texting with?"

"Knox."

"Knox?"

He nods. "I have a friend who lives in Philly," he says.

"Really?"

"He's not here right now. He's working at a camp this summer, about an hour away." Jack looks up. "He's willing to host us."

It seems strange to run away from camp to go to . . . camp. "It's not a dance camp, is it?"

Jack laughs. "I don't think so."

"Then that'll work."

"Should we go pick up that tiny canine of yours?" He stands up and extends his hand to me. I let him pull me up.

"Okay."

On our way to get the Volvo (which, when you think about it, is basically Jack's pet), we pass a natural foods store called Gaia Groceries. There's a girl out front, red-cheeked in a red apron, holding a basket of apples.

"Want one?" she says. "We're offering samples. These are the best apples you'll ever have."

Jack shakes his head and says, "No thanks," but she holds the basket so close to me—almost blocking my path—that I can't really pass without taking one.

"Thanks," I say. I put my hand into the basket and close my fingers around the piece of fruit.

I keep walking, looking at the apple. It's beautiful: cool and round, red and glossy. It's heavy in my hand. And I'm hungry, the kind of hungry that comes from not having eaten since breakfast.

But I've come this far. If fairy tales teach you anything, it's that apples from strangers are never a good idea.

When I get to the corner, I pitch the apple into the nearest trash bin.

Never Make Me Cry

THE CAMP IS CALLED CAMP Wildflower, if you can believe it. An hour and a half later, Jack and I stand under the huge wooden sign, waiting for Knox to come and get us.

"Wildflower. Sounds like a real rough-and-tumble place," I say.

"Oh yeah," Jack says. "Caters to a very tough crowd, obviously."

"Only the wildest flowers," I say. "My kind of people."

Knox appears then—tall and grinning, with pale wavy blond hair and hazel eyes. He's basically the human version of a Labradoodle.

He immediately folds Jack into a huge hug. Pavlova barks at him, so when he lets go he kneels down to pet her.

"Hey, you," he says. I swear she bats her eyelashes at him.

When he looks up at me, he smiles. "You must be Jack's traveling companion."

"Yeah," I say. "I'm Sylvie." I put out my hand, but he hugs me too. I let him. I even hug him back. I'm a little overcome by his Muppety energy. When he lets me go, I look over at Jack, who's grinning.

"See?" he says. "This is way better than going to Richmond."

Knox leads us toward a cluster of cabins across a wide-open lawn, at the edges of which are a bunch of little kids playing freeze tag. Beyond that, cabins, and then the dark green edge of the woods. My heart squeezes a little to see all those trees.

"So where did you get your name?" I ask.

"Oh," he says. "People always ask this. My mom was on bed rest before I was born, so she was watching a lot of soap operas. There were two characters on two different shows with that name." He shrugs. "She thought it was a sign. But I think it was an unfortunate choice, because one of those Knoxes had amnesia and the other eventually plotted to kill his twin brother." He smiles. "I've seen the reruns."

I laugh. "Well, you don't seem to have amnesia, and I'm just going to assume you're not a murderer."

"Good assumption," Knox says. "Camp screens pretty hard for that sort of thing."

"Are you sure it's all right if we stay?" I ask.

"Oh, totally." He's nodding his head. "There aren't really any grown-ups here." I must look surprised, so he starts shaking his head. "Or, rather, we *are* the grown-ups. This is a hippie-ish nature camp. It's pretty hands off."

I'm nodding. "Okay."

"I mean, we're very responsible. But I can vouch for Jack, and he can vouch for you." Knox makes a game-show-hostess type of gesture. "And anyway, we have a couple of empty cabins right now, so you won't be staying with the kids. You are very welcome to stay for the night."

He waves across the lawn to a tall girl with her hair in a smooth black bob. Like Knox, she's wearing a navy-blue polo shirt. She smiles and starts heading over.

"Allie!" he says. "We have guests. Can you show Sylvie to Bluebell Cabin?" He looks at me. "It's empty," he says. "All yours." He points to Pavlova. "Along with this little dude."

"Dudette," I say.

"Oh, sorry," Knox says, not really to me but to my dog.

"Hey," Allie says. She puts out her hand and I shake it. "Alexandra Kim," she says. "But you can call me Allie."

"I'm Sylvie Blake," I say. "Friend of Knox's friend Jack."

She smiles. "Then you're a friend of mine." She points toward a cabin with a blue-painted sign. "Let's go drop your bag before dinner."

At the cabin, Allie holds the door open for me.

"It's a little dusty," she says. "We're not using it this summer." The inside of the cabin is all wood, trimmed in bluebell blue. It's so cozy and sweet I almost swoon. When Allie leads me to an empty cot on the far side of the room, I drop my bag on the floor and sit down on the mattress.

"You look like you've had a day," Allie says. She sits down

on the cot opposite from me.

"You could say that."

She tilts her head. "Are you on some kind of quest?"

I laugh. "I guess so. Why do you ask?"

"I don't know," she says. "You just have that look about you."

"I have the look of not having showered in a while, I think."

She smiles. "Well, you can certainly do that here. I'll show you where."

I absentmindedly scratch my tattoo, and I see Allie's eyes are on it.

"You have a tattoo?" she says. "How old are you?"

"Sixteen," I say.

"You're a badass. Let me see."

I hold my wrist out to her.

"'Twenty-six bones'?"

"The number in each of our feet." I lift one of mine as if to demonstrate. "I'm a ballet dancer."

"Oh, I've heard." Allie smiles. "So who's Jack to you?"

You ask a lot of questions, I think. But Allie seems so nice, so interested, that I don't have a reason to avoid her.

"Jack is my—" I struggle to finish this sentence. My what? Driver? Chauffeur, maybe, if you want to get all fancy-French about it? My traveling companion, as Knox said? My friend?

I settle on the clearest answer. The old one.

"My best friend's brother," I say. "He's giving me a ride."

Allie nods, slowly like she's considering things. "That's all?"

I pause for a moment. "Pretty much," I say.

* * *

When Allie leaves to go wrangle some campers, I sit down on the edge of the cabin steps. There's a trellis to my right, wound with red honeysuckle, and all the air around smells fruity and warm and honeyed. A girl with wildly curly hair sits down against the opposite railing.

"I'm Celia," she says in that up-front, just-so-you-know way little kids often have. "Can I pet your dog?"

"Sure." Pavlova trots across the stair and puts her head under the girl's hand. As always, she takes an active role in her own petting.

It's so calm and quiet here that I feel far from my old life, far from my search from Julia. Just now, I wouldn't mind settling into the empty cabin and staying for the rest of the week. Building bonfires and playing capture the flag and doing whatever else you do at normal camp. Or maybe going to Richmond and eating a fancy meal at Mr. Allister's restaurant, Sadie and Jack and I all lit by candlelight. I wouldn't even mind eventually going home, as much as that surprises me.

The honeysuckle's perfume is so sweet and heavy that I feel a little drunk. I hear a low sound suddenly, a whirring. When I turn, there's a hummingbird to my left, hovering in front of a honeysuckle cluster. I hold my breath. The bird is tiny, iridescent green with a bright red throat. Its wings move so fast they're a blur.

"That's a hummingbird," Celia says.

"I know," I say, half whispering.

"Hummingbird hearts beat twelve hundred times a minute," she says softly. "Did you know that?" I shake my head, still watching. I can't take my eyes off this bird.

"That's really fast," Celia says.

I'm nodding. "It sure is."

Three more birds rise over the top of the trellis, float slowly down and start their own dance with the blossoms. I look at Celia and she's just watching them. She doesn't look especially impressed.

"Is this normal?" I say.

She nods. "Yeah, they love the honeysuckle. We get tons of them around here."

"You're lucky."

Jack appears now around the honeysuckle.

"Don't scare the hummingbirds away!" I say.

He takes a step back. "I'll do my best," he says.

I wave him forward. "This is my friend Jack," I say. "Jack, this is Celia."

"Hey," Celia says, then looks at me, considering something. "I hear you're a ballerina," she says.

"Boy, word sure travels fast around here," I say.

"Will you dance for us?"

I lean back on the stairs. "Oh, I don't know."

Jack is smiling. "Uh, I may have neglected to mention, it's part of why they're letting us stay. I told them you'd perform for the camp, so I think you have to now."

"Shit," I say, and Jack keeps smiling.

TRACK 21:

Songbird

AFTER DINNER, MOST OF THE camp sits out on the lawn in front of the main cabin, which has a wide front porch. I sit on the porch stairs with my nearly wrecked pointe shoes, the ribbons between my fingers. I look out on all those kids in their flower-fronted T-shirts, the other counselors, plus Allie and Knox and Jack up front. Allie waves to me, grinning. I lift my hand in reply.

I used to get nervous before dancing, but since Julia's gone, I don't. Or maybe it's that I feel nervous all the time—that galaxy feeling—so I don't notice anymore. I feel a little weird about this, the same sort of weird I felt about doing the lift with Tommy in the meadow near Fancy Dance Camp, but I don't really mind. Especially since the girls sitting closest are watching me tie up my shoes so intently they must be trying to memorize how to do it themselves.

I've decided to dance my solo from *Chrysanthemum*, the one

I've been practicing for two months. The one Julia danced years ago, for which Miriam's sewing my costume. Later this summer, I'll dance it in front of a bunch of very rich donors in hopes that they'll give the Academy more money. To be honest, I'd rather be dancing here. I've pulled the song up on my cell phone, and I step out on the porch to it playing on the small camp speakers along with the crickets outside, the creak of the floorboards, the hum of the porch light above me.

I've practiced this dance hundreds of times, but on the uneven floorboards of a cabin porch it's so different. It *feels* different, in my feet and my legs and my arms and my heart. My body is a little looser than normal, but I still have to keep an eye on the floor in a way that I wouldn't if I were in the studio, or on a real stage. I don't even go up on pointe at first. I dance on the balls of my feet instead, which feels safer, closer to the ground.

When I first saw Julia perform this onstage I'd already seen her dance it in the studio a dozen times, and when she danced, it was so hard to stay in my seat. I knew the choreography, and I wanted to do it too. Of course I didn't know that by the time Miss Diana would choose me to dance it, Julia wouldn't be dancing at all. Until today, dancing it made me feel like a ghost.

Ballet, Miss Diana would say, is about the relationship between movement and stillness. It's about those twenty-six bones. That galaxy-spinning feeling comes back now in a way I can use. I'm powered by it, actually. When I dance, there's a place to put that spinny, vibrating feeling. Maybe that's why I like it.

Or maybe I like it because it's incredible to see the looks on the faces of the audience, to do something that they absolutely believe is magic. Right now, I can see the kids on the lawn in flashes, and Knox and Allie and Jack behind them. Jack, who right at this moment might understand me more than anyone else does, because he's been there with me with Rose and Thatcher, and because, right now, he's seeing this.

So I make a deal with gravity, mid-dance on this creaky porch. I convince it to let me go. I rise up arabesque on pointe and then I start the series of fouettés that ends the dance, sixteen of them in a row. So many fewer than I did in the studio with Tommy the other day, but here on the porch, getting through them without losing my balance feels like a victory. It's totally different: the wind and the leftover light of evening and the smell of grass and old wood. The crickets and the floorboards and the kids, who aren't talking at all but who I can hear gasp from time to time. Just like my classmates and I did years ago, when Julia came to teach us about gravity.

When I finish, breathless and panting, I look up and I see Jack looking at me like he's never seen me before, over the heads of the kids, who've crowded toward me on the porch.

"It wasn't perfect," I say to him.

He's grinning. "You're impossible," he says. His smile could light a whole house, and I feel mine glowing too. So I sit straight down on the porch bench.

I untie my shoes and set them down next to me. Normally I don't love strangers seeing my feet with their blisters and busted toenails, but for some reason I don't completely mind today. It feels like one kind of truth I can tell these kids, especially the girls.

"Ballet is hard on the feet when you do it as much as I do," I say, raising one foot. "It hurts."

Jack is down on one knee on the ground with my pointe shoe in his hand. He's looking at it, examining it, really, his engineer brain trying to take it apart. Those particular shoes are pretty gross, which makes it embarrassing. But there's something really sweet about it, as if he's holding a part of me. As if he's trying to figure out how I work too.

Knox sits on my other side and sighs loudly. I look at him.

"He's got it bad, you know," he says. A half-dozen birds shoot up in the sky behind him like someone's tossed a handful of confetti. I watch them arc off in different directions, then I look back at Knox.

"Got what?"

Knox just looks at me then, a small smile on his lips. When I figure out what he means I blush so hard I can feel my cheeks warm.

"Go easy on him, okay?" Knox looks at me then, and I can see that his eyes are kind. I'm smiling before I realize it, and my heart's beating so fast it might as well be a hummingbird's.

TRACK 22:

Angel

BLUEBELL CABIN IS LIT GOLD by the paper lampshade in the center of the ceiling, and I'm alone for the first time in days. Well, Pavlova's here, but she's asleep on one of the empty cots. Jack's across the yard in a staff cabin, bunking with the camp cook, I think.

There's a moth circling the lantern, all flutter and lit-up wings. Every once in a while it lands on the paper sphere and folds and unfolds its wings a few times, but it always takes off again. The problem is that it can't get close enough. The problem is, if it did, it would burn up.

Somehow everything feels like it's about Julia, in ways that are impossible to explain.

My phone dings, saving me from my moth-watching. It's Jack.

Want to take a walk?

I answer before I have time to think about it.

When I close Bluebell's door behind me, Jack is already standing down on the grass. I guess he knew I was going to say yes.

"Should we try the woods?" he says. "Knox says there's a path that leads to some clearings. He says it's a pretty walk."

What else did he say? I wonder, but I just say okay. We start walking. I don't know if we're supposed to be holding hands or what. I don't know what's supposed to be happening.

The sky above us is pitch-black and star-dusted, but I can only see a narrow strip of it between the tops of trees. Here I am in the middle of the actual woods—a strange thing for a city girl, period, and even worse when you consider what's been happening to me lately—but I don't even mind. I don't know what the hell I'm doing, but for once I'm not scared.

When we come out into a clearing, it's like we've walked into a bowl filled with sugar-stars and sky. It's breathtaking, and by that I mean it literally takes my breath. I stand there, staring, and then I hear Jack's voice.

"Come here," he says. He's maybe twenty feet away, his back to me, looking up toward the sky. I walk toward him.

"Over there," he says. "See that light?" He points to the sky and I do see it, a bright white light traveling slowly, steadily across the sky.

"Airplane?" I ask.

"No." He turns to me, smiling. "That's the International Space Station."

"Really?" I look back at the light. It doesn't look like a space station. It looks like a plain old white dot. Another thing that must be magic but is real at the same time. "How do you know?"

Jack taps his pocket. "I get alerts by text when it's going to be visible."

I raise my eyebrows.

"It's less nerdy than it sounds," he says, still looking up. He glances down, then, smiling. "Or maybe it's not. But it amazes me, every time I see it. There are people living on it, orbiting the earth, and they don't know we're down here. Well, they know lots of us are, but they don't know about us. Specifically." He looks at me. He might be blushing.

"I get it," I say. My voice is soft. We both look back up, just as the space station passes to the edge of the sky-bowl.

"West-northwest to northeast," Jack says. "Four minutes."

When it's gone, I sit down in the grass. I don't know what else to do. Jack sits down too.

"You don't want to be an astronaut?" I say.

He shakes his head. "I want to design things. Bridges. Like Sadie said."

I nod. "So what's the deal with you and UVA?"

"My dad. I don't want to be near him."

"You're going to let your dad ruin that for you?"

Jack shrugs. "He's a jerk. I don't want to give him the idea that he's forgiven."

I roll a leaf between my fingers. "It doesn't mean you can't be in the same state as him."

"He'll think he owns me again." Jack picks up a twig and pulls a piece of bark from it. He puts it back down. "He'll want me to come for dinner all the time. I don't even want to go once."

"You can say no to a dinner invitation," I say. "You don't have to say no to the college acceptance."

"I already deferred," Jack says. "It's over."

"You didn't just turn them down?"

"Sadie wouldn't let me."

I know as well as anyone how hard it is to say no to Sadie, but this seems like a sign that he doesn't want to give up.

"Maybe you'll change your mind someday," I say.

Jack shakes his head. "I won't. He lied too much."

That word—*lied*—echoes around my head. Julia lied over and over, near the end. About everything. Once upon a time I believed Julia even when she told me a girl could sleep a hundred years and wake up happy, or be cut, still alive, right out of a wolf's belly. But by the night she left, it had been a long time since I believed much of anything Julia said. That she was fine. That she was going to rehab again. That she hadn't taken my mother's gold necklace, the one with the star-shaped charm I had always loved, and sold it to buy her pills.

This is when I decide to tell Jack about the fairy tales.

"I want to tell you something," I say to him.

"Okay," says Jack.

"But it's going to make me sound loopy."

He smiles. "Even better."

A firefly blinks at the far side of the clearing, behind Jack. He can't see it, and I don't point it out. I watch for a moment as it blinks itself into existence every few seconds, in different spots. Then I push on. "I've been seeing things," I say.

Jack's face doesn't change. "What kind of things?"

I'm not sure where to start. "It's hard to explain," I say. "There was a fox, and a bluebird, some pigeons on the roof of your building. All those seagulls back in Jersey."

Jack is looking at me. I can't tell what he's thinking.

"I mean, you saw those, right?"

"Sure," he says. "Of course. But I don't know what you mean. Those are just animals."

"Not 'just,'" I say. "There were girls too."

"Girls?"

"Girls in trouble." I know he has no idea what I'm talking about, so I need to show him the book. It's in my bag, which is slung crosswise over my body, because I can't bear to leave the book behind. I take it out. "Julia sent me this."

I give it to him. He holds it in his hands. More fireflies appear behind him, sparks in the air. The clearing—or one side of it—is alight. Warmth spreads from my belly to my arm to my wrist. My tattoo throbs.

"The book," he says. "Sadie told me about that. But not the other stuff."

"She said the bluebird was a sign from the universe," I say. "That I was supposed to go see Julia."

Jack flips through the pages of the book. He still doesn't notice the fireflies, blinking their glowing selves at each other.

"What if it's not the universe?" he asks.

"What?"

"Sending messages. What if it's your subconscious? Maybe you were missing Julia so much you just started noticing these things that were already around you. Your brain sees them as fairy tales."

"I didn't imagine the birds," I say. *And I'm not imagining these fireflies*, I think.

"I know. But seagulls can be aggressive when they think you might feed them."

"I don't know," I say. "What's the difference between coincidence and magic anyway? Both are unexplainable."

Jack moves so he's sitting crosslegged in front of me, looking right into my face.

"When my dad first left," he says, "I saw his car everywhere. The Volvo. I'd see it while I was sitting next to the window at Class Coffee, and I'd try to catch my mom's attention so she wouldn't see. I'd see it on Broadway, waiting at a stoplight in between two taxis. He was in Virginia by then, so it wasn't really him, but every time I saw it I was convinced it was."

I'm shaking my head before he even finishes. "So you think I'm just making this up?" I ask. "Hallucinating?"

"No," he says. "I don't know what's going on. Maybe it's magic. But maybe it's just a matter of how your brain is perceiving the things you see."

"I'm perceiving just fine," I say, but that's a lie. I'm not sure what I'm doing here on this road trip. I'm not sure what anything means. Suddenly I feel exhausted, just straight-up bone-tired. Behind Jack, the fireflies are dimming, blinking out like flashlights switched off.

He's looking at me. "So if it's magic, then what?"

If it's magic. I almost echo his words out loud.

"I don't know," I say. My heart is falling again, like a lead weight through water. "Maybe it can help me forget."

"Forget what?" he asks.

The breeze kicks up then, and all the leaves above me whisper the same thing.

"All of it."

TRACK 23:

Storms

LIKE THIS. ONE NIGHT IN April, when my parents were at a faculty party, I could hear Everett rummaging in the kitchen, opening the cupboards, the fridge. I had barely talked to him in weeks because he either wasn't home or he wouldn't come out of his room. There were sheafs of sketches piled on every surface of his room, as far as I could see through the cracked-open door. He couldn't even look at Julia since the day we'd had to call the ambulance, so he was avoiding her, I guess, but it felt like he was avoiding me too. I hovered just before the kitchen for a few moments, listening to him opening and closing things, not eating anything. Then he turned down the hallway. He looked unsteady, like the floor beneath him was uneven. His face was ash gray. I didn't say anything. I couldn't.

"I'm fine," he said, answering a question I hadn't asked. He rubbed his forehead.

"You're not," I said.

"I just need to sleep, Sylvie." He was already turning away. "Please let me sleep."

He shut his door hard behind him. I heard him switch on his turntable.

When I turned around I saw Julia, standing like a ghost in the doorway of her room. I couldn't really see her face clearly in the half-light, just the shadows in the hollows of her cheekbones. Her beauty was spectral. She stepped toward me and I took a step back.

"Can't you just get better?" I asked.

Her eyes were glassy with tears. She took another step toward me, and without thinking about it, I backed up just a little.

"I used to read you 'The Red Shoes,'" she said. "Do you remember?"

I did. It was a Hans Christian Andersen story and we'd had an illustrated edition. In it, a little girl wishes for a pair of red shoes and is forced to wear them forever as a punishment for her vanity. The shoes keep dancing, whether she wants to or not. She can't take them off. She eventually asks an executioner to chop off her feet. It doesn't help.

"Sort of," I said. I was lying. I remembered.

"It's like that," Julia said. "I want to stop. I don't know how." She was standing right in front of me, but her voice sounded small and far away.

Rage moved through me like a comet, fire on the outside and dirty ice at its core.

"Well, figure it out," I said. "Don't you see? You're wrecking everything!"

I didn't wait to see the look on her face. I whirled around and went back into my own room, slamming the door behind me. And two days later, Julia left.

Now, in the forest, that feeling is back, the one where my molecules are spinning and I'm a galaxy again, full of stars and wide-open space. I'd give anything to settle myself, to stand on the edge of something, do a hundred fouettés. But what can I do in the middle of the forest?

"I don't know what I'm doing out here," I say to Jack. I stand up and turn to leave, to head back toward the cabins, but he catches my wrist in his hand. Under his fingers, my tattoo feels hot.

"Wait," he says.

When he pulls me back toward him, it feels like choreography. It makes me think of my physics teacher's favorite rule: *to every action there is an equal and opposite reaction*. I pull away, he pulls me back, and we end up in the place we're supposed to be, right in the middle. Then we're kissing and I don't even know how it happened.

I'm certain the stars are exploding above us, that woodland animals are forming a circle around the spot where we stand. (Creepy little jerks.) But it doesn't matter because I don't open my eyes, so the only magic is here, inside us. Between us.

In fairy tales, everything changes after the kiss, but that's mostly because the heroines are unconscious directly before. Jack lets me go and I step back a little, unsteady, still holding his hand, my eyes open now. The stars are a glittering canopy over our heads, the trees form a soft, shadowy barrier around the clearing, and the last firefly goes out. For this one moment I feel completely, perfectly safe. And here's what I'm thinking in this exact moment:

This is what it feels like to wake up after you've been asleep your entire life.

TRACK 24:

Never Forget

"ARE YOU OKAY?" JACK ASKS.

"Yeah," I say. "You?"

"I am very okay." He's smiling. "I've wanted to do that since we crossed the New Jersey state line. Maybe before."

"I thought you hated me." When I say it, though, it doesn't feel true. Or it feels like it's been a very long time since I believed it. And I believed it in a place far, far away.

Jack shakes his head. "I never hated you. I . . . felt confused when I looked at you, and that made me mad."

"That's perfectly normal," I say, smiling.

He smiles back. "I thought so," he says, and kisses me again.

When we come out of the woods I'm surprised to see the cabins still there, each with a round white lamp glowing like its own personal moon above its door.

"Civilization," I say.

"I preferred the woods," Jack says. He leans close and presses his shoulder to mine. Even though I feel my molecules rearranging themselves again, I don't mind it this time. Nothing disturbing or scary has happened in the outside world since we got to Philadelphia, and I'm thrilled about that. I may be carrying the fairy tale book around, but I want the stories to stay safe inside it.

When we part I walk up the stairs, keeping my footsteps quiet. I wave to him from the doorway.

"Pssst."

I turn and see Allie sitting on the stairs of her cabin next door. She's lit up by the bulb above her and has a novel facedown in her lap.

"Hi," I say. "I snuck out. Am I busted?"

Allie smiles, showing all her teeth. "If I had someone as cute as Jack to sneak out for," she says, "I'd be right there with you."

I can feel my skin get hot. I shiver a little, shaking it off. "You totally do," I tell her. "Hello? Knox?"

Allie looks toward the ground. "Well, he's got to ask me first."

"It's going to happen," I say. She smiles.

"How was it?" she asks. Her voice is just above a whisper but she's watching me with interest.

There are so many possible answers to that question after what I've seen the past few days. But I just choose the easiest one.

"Magic."

That's the Way Love Goes

THIS MORNING IS FAIRY BREAKFAST, and Allie has a pair of wings for me to wear. They're made of silver wire and tulle, tied with sky-blue ribbons at the bottom.

"These are amazing," I say when she hands them to me. "You just have extra wings lying around?"

Allie shakes her head. "I made them this morning. I've made so many at this point, I could make them in my sleep."

"Have you ever thought of a future in costume design?" I say. "We could use you at NBT." I flash back to standing on a stool in the middle of our wardrobe room last week, Miriam fussing with my skirt below me, her mouth full of pins. It seems like a lifetime ago.

"Maybe," Allie says. "Actually, I think I'd like that."

I slip the straps of the wings over my shoulders and stand with

Allie in the front of the cabin. All the small fairies line up in front of us, smiling, their own wings covered in glitter and silk.

"All right, fairies," Allie says. "Sylvie has to leave this morning."

A collective sad noise rumbles through the room. Allie raises her hand and they quiet.

"But first we're going into the woods to make our fairy houses," she says.

The girls cheer. I can't stop smiling. They're so cute, and it's so easy to like them. It's so easy to be here.

Allie has already explained this to me: the kids will use sticks and leaves and bark to make little houses in the middle of the forest, making the fairies' real estate dreams come true.

Across the yard I see some of the boys coming out of their cabins, in full fairy attire. I don't see Jack, and honestly, the idea of seeing him makes my blood spin. What the hell was I thinking, kissing him?

Oh my god.

But I don't say this to Allie. I just ask her about the wings. "The boys wear wings too?"

Allie nods. "Just as much glitter over there, if not more. Definitely a little messier."

I run my fingers over the edge of Allie's wing. "I love this place."

"It's pretty magical," she says. There's that word again—*magic*—but I like it better this way. Not creepy. Just real.

"If you're interested in being a counselor next summer," Allie says, "let me know. I know the boss."

"I'd love that," I say. And I wonder, again: *What would it be like if I weren't always dancing?*

I turn around and Knox appears in front of me, huge dark blue wings on his back. They're covered in sequins big as quarters, shiny like the scales of a fish.

"Your wings are enormous," I say.

Knox looks at me. He presses his lips shut. Then he opens them.

"This is me," he says, "resisting the urge to make an off-color joke."

I laugh. "Thanks. Where's . . ." I let my voice trail off.

Knox smiles. "Your dashing consort?"

"Yeah."

"He's coming. He's not quite as comfortable in his wings as I am. Give him a little while to let go of stereotypical gender roles."

I see him then, across the grass. Jack, his wings wide and green. They're covered in iridescent fabric and shaped like a drag-onfly's, but a little smaller than Knox's. He can still fit though a doorway without turning sideways.

My heart butterflies inside my rib cage. Panic rises in my blood. Here's the guy I made out with last night: my best friend's crabby brother, my chauffeur, a guy who is presently wearing drag-onfly wings. Which, honestly, is a pretty good look for him.

When he sees me he smiles, a slow, warm smile like a sunlamp angled in my direction, and my heart straightens out, settles back into its spot. And beats so hard I think he must be able to hear it.

"Hi," Jack says. His hand comes up like he wants to take my hand, or otherwise touch me, but then he pulls it back to his side.

"Hi." My hand wants to hold his too, but I keep it at my side. I don't really know the new rules.

"Nice wings," Jack says.

"You too." I can't stop smiling.

"I'm trying to play along."

I tilt my head and look at him. "I never really saw you as a dragonfly."

"I'm not," he says. "I'm a fairy like everyone else. Or is there, like, a male word for fairy? Like you have mermaid and merman, for example."

"Fairman."

"Something like that."

We watch the kids gather pinecones and sticks and leaves, then form them into delicate houses they lean against the bottoms of tree trunks. Jack leans down next to a boy with shiny black hair and huge dark eyes.

"That ought to last through any storm this forest can throw at it," Jack tells him. "The engineering is very sound." The boy grins.

My heart is getting kind of melty, so I take a few steps toward Allie, who's helping one of her girls make a freestanding fairy house out of twigs.

Past her, Knox is watching Jack help a boy named Leo arrange a pile of pinecones in a "fence" around a fairy yard.

I lean close to Knox.

"Want some advice?" I ask. He nods. "Ask her to sneak out some night. Do something romantic." I poke him in the arm. "She'll love it."

"Yeah?"

I smile. "I'm sure of it."

Knox looks at Allie, who's standing a few trees away.

"Fairies!" she shouts. "Are you all finished?"

There's a chorus of *yes* from all the tiny people, and Allie climbs up on a tree stump like it's a soapbox.

"Okay!" she says. "Then it's time to call the forest fairies. The tiny ones. But here's the deal: you have to close your eyes while they come, because if they see you looking, they'll stay away. And then we're going to leave once they're safe in their new houses."

Jack and I stand there and watch the kids shut their eyes tight, fully believing. He squeezes my hand and closes his own eyes, so I do too. With places like this in the world, it's no wonder I can't figure out where magic ends and the real world begins. But I know what I'm choosing: real world.

So of course this is when I hear it, the bright song of a bird from the tree above me. No one else seems to notice, but I look up, listening, trying to glimpse the bird through the branches. I can see flashes of it moving in the leaves. It's red, of course, singing its song over and over, a song I know because I've heard it dozens of times. It's the Dance of the Firebird, from the Stravinsky ballet. I close my eyes and I see it: the long crimson tutu, the feathered headdress.

I figure it out before I open my eyes. I remember who my fairy godmother has been all along.

Landslide

MISS DIANA ANSWERS ON THE first ring.

"Hello," she says, like a normal human. I can't quite manage it myself.

"Who's Daniela?" The words just tumble out of me.

"What?"

"It's Sylvie," I say. "I need to know. Do you know who Daniela is?"

She pauses. "Where are you, Sylvie?"

Well, I'm in the woods, obviously, both literally and metaphorically, but she doesn't need to know that. "It doesn't matter."

"It matters to me," she says. Her voice is soft. "I know you're not at camp."

Shit. "They called you?"

"No. I called them. I had a feeling."

Because you're magic too, I want to say. I look down at my feet, my sneakers sunk into the grass. I'm always attached to the earth.

"Tell me," she presses.

"Fine." I look around the clearing. Past the trees I can see flashes of the campers finishing up their fairy houses. I can hear the hum of their voices too, punctuated by little shrieks of joy. "I *am* at camp, actually, but it's a different camp, in Pennsylvania. I'm with my friend. I'm safe."

"Okay," she says. "I'm listening."

"You knew that package was from Julia." This isn't a question.

"Yes."

"Did you know what was in it?"

"No."

I turn away from the clearing, start to walk back on the path a little. "It was a fairy tale book of mine, from when I was a kid. Julia made a list of names in the back. Grace Akua was the first. I mean, it didn't say her last name, but you know Grace." I'm rambling.

"I know Grace," she repeats.

"Then my cousin Rose, and then Julia's ex-boyfriend Thatcher."

"Okay," Miss Diana says, carefully, slowly.

"I went to see them," I say. "All of them. I'm going to tell you all this, and I really hope you won't call my mother."

"I'm not going to call anyone right this second, Sylvie," she says.

"Great. So here's the problem. Thatcher doesn't know where Jules went next, but I'm thinking it must have been to Daniela because Jules put her name right on the list. But I don't know who she is. And this is where I think you can help me."

"Sylvie," Miss Diana says. She doesn't say it like it's the start of something, or the end of something. She's just saying my name. And in this moment the world cracks open a little, just a little fissure at its edges, and I don't know if light or darkness is going to leak in. I'm so afraid that she won't be able to tell me where to go next.

I sit down with my back against a tree trunk, fill the space with words instead of fear. "I got a tattoo," I say.

"Really?"

"Yes. For Julia. And for you too, I guess. It says 'twenty-six bones,' like you always say." I pause for a moment. "Did you ever see hers?"

I can almost hear her smile. "I did."

"I always wondered if you had. She thought it would keep her safe. But it didn't. I don't think there's anywhere that's safe in the whole world." I'm crying now and I don't know when I started. I don't know how to stop.

"Sylvie," Miss Diana says again.

I let empty space fill the line for a moment. "What?"

She doesn't say anything right away. I hear her breathe. "I thought about keeping that package. I thought about opening it, to see what it was. I should have, probably. I wish you had talked to me."

"I didn't know you knew anything," I say. "You didn't tell me. So tell me now. Who is she?"

"Daniela Rojas," she says. "She's a former student of mine who dances for the Washington Ballet." She takes a breath. "Julia was afraid she'd keep hurting you and your brother if she stayed in New York. She told me that she was sure if she just got out of town for a few months, she'd be able to get herself under control. She'd go to her meetings. She'd stay clean."

Through the trees, I can see the campers heading back toward the cabins with Allie and Jack and Knox. "Did she?" I ask.

"I don't know. Your sister made me promise to stay out of it from that point forward, and I agreed." She sighs. "Julia had lied to me, fooled us all. She put the whole company at risk, really, since she was such a high-profile member. I mean, they covered her accident in the *Times*."

I remembered. It was only one paragraph in the Saturday Arts section, but it ran next to a small photo of Julia's face, a close-up from the feature they'd done on her and her friends earlier.

"We could have helped her, if she had asked. Or at least I think we could have." Miss Diana pauses. "In some ways, it was easier to let her go."

When she says this, something cracks inside of me, loosens and floats up to the surface. I lean my head back against the tree and look up. Branches and blue sky, and way up there: the Firebird, watching me. It ruffles its feathers, then settles them back. The bird keeps quiet, and somehow, that makes me open my own mouth.

I tell Miss Diana the story I haven't told anyone, and something breaks open in me when I do.

PART THREE

Ever After

The Tale of Her Leaving

THE NIGHT JULIA LEFT SHE came into my room just before midnight, her voice lifting me straight out of a dream. I opened my eyes
into the room's half black and saw my sister on the edge of my bed,
her hands clasped in front of her. Her palms were pressed together,
thumbs hooked. The way you'd hold on to a person if you didn't
want her to fall.

As soon as I saw her, I knew what was happening. It was there
on the breeze coming through my window, lifting my curtains away
from the sill. She was going to leave. It was in the streetlamp light
seeping through my blinds, making gold stripes over the windows.
I pushed myself up on my pillows.

"What," I said, not quite a question. Julia shook her head (not
an answer), her dark hair brushing her shoulders.

"I have to get out of here for a while," she said, leaning

forward. "So I can get better. But I'll come back." Her voice was a whisper over the hum of my ceiling fan.

I tried to answer but no words came out. Instead they floated in front of me like butterflies in the air.

don't go
get clean
this is all your fault

I was so tired of all this. So sick of waiting for Julia to get better or not. To ruin all our lives again. Because it didn't feel like this would ever be over. We'd always end up in the same spot.

I took a breath and the word-butterflies scattered, leaving only one in the air between us.

go

Then I said it out loud.

"Go," I said.

Julia flinched a little, then looked at me like she was trying to solve a riddle. Then she stood up and walked straight out the door.

How to Save Yourself

"IT WASN'T YOUR FAULT," MISS Diana says. "None of this was."

"You're wrong," I say, my voice hard, and for just a second, my heart gives a twinge at my tone. She's my teacher, one of my idols. I've never spoken to her like this before. "I knew what she was doing. At least a little. And I didn't do anything. I didn't tell anyone."

"Sylvie, plenty of people knew about it to one extent or another." Miss Diana's voice is still calm, still quiet. "And the rest of us probably should have known."

"Maybe, but once you figured it out, you helped her."

She breathes in, lets it out. "She helped herself. I just found her a place to go."

I lie down in the cool grass then, tip my face up toward the clouds. Above me, the Firebird makes a soft shrieking sound, then takes off for the sky. I watch it get smaller and then disappear, a red flash disappearing past the trees.

"Did it break your heart?" I ask.

"What?" She says this absentmindedly, half to herself.

"When Julia had the accident. When you found out about the pills."

Miss Diana waits. I strain to hear her answer, but I only hear the sounds of the forest: leaves rustling, anonymous birds singing, branches shifting in the wind. Then she answers. "Yes. Of course it did."

"I need to see her," I say.

Miss Diana starts to say something, but she stops.

She gives me the address. I write it down.

Return to Sender

WE MAKE IT THROUGH THE ring of traffic hell around DC by two o'clock, and so at two-thirty we're standing outside Daniela's apartment, blinking into the golden sunlight. It's a row house made of gray stone, two doors side by side at the top of a short flight of stairs. Before I head up the stairs, Jack squeezes my hand and then lets it go.

I take the stairs two at a time and ring the doorbell. Nothing happens. I press my ear to the door. I turn back toward Jack.

"I'm just going to ring her neighbor," I say.

"Okay," says Jack, but his voice doesn't sound sure.

The door opens, and it's a tall man in a blue button-down shirt.

"Girl Scouts?" the man says.

"Um," I say. "What?"

"Are you selling cookies?"

"What?" I say again. I picture the badges I might earn lately: one in Running Away from Fancy Dance Camp without Getting Caught, one in Holding On to Your Sanity When the World Turns Magic. Another in Fleetwood Mac's Greatest Hits.

"No," I say, "I'm not a Girl Scout." I gesture toward Jack as if that explains it. *I'm traveling with a boy. Therefore I can't be a Girl Scout.*

"They sell cookies in the winter," Jack says from down on the sidewalk. I look at him. "Not the summer." His voice sort of trails off. "What?" he says. "I'm really into the Samoas."

I look back at the man, and he looks at me.

"Okay," he says. "Then who are you?"

"I'm Sylvie," I say. "I'm looking for Daniela. I think she lives upstairs."

"She used to." This is a different voice, from behind the man. A shorter man who steps up to lean in the doorway. "She moved out about two months ago."

Jack steps up on the landing with me. "She was—friends?—with another girl named Julia. She was here about a year ago, we think."

I pull up a photograph of Julia on my phone and hold it so the men can see.

"She's my sister," I say. "She's the one I'm really looking for."

"We just moved here six months ago," the first man says. "I'm sorry." He really does sound sorry, and I feel my lungs contracting.

"Do you think you could call your landlord or something?" Jack asks. "Get her forwarding address?"

"We just bought this house. It was an estate sale," the second man says.

I almost expect him to say that all the records of the sale were destroyed in a fire, and that the firemen all moved to Tallahassee immediately afterward, because it's that clear the universe isn't giving Julia up easily.

I take a big breath, and my eyes well up with tears. The man looks alarmed.

"I'm sorry," he says again.

"I'm fine." *Fine fine fine.*

One of these times I'm going to tell the truth.

Experts on This

WE'RE SITTING ON A BENCH across from a bakery called The Yeast We Could Do. I can see loaves piled in the window, and even though I feel like I should be hungry, I'm not.

Jack tries to take my hand, but I clasp my hands at almost the same time. I press my palms together, fingers clenched around each other.

"I'm sorry, Sylvie," Jack says. That's all anyone can say to me today, apparently.

I shrug and put my right hand in Jack's. "I just have to figure out the next step."

Jack waits a second, his eyes on the bakery window. "Do you?"

I look at him and he turns toward me. "What?" I ask.

"Listen," he says. "You're looking for signs everywhere.

Maybe this is a sign. Maybe it's time to let this whole thing go." He's still holding my hand, and when he says that last part, he squeezes it harder. "For now, I mean."

My pulse quickens. "How am I supposed to do that?" I ask. "We came all this way. She's here, in this city."

"She *was* here," Jack says. "A year ago."

He's right, of course. There's no reason to believe she'd stay.

"Okay," Jack says, his tone neutral. He's problem solving. "For the sake of argument let's say Julia *is* here. If she is, we'll find her. We'll figure this out. But in the meantime, maybe we could just step away from this for a moment? Clear our minds? See the sights?" He makes a little gesture in the air with his left hand. "What have you always wondered about our nation's capital? We can find out." He's smiling, trying to be silly, trying to distract me from my failure. It doesn't work.

"The only thing I'm wondering about," I say, "is the where-abouts of my sister."

Jack nods. "I know. But here's the thing: you might find her. You might find her and it might not change anything. She might still hurt you again. In fact, she probably *will* hurt you again." His voice turns hard on these last words, brittle like cold glass.

I try to catch his eye but he won't look at me. "You don't know that," I say.

"No, but I've been with you for three days. I've watched you talk to these people who loved Julia." He turns toward me. "I've seen this before. When people leave, sometimes they just want to be gone."

Something in his voice tells me where this is coming from.

"You're not talking about Julia," I say.

He looks away from me and reaches down to pet Pavlova. "I think it applies in both cases. And that's why I need to tell you this." He sits up, leans back against the bench. "I've decided that I'm not going to my dad's. Sadie will be mad, but I just can't do it."

"You have to!" I say. "You promised her."

Jack looks straight at me. "I can't. I'm not going to pretend things are okay when they're not."

"I know you think you're an expert on this," I say, "but what if Sadie's right? Your dad seems to want a fresh start. What if he's different now?"

"I don't want to know!" Jack says.

I fold my arms over my chest. "Exactly. It's easier to put people in boxes and leave them there. Isn't it?"

"No, that's not right." He leans back on the bench. "That's not what I'm doing. And anyway, this isn't about me and my dad."

I can feel my face getting hot, my heartbeat swell in my chest. I move my body so I'm facing Jack, and he turns toward me too. His brow is furrowed.

"Listen," I say. "You've known me for, like, three days. I mean, yeah, you've been around half my life, but you never paid any attention to me before now." The words are unspooling so quickly I can't stop them, and I don't think I want to, anyway. "All I'm saying is that you don't know me, and you don't know Julia either. So don't put *your* shit on *us*. Okay?"

Jack opens his mouth. He closes it. Then he shakes his head.

"Okay," he says. "I'm going to give Pavlova a walk around the block. Just think about what you want to do next."

Before I can say anything, he walks away, following Pavlova on the sidewalk. She doesn't even turn to look at me.

So I sit on a bench in Georgetown, trying not to cry. I still feel the heat of anger in my blood, and my fingers are wrapped around the edge of the bench so firmly they're turning white. But I already know that anger is going to fade to sadness. That's what always happens, the way even a meteor, red-hot from its trip through the Earth's atmosphere, eventually ends up just a plain old rock.

A girl passes me, or rather she cuts across the sidewalk in front of me and begins to cross the street. She has black hair in a hundred tiny braids and brown skin, and she's wearing a dark purple dress. I mean, she's just some girl. But something makes me look at her, watch her, and when she turns toward the bakery, I see that she has a goose.

As in she's carrying a goose, an actual pearl-white goose, under her left arm. She walks straight into The Yeast We Could Do, opening the door so quickly I can hear the bell on it ring from across the street. I watch her disappear behind that glass, behind all that bread. I'm up on my feet crossing the street before I even know what I'm doing.

Gone Goose Girl

THE BAKERY IS COOL AND dim, with walls painted china blue. It's empty inside. There's no one behind the counter, just loaves of bread lining the shelves on the wall. Next to the counter is a glass-fronted case full of pastries dusted with sparkling sugar. I crane my neck to see into the back room, but the girl is already gone, as far as I can tell. I follow.

In the back, the air is warm from the ovens and hazy with flour. To my right there's a guy in a white T-shirt kneading a pile of dough.

"Hey," he says, seemingly unfazed by the presence of a strange girl—me—in the bakery's kitchen.

"Did a girl come through here?" I say. "She was carrying a goose."

He smiles, slowly. Maybe he's on major Valium, or perhaps the warm-bread smell just has a tranquilizing effect. I could believe that.

"If she did," he says, "I didn't see her."

This is when I see the glimmer of a white feather on the tiled floor just in front of the door. I lean down and pick it up. It's real, here between my fingers. I push the door open and walk out into the sunlight.

There are more feathers out here, lots of them, tiny downy ones and big curling ones, drifting around on the concrete like fake snow. *The Nutcracker* flashes through my mind again, just like it did a week ago while I stood on the stool in front of Miriam. *Sugarplum.* I sweep my right foot, toes pointed, in a sort of rond de jambe on the concrete, and feathers stick to my sneaker, the same way fake *Nutcracker* snow always sticks to my slippers.

The feathers are in the street too, and when cars drive by the feathers swirl into the air. When the light turns red, I cross to the other side. There are more of them over there. I don't really understand where that girl could have gone, or what could have happened to the goose between there and here to make it shed so many feathers. I stand on the curb for a moment, and a bus pulls up in front of me, groaning to a halt. I step back, and then I see the poster spread across the bus's side.

It's for the Washington Ballet.

I stand there, staring, on the corner. The bus driver opens the door.

"Are you getting on?" he says. He sounds part-friendly, part-bored.

"The ballet?" I say this as if it's an answer, and I point toward the side of the bus.

"Yeah, that's on the route. Farther down Wisconsin. Maybe twenty minutes away."

My molecules start to spin. *Sorry, Jack,* I think.

I get on the bus.

Where I Am

I FEEL CALMER ON THE bus, on my way somewhere. I put my bag on the seat next to me and watch the buildings go by.

My phone chimes a text. From Jack, of course.

Where are you? it says.

Don't worry, I type. I'll call you in a couple of hours. It's not an answer, but I'm not sure how to tell the truth right now. And I don't need anyone who doubts me along for this ride. After all, our patron saint, rock-and-roll princess Stevie Nicks, spent years hoping some guy might save her, and then she figured out that she was absolutely capable of saving herself.

My phone chimes again. **Sylvie**, it says. **Are you all right?**

Out the window is a clear blue sky. We're twenty minutes from the ballet (and Daniela? and maybe, my sister?). From the possibility that I'm going to figure all this out.

I'll be fine, I type.

Then I press Send, hoping that makes it true.

A Stone, a Tree

THE WASHINGTON BALLET IS HOUSED in a boxy, cream-colored building you'd never guess held a ballet company inside it. It seems about right, though. You might think of the feathers and beads and tulle when you imagine ballet, but what matters most are the practical things: the firm, even stage floor; a dancer's bones and muscles. This building seems like it could hold it all.

I walk straight through the door and toward the reception desk across the room.

"Hi," I say. "My name is Sylvie Blake, and I'm looking for Daniela Rojas." I take a breath. "Is she here right now?"

The receptionist looks at me. She blinks. I realize what I must look like, wild-haired and exhausted, holding a small book of fairy tales in my hand. I smile, try to look normal and calm. I fail at it, probably.

"If she's in class," I say, "I'm happy to wait until she's done."

"I'm sorry," the woman says, and she really does look sorry. She's seen a lot of ballets, I imagine, so she feels sorry for poor waifs or street urchins like me. "You can leave your name, but I can't let you into the building."

"The thing is," I say, "you don't have to let me in. I'm already in. I came right through that door." I point my thumb backward toward it.

The woman looks at me.

I look at her.

We seem to have reached an impasse. Or maybe she's telepathically summoning a security guard. That's possible too. But I'm not even close to giving up. In fact I'm mentally preparing my next line of argument.

"Please." I take a step closer to her desk, and repeat myself. "I'm Sylvie Blake," I say, like that means something. "I'm a student at the NBT Academy in New York." I pull my phone out and scroll through the pictures, showing her. "My sister was a dancer in the company. I'm just trying to find her. She's a friend of Daniela's." I know I'm getting loud, and I don't care.

The woman is looking at my phone with interest, though she looks a little worried too.

"I'm sorry," she says. "I really can't help you beyond taking your name." She hands me back my phone and exchanges a glance with someone behind me. I turn around and see half a dozen dancers leaning out of the closest studio.

"You *can* help me," I say, my voice breaking. "You just don't want to." I square my shoulders. "Well, I'm not leaving."

The woman picks up the phone. She must not be any good at telepathy. "I need some assistance at the desk," she says, to who-knows-who.

"I need some assistance too," I say. "And honestly, if I call for it, it'll probably end up being a talking cat or, like, a horse with wings, so watch out."

Arguably, this is not the best thing to say, because it just makes me sound unhinged. And even though the guy walking fast down the hallway doesn't hear, he sees the look on the receptionist's face. It's not a good one.

"You have to leave," he says. He puts his hands on my shoulders and starts to guide me toward the door. I try to plant my feet—to be a stone, a tree with roots deep in the ground—but he's already got momentum, and I'm moving.

Then someone saves me, with only her voice.

"Wait!" she says, we hear from behind us. "I know her. It's okay."

I turn around. The man's hands are still on my shoulders, but he loosens his grip a little. The dancer standing in front of us is tiny, maybe five feet tall, really beautiful, with long black hair piled on her head and thick, smudgy eyeliner around her dark brown eyes. She looks amazed.

"Shit, Sylvie," she says. "What the hell are you doing here?"

Pain and Power

WE SIT OUT ON THE front lawn, under the spread-out branches of a maple tree. Daniela splays her legs out into a V shape, pressing her head toward one knee. Seeing it makes me want to do it too. It's so familiar, that type of movement, even though she's in a leotard and I'm in cutoff shorts. She sits up straight then, and I lean forward, waiting for her to tell me a story. To tell me where Julia is.

"You came all the way here?" she asks. "From New York?"

I nod. "I went to Princeton first, and Philadelphia. Saw my cousin and Julia's ex-boyfriend."

"How, though? I mean, how did you get here?"

"My friend drove me." Daniela is watching my face as I say this and I'm sure she can tell there's more to it than that, but I don't feel like explaining it right now. I don't even know how to explain it to myself.

"All right." She rolls her shoulders, then tips her head to stretch her neck. "Julia stayed with me for two weeks. Then she got her own place."

"Where? Here in DC?"

Daniela nods. "She could have stayed longer, but I think she wanted to try to forget about ballet. Which is hard when you're living with a dancer." Daniela smiles, and I feel the muscles in my shoulders relax a little. She wouldn't be smiling if my sister were still taking pills. Though maybe she doesn't know.

"Is she okay?"

"I think so," Daniela says. "I haven't talked to her in a while." She pulls up a handful of grass, lets it drop. "I feel bad about that, but I think it's what she wanted."

"It's what she does," I say. "She leaves."

Daniela looks at me for a long moment. "Yeah, I think people would have said that about me a few years ago."

Something clicks in my head, like a key turning a lock. "You were . . ." I can't say it.

"An addict," Daniela says. "Yeah. Diana sent Julia to me so I could be her role model." She laughs a hard laugh. "To prove she could get clean too."

My next words are out of my mouth before I can stop them. "What's it like?"

Daniela doesn't seem surprised or bothered by my asking, but she thinks about it for a second before she answers.

"I think being a dancer prepares you for it, somehow. You're used to pain, and you're used to power." She looks at me. "Right?"

I nod.

"And you're used to giving up everything else in pursuit of your goal." She lets out a small laugh. "You're used to being an asshole. Anyway, I screwed my life up for a while, but somehow my body made it through mostly okay. Unlike Julia."

I shut my eyes tight and see in a flash: my sister on the studio floor, sobbing. Her leotard soaked with sweat, her leg at an angle that wasn't quite right.

I open my eyes.

"So why did you stop?"

"My mom," Daniela says, nodding a little. "I did it for her. Plus, she pulled me right out of here and took me back to New Jersey. To rehab. I didn't have a choice." She looks down at her hands in her lap. "I could have run away, but I figured . . . I don't know. I figured I was already there. I could give it a shot."

A dark gray squirrel runs down the other side of the maple tree and halfway across the lawn. I watch it. I know Daniela is looking at me.

"You have to be prepared, Sylvie. She might not be ready to see you."

"Ready to see me?" I say this too loudly. "I'm her sister. It's been a whole year. How long does it take to get ready?" I mean this as a rhetorical question, but Daniela answers it.

"It's different for everyone."

"She sent me a book with a list of names in it," I say. "Mine.

Yours. My cousin's. Her ex." I lean forward. "She wants me to find her."

Daniela resettles herself on the grass, folding her legs in front of her. "Okay," she says. "But why wouldn't she have told you where she is?"

"Maybe . . . maybe she can't," I say. "Maybe it's like a fairy tale: I need to prove myself, show what I'm willing to sacrifice. Show that I'll do whatever it takes to get to her."

Daniela shakes her head, her piled-up hair swaying a little on her head. "Kid," she says, "that kind of thinking will get you into trouble."

"Exactly," I say.

Daniela looks down at her hands. The squirrel comes back toward the tree, but just runs straight up the trunk.

"Listen, I worked really hard to find you," I say. "You can see that, right?"

She nods. "I can see that."

"All right, then, you can imagine how hard I'll work to find *her.* Even if I have to wander around this city for days on end, I'll do it." I make a wandering motion with the first two fingers on my right hand. "I'll sleep out on the National Mall. Can you do that? Or will the Secret Service come and cart you away?"

She smiles. "I don't think it would be the Secret Service," she says. "Probably the National Park Service."

"Whatever," I say. "I know she needs me."

"Sylvie," she says, and the first thing I think is: *I've got her.*

"Yeah?"

Daniela pulls her phone out of her bag and looks at it. Then she looks up at me.

"She was going to meetings every afternoon when she got here at a place a few blocks away." She gives me the address. "You might be able to make it," she says, "if you run."

So I do.

Migration

THERE'S ONLY ONE WOMAN LEFT in the room by the time I get there, gathering the folding chairs into a pile in the back. She's white, tall, and thin, with frizzy platinum-blond hair falling over her shoulders. There are deep lines in her tanned skin. She might be the villain of the fairy tale or a heroine who never got to the Happily Ever After. I'm not sure yet.

"Hi," I say. I take a step through the doorway. "I'm wondering if you can help me. I'm looking for my sister, Julia."

She looks at me for a long moment, sizing me up. "The ballerina?" she says.

I feel relieved when she says it, because it means she knows Julia, but I feel a twinge right in my heart, as if a shard of glass has found its way in there.

She used to be, I want to say, but instead I just nod. "Are you the leader?"

She laughs in a way that isn't exactly nice.

"I'm just part of the group," she says. "And I'm on my way out." She goes, then, just walks out the door, but I follow her outside. The sky is even bluer than when I came in, if that's possible. A cartoonish blue sky from a Disney movie.

"Please," I say. "I've been trying to find her for days. This is my last lead. *You're* my last lead."

She lights a cigarette with a silver lighter, takes a drag. "They call this *anonymous* for a reason," she says.

"I know that. But I already know she's here, and honestly, I think she needs my help. If you could tell me something, anything, I'd be so grateful."

The woman stops moving away from the door and faces me. She looks at my face and then down at the rest of me: tank top, cut-off shorts, silver tennis shoes on my feet.

"You think she's different from the rest of us."

The way she says it, it isn't a question, and I'm not sure what to say. She's right, I guess. But how could Julia not be different from the rest of the people at her meeting? She was different, *is* different, from anyone else I've ever met.

"What you need to understand," the woman says, "is that the things that make you different are the things that get obliterated when you're an addict. Okay?"

She looks at me expectantly, and I nod.

"She isn't different anymore." The woman says this and

then takes a step back from me. She doesn't look angry. She looks sad. "She's just an ordinary junkie."

My tattoo twinges then, and I press the fingers of my other hand onto it. This is when I hear a sound above me, a flutter of wings—and then a small crash, something hitting glass. I look up and see the window: a reflection of the building across from it. Whatever the thing was, it falls in a flash of blue like a piece of the sky.

A chill spreads from the sidewalk into my body, up, up, up to my heart. I walk over to the small blue thing on the pavement.

It's a bluebird. Its wings are half-spread and its head tilts to the side, beak pointing toward the sky. I can see in its crumpled shape the bluebird on the High Line from days ago.

"Shit," the woman says. She walks over too and stands next to me, so close that her sleeve touches my arm. I don't think I'm breathing.

"I read about this," she says. "They're migrating, and they get disoriented by the lights and the glass. Stupid humans."

She's a bird expert or something. A freaking birdologist. My eyes fill with tears.

"It's just a bird," she says. Her voice is much softer now, something close to kind.

It's not just a bird, though. Or at least I don't think it is. It's a sign, a warning. I can feel the tears spill out on my cheeks now, and I don't try to stop them. "I *know* this bird," I say.

She lets out a small laugh. "Well, I'm sorry for your loss."

My tattoo is burning, and I encircle my left wrist with my right hand. I know Julia's not imprisoned in a castle somewhere—at least I think I do—but that doesn't mean that she doesn't need me. "Please," I say. "I mean, I know why Julia comes here. She's not anonymous to me. I'll just find out when the next meeting is and wait for her."

I'm watching her face. Out here in the bright sunlight, it doesn't seem as wrinkled. She was pretty once, I can tell. Life and years did this to her. And drugs, I guess.

"Fine," the woman says. She drops her cigarette on the sidewalk and crushes it with her heel. "She works at a diner in Capitol Hill. It's called the First Lady."

"Thank you," I say.

"But you didn't hear it from me."

I try to smile. "I don't even know who you are."

"Exactly." She shakes her head. "I don't know who I'm helping here. Maybe neither of you."

"Maybe both of us," I say.

Maybe.

Stakeout

AN HOUR LATER I'M STANDING on C Street in front of the First Lady, enveloped in the hazy blue light of its neon sign. The air is so humid I might as well be in the rain forest, and my tank top is stuck to my back with sweat. I turned my phone on long enough to find this place, and I see that Jack has sent me three text messages, and Sadie's sent me five. He must have told her. I don't know what, but something. I turn off my phone again without reading them.

When I open the door the bell above me rings, old-fashioned and metallic. Chilled air raises goose bumps on my skin. The seats at the booths are dark blue vinyl and the tables are Formica. Portraits of the ladies line the walls, many of them photographs—Eleanor Roosevelt with her kind-eyed smile, Jackie O. with her dark bob and slim sheath dress—but a few prints of paintings too. I recognize Martha Washington by her powdered wig, and I have a sneaking suspicion that the brunette across the way is Mary Todd Lincoln. My favorite, Michelle Obama, smiles in a deep green dress just across from the door.

I don't see my sister anywhere, but a cheerful blond in a navy-blue shirtdress walks toward me from the back of the restaurant.

"Hi," she says. "Table for one?"

I take a deep breath. I'm just a customer.

"Sure," I say. She seats me in a booth and places a menu in front of me. I flip through it for a second and see Eleanor Roosevelt's scrambled eggs, Abigail Adams's raspberry waffles, Dolley Madison's blueberry French toast. If I had an appetite at this point, I could really get into this famous-lady breakfast food. I could order one of everything and have a first-lady feast. Maybe *after* I find my sister. Maybe then I'll have first-lady-feast seconds. I imagine what that would be like, sitting across the table with her at last, having pancakes. I can't quite picture it.

I look up from my menu and this is when I see her. She's facing away from me, standing in front of the window, awash in a sunbeam. She's wearing the same navy-blue dress as the hostess, and her hair is cut into a long, wavy bob. She's chatting with an elderly couple at the table, regular customers, maybe, putting their ice waters down and pulling straws from her apron. She's any old waitress.

She's the bright star that has guided me all this way.

She's my sister.

Julia turns then and walks right by my table, but she doesn't see me. Or she doesn't see that it's me, sitting here. I'm just some teenage girl in a vinyl booth.

I'm so hopeful in this moment. Everything that has happened has brought me here.

"Jules," I say. I slide out of the seat and stand up. She stops for a beat, then turns toward me. Her eyes are wide. She drops the empty tray she's holding, and it bounces across the tiled floor.

Then she says my name.

"Sylvie."

It's followed by the last word I want to hear.

"No."

Okay

"SYLVIE," SHE SAYS. "WHAT ARE you doing here?"

"Finding you," I say, and then I say it again, as if I have to. "I found you." She stands there, her brow furrowed, looking at me. I keep talking. "Isn't this what you wanted?" I say. "You sent me the book."

"I didn't know what else to do with it," she says. "I found it. In a bookshop." She crosses her arms in front of her chest, and I swear she shivers. "I don't—I don't understand how it was there. But it was."

"Magic," I say.

She shakes her head. "There is no magic."

"Oh, but there is!" I say. "You don't know." I'm about to tell her, but she says, *"Shhhhh."* She goes to sit in the booth and pulls me along. I slide into the seat across from her.

I reach down on the booth's seat and pull the fairy tale book out of my bag as if I need evidence. I hold it out to her.

She looks down at it, and then back up at me.

"What?" she says.

I push the book closer to her. "You drew me a map."

"I drew a *flower*, Sylvie." Her voice is louder than it should be, and I can see the couple she'd just been serving across the aisle turn to look at us. Julia doesn't notice, but she lowers her voice anyway. "I didn't mean you should follow me here. I just wanted you to know where I went. That I was safe."

"Maybe you should have just written, 'I'm okay,' then. Instead of this." I'm fighting off tears now, and the last thing I want to do is cry in front of my sister. I want her to think I'm strong.

"Maybe," she says. But she doesn't sound convinced of her own words. "Listen, I'm sorry. I had to take care of myself. I couldn't worry about you or Everett. Or Mom or Dad. I had to start over."

"I see you've done well at that," I say. "You have a job. You have friends, I'm sure. So, what? You don't need us anymore?"

Julia rakes her hand through her hair. I see her tattoo in a flash on her wrist.

"Of course I need you," she says. "It's not that. It's that here, I'm not a screw-up. Here, I'm not someone who let everyone down." She's speaking so quietly I can barely hear her over the clatter of dishes coming from the kitchen.

"I want to go to school," she says. "I have to figure out what I can be, since I can't be what I thought I was meant for." She looks down, clasping her hands together hard.

My memory flashes on a girl dancing, reflected in a mirror, but it's not Julia. It's me.

"I'm dancing the same solo in *Chrysanthemum* that you danced," I say. "For the donor dinner."

One little twinge of pain crosses her face meteor-quick, then disappears.

"*Chrysanthemum*," she says. "You must be doing really well."

"I'm trying," I say.

Julia catches sight of my wrist then. Her eyes widen, and she grabs my arm.

"Where did you get this?" She touches the tattoo so gently with her fingertips—to see if it's real, I guess—but I pull my arm away. I don't even want her to see it. For the first time since I ended up at Butterfly and Bee, I wonder if the tattoo was a mistake.

"Was it Toby?" Julia asks. "I'm going to kill him."

"Why?" I say. "It's not your job to protect me, right? You left. You didn't come back. You needed a fresh start."

"I was going to come back," Julia says. "I miss you so much."

"When, Julia? I was moving forward, you know? One foot in front of the other. Then I got that book and it broke the world. Or it fixed it. I can't really tell."

Julia sighs. Her cheeks are flushed. "I'm sorry, Sylvie. I didn't mean for any of this to happen."

"Julia." Someone else has entered our conversation. I turn, and there's a man standing at the end of the table. He's wearing a dark blue polo shirt with a name tag that says *Ken* pinned to his chest.

"You have an order up," he says.

"Okay," Julia says. "One second."

He looks a little baffled at her answer, and then something changes in his face. If I didn't know better—I know better, don't I?—I'd say that this is when he turns into an ogre.

"Now," he says.

Julia takes a shaky breath. I hold her gaze.

"You don't have to let him talk to you like that," I say. I want to tell this Ken who Julia really is. I want to tell him what she can do.

Or rather: what she used to be able to do. I want to tell him a once-upon-a-time. But I can't find the words.

"Sorry, Ken," Julia says. I glance up at him quickly. He looks bewildered. I grab my sister's hand across the table.

"Just come with me," I say.

"I can't," she says. There are tears in her eyes. "I'm sorry."

I pull my hand away as if she's burned it. I can see the magic cracking, this world I've built falling apart. It wasn't that she *couldn't* call me. It was that she didn't want to. My sister, who doesn't need me, who didn't want me to find her, who was just trying to send me the book so she wouldn't have to feel guilty. Sadness bubbles up in my chest, golden and frothy.

This time, I'm the one who leaves.

Seven Little Men

AN HOUR LATER, I'M SITTING on the Lincoln Memorial, on a ledge near the bottom of the stairs. Somehow I ended up here, seeing the sights like Jack suggested all those hours ago. I wandered in the general direction of the Washington Monument and then kept going. And now I'm here. I haven't turned on my phone yet, but I'm going to soon. I'm going to text Jack and have him come get me, and I'm going to tell him I'm sorry. I'm going to buy him an ice-cream cone. Or something.

"Do you mind if I sit here?"

I look up. It's a girl in an emerald-colored sundress, pale-skinned with a black bob.

"Sure," I say.

"This is like, the farthest I can be from over there"—she gestures in the direction of a small crowd in front of Lincoln's statue—"and still be *at* the memorial. I'm in charge of those seven little boys over there. In the green shirts." She points, and I look. They're shoving each other at the top of the monument.

"They look like fun," I say. She just sighs and takes out a flat green package of candy. Laffy Taffy.

"Want some?" she says. "I know it's, like, fluorescent, but it's pretty good. It's apple, not lime."

"Thanks," I say. She breaks off a piece and hands it to me.

"*This* is the problem," she says, waving the candy above her head. "They give the kids tons of sugar and they wonder why when they're bouncing out of their skins." She looks right at me, her green-eyed stare intense.

"I'm giving out free advice, if you want it." She pops a piece of candy in her mouth and chews.

"Okay," I say.

"Don't ever agree to be a day camp counselor."

I laugh. "I just spent some time at a sleepaway camp," I say. "It seemed pretty great, actually."

She shrugs. "Maybe it's different if they're with you twenty-four/seven. Some kind of survival instinct kicks in if they know they're dependent on you for food."

"Right."

"My boss offered me a brief reprieve." She laughs. It sounds the teensiest bit maniacal. "I think because she could see I was going to lose my shit. "Being ordered around by tiny . . ." She waves her hands in front of her face—she does a lot of hand waving—as if it'll help her think of the word. "Tiny dwarves! Even seven-year-olds can mansplain, did you know that? They already know everything there is to know about Abraham Lincoln and they're really happy to tell me. All. About. It."

"Well, now you're here, and you have Laffy Taffy," I say.

"True." She's nodding. She breaks off another piece. "So what's your story?"

I take a breath, let it out. "I was trying to save someone."

"What happened?"

"She didn't need saving."

She shakes her head, turning to look at the reflecting pool. "Isn't that how it always is? Boys go on adventures! Girls get *into trouble.*"

I breathe in fast. "What?"

"Girls. In. Trouble." She says it slowly, one step away from spelling out each letter. "You know." She doesn't elaborate, but she's right. I do know.

"Seven seven-year-olds," she says, half to herself. "There's a terrible symmetry to it." She squints in the direction of her people. "Oh, crap. They're calling me back." She smiles at me.

"Wish me luck," she says. I do.

When she leaves, I look out over the water. I keep waiting for the sun to set. Even though this day seems like it's been twenty hours long, it's only six o' clock.

I stand up, even though I can't see much farther that way. The sun is behind me, and my shadow spools out on the dirt in front of me, on the leaves of the bushes below and the concrete just past. A V-shaped flock of geese sails down toward the reflecting pool, not even flapping, wings spread wide on a current of air. They touch the water so softly the surface barely ripples.

I feel a little funny, all of a sudden. My heart beats hard and my blood starts spinning. The world erupts in sparkles around me and for just a moment, it's beautiful. And then I fall into the dark.

Gold Dust Woman

THE SUN IS CROOKED IN the sky, and I'm looking up at it. I'm lying on the ground. I sit up slowly, gingerly moving my arms. I'm a little scratched up, but I seem to be in one piece. Something feels off, though. Tilted. But before I can figure it out, a shadow falls across my body. I look up and see the silhouette of a person blocking the sun. Long black skirt skimming the pavement. Long blond hair, lit up from behind like the sun's corona.

I figure it out from its pieces the way I'd recognize a constellation in the sky. It's Stevie Nicks.

I am not kidding.

Actual Stevie Nicks. Singer. Songwriter. Member of Fleetwood Mac.

Stevie puts out her hand and I take it. She pulls me to my feet.

"You all right?" she asks. Her voice sounds like the inside of a geode: secret sparkle, lowlight glitter. Hearing it out in the open, not in Jack's car in the middle of a song, is startling at first.

I just nod. I can't seem to make my mouth work. Truthfully, I feel a little woozy again, but I try to stay upright. I've done enough falling for one day—right off that five-foot ledge. Which, I see when I turn around, isn't quite the same as it was when I fell off it. The whole memorial is different now, built of dark, gleaming gray-blue marble, and it's not Abe Lincoln in there. It's a woman, I think—I just have this feeling—though from here I can't quite tell who. And when I turn back around, I can see that the water in the reflecting pool is deep purple, and it's full of flamingos.

Yes.

Flamingos.

Totally normal. Nothing to see here.

"What's wrong with everything?" I ask Stevie.

She shrugs. I have to tell you this: a Stevie Nicks shrug is a thing of beauty.

"Who says anything's wrong?" she says. "And anyway, you should know. You made this."

There are honeysuckle vines trailing the wall next to me, and I can smell the heavy sweetness of the flowers. "I didn't make anything," I say.

"You underestimate yourself," she says. "We build the world we want," she says. "We see what we want."

I look at the monument, glistening in the sun, the purple pool, the flamingos. This is what I want?

"Wait," I say. "Do you mean the magic?"

She shakes her head.

"No," she says. "The magic just gives you what's missing from the world. I was talking about the way you thought you had to save Julia."

"I didn't," I say, too quickly.

Stevie looks at me pointedly. "Didn't what?"

Good question. I think my first impulse was to say that I didn't think I had to save her, but that would be a lie. She was the princess in the tower with a dragon outside the door, and I was the one with the sword. Or at least that's what I thought.

"I didn't save her," I say.

Stevie smiles just a little. "That was never your job."

We start walking toward the main set of stairs up into the memorial. We're the only ones here; the steps are empty otherwise. Stevie starts walking up the stairs and I follow.

"Who's in there?" I ask.

"Aretha."

"Aretha Franklin?"

"Is there another Aretha worthy of a monument?" Stevie asks.

"No," I say. "But Aretha isn't dead. She's my mother's favorite singer. I would know."

"Who says you have to be dead?"

I'm certainly not going to explain to Stevie Nicks that *memorial* literally means something made to preserve the memory of someone who's gone. But I guess that doesn't mean dead. After all, that's what I've been doing for Julia for a whole year. I built her a memorial out of my own life. Everything I did was what she would have done. Or what she *should* have done.

We're standing at the top of the stairs now, looking out on the reflecting pool. The flamingos move slowly across the purple mirror-water, their necks in graceful S shapes. They dip their whole heads in the water and then pull them up again, black beaks dripping. They are the beautiful weirdos of the bird world, and I wouldn't blame anyone for not believing they exist. Like I said at Camp Wildflower: it's so hard to tell with this world sometimes.

"So is it real?" I ask. "The magic?"

"Honestly?" Stevie turns her gaze toward me. "Does it matter?"

I open my mouth to answer, but before I can, Stevie smiles and raises her hand to stop me.

"It's time to go," she says. The world shimmers apart then, dissolving into molecules and sparks. The whole place goes galaxy around me.

Then I'm falling again, or maybe I'm waking up.

Can I Get a Witness?

WHEN I COME TO, EVERYTHING is hazy around the edges, and my head feels like it's made of glass, a hundred cracks spiderwebbing through my skull. I'm lying flat on my back, indoors, and the room is shaking.

No. It's not a room. There are windows at the far end of the space, and medical supplies in bins lining the walls. There's no siren that I can hear, but this is definitely an ambulance.

There's a paramedic sitting next to me. I grab his hand and try to sit up.

"Whoa," he says. "Lie back down."

The world is tipped and spinning, so I do.

"I don't need an ambulance," I say.

He gives me a capital-L Look. "Miss, you're *in* an ambulance," he says. "So I think that's already been decided."

He has a point. I try a new strategy. I take a deep, calming breath and put a sweet smile on my face. I am definitely not a person who is panicking. I definitely didn't just see Stevie Nicks at the Aretha Franklin Memorial.

"What happened?"

"Witnesses said you fell off the memorial," he says.

"Witnesses?" I say.

"Yeah," he says. "The people standing around you. The people who called us."

I squeeze my eyes shut. I open them again. "Stevie Nicks?"

"Um." He narrows his eyes. "No, I didn't see her. Or any of the other members of Fleetwood Mac."

I lean back a little and look at the ceiling. "Dammit," I say. "I would have liked to meet Lindsey Buckingham too. I'd tell him he should have let Stevie put 'Silver Springs' on *Rumours*. That asshole." I smile, trying to show him that I'm being funny, that I'm not actually hallucinating 1970s rock stars outside the Lincoln Memorial (though that matter's still up for debate). He isn't having it.

"Can you tell me your name, please?"

"Sylvie Blake."

"Good," he says. I see he's got my purse right there, and he's already read it on my ID. The ambulances lurches a little, then stops. He stands and, when the driver opens the back doors, starts to move my stretcher toward the opening. He and the other guy bring me down in one quick, smooth movement. For a moment, I look up at the still-blue sky and feel like I'm flying. Then the wheels of the stretcher touch down on the pavement.

"I'm sure I don't need a hospital," I say.

"Well, we're already here," he says and smiles, not unkindly. He points toward the doors, whooshing open for some people in scrubs walking out. "You're going to have to tell them that."

Sara, Like the Song

I DO. AT LEAST, I try to. But the nurses with their calming voices just want me to get out my insurance card, and have my blood pressure taken.

The doctor has a badge clipped to the pocket on her scrubs. Her first name is Sara, and she's young, with curly blonde hair pulled back from her face. A resident, maybe. Just a few years older than Julia.

"Sara," I say. "Like the Fleetwood Mac song."

She straps the blood-pressure cuff around my upper arm. "Okay."

"Haven't you heard it?"

"I'm not sure," she says. Her eyes are on the dial. The cuff starts to inflate.

"Oh, you should," I say, because apparently, I am now a person who recommends the Mac to random strangers.

I am also now a person who calls the band "the Mac."

"Okay," she says again. There may be a tiny hint of a smile on her lips. "Your blood pressure is normal."

"Good," I say.

"You know your name—"

"Sylvie."

"—and who's president and all that, right?"

"Of course," I say. "But please don't make me talk about that guy."

Dr. Sara smiles, finally. "I sure won't," she says. She looks down at her clipboard and then back up at me. "To be honest, I think you're okay. I don't know why they even put you in an ambulance. You're a little scratched up, but I'm not convinced you hit your head. I think you just fainted. When did you last eat?"

"Breakfast." Suddenly I'm craving whatever Dolley Madison and Eleanor Roosevelt have to offer.

"Right. And it was hot. Probably a combination of hunger and heat." She hands me a paper cafeteria menu. "You should call down and get some food sent up here. The grilled cheese isn't bad. Maybe an orange juice too."

"Can I text my friend?" I hold up my phone. "He'll come pick me up."

"Sure," Dr. Sara says. "But you have to stay three full hours, okay? Just to make sure you're okay."

She's already walking out the door when she says it, so I don't bother to argue. I text Jack the whole story, stripped down to the essentials, which are basically I found her and she doesn't want to see me. I try to play down the falling-off-a-national-monument angle. Then I wait for his reply. It only takes a second.

I'm coming, he says.

Knight, Shining

JACK GETS THERE IN RECORD time, maybe a half hour from the moment I pressed Send. He's breathless, flushed, Pavlova in her travel bag slung over his shoulder. When I see him, a bottomless well of relief fills my stomach. (It probably helps that I've already eaten my grilled cheese.) We look at each other for a moment, smiling wide enough for the International Space Station to see us.

Dr. Sara pokes her head into my room.

"Is that a dog in there?" she asks.

"Um." Jack looks at me. "No?"

Dr. Sara shakes her head and sighs theatrically—I love her—but she doesn't tell him to leave. So he sets Pav in her bag down on the ground and folds me into his arms. I let myself exhale fully for what feels like the first time in hours.

"I'm sorry," he says into my hair.

"I know." I put my nose against his shoulder and breathe in his scent like a weirdo. "Me too. I want to get out of here but they told me I had to stay."

"Well, they're not just going to let you wander out of here by yourself. But maybe they'll let you go with me."

I flag down Dr. Sara as she passes the room.

"I have someone to pick me up," I say. I point at Jack. "Him. I have a chaperone. Can I go now?"

"I told you, Sylvie. You have to stay." She's shaking her head. "You need at least three hours of observation."

"I guess." I look at Dr. Sara. "Can we at least take a walk around the floor?"

"Sure," she says. "But you"—she points to Jack—"need to stay next to her in case she gets unsteady. Hold her hand."

Jack smiles then, a straight-up grin, and holds out his hand. I take it. Just before we go, I grab my bag and slip it over my shoulder. Jack picks up Pav's bag.

When I smile—he's carrying my dog!—he says, "Well, I'm not just going to leave her unattended."

We walk through the doorway and out into the hall, straight into the bustle of the hospital floor. There's a desk in the center and Dr. Sara's already sitting there, filling out paperwork. My paperwork, maybe. I wave to her and mouth the word "thanks." She smiles.

Jack is still holding my hand. "You were right, you know."

"About what?"

"Well." He pauses. "We don't really know each other that well, despite having known each other for a long time. But there are things I know about you."

Jack is looking ahead of us, and I'm looking at him.

"Oh yeah?"

"Yeah," he says. He turns his face toward me. "I know how kind you are, and how smart you are. I know that when you want something, you find a way to make it happen."

"Is that a good thing, though?" I glance down at the lino-leum, which is shiny and pearl gray. "All it meant was that I broke my own heart."

Jack nods his head one time, emphatically. "Yes," he says. "It is a good thing. You found out what you needed to know."

"I guess." There's a little girl in a wheelchair to my right, waiting for her mother to fill out some paperwork. Her leg is in a dark pink cast right up to the knee. I smile at her, and she smiles back. She waves, and I do too. Ahead of me, at the end of the hall, I see a woman push the button for the elevator and a little spark goes off in my brain. *Save yourself*, I hear. (In the voice of Stevie Nicks, if you really want to know).

"Do you think we could make it?" I ask Jack.

Jack looks at me. "Make it?" he asks. I nod in the direction of the elevator. I'm afraid he'll say no—that we couldn't get there in time, that someone would stop us, and anyway, I should stay to make sure I'm okay. He's cautious like that. But I can see the pos-sibilities unspool in his brain, see him calculating the risks. For a moment, I can't tell which way it's going to go.

He squeezes my hand. Ahead of us, the elevator doors slide open, and Jack leans a little closer to me, puts his lips by my ear.

"Run," he says.

Where We're Going

THE DOORS TO THE STREET whoosh open for us and we run straight through them, then all the way down the block. We don't stop until the flashing lights of the ambulance out front look like snow-globe glitter when we look back.

"We may have made that exit a little more dramatic than it needed to be," Jack says.

"That was so much fun," I say. Or I try to say it. I'm basically panting.

"*You* are so much fun," Jack says. He reaches for me and pulls me toward him. We kiss in the street and I feel my molecules swirling, but I don't mind. Someone honks, and we pull apart. We hop up on the sidewalk, both smiling like someone has given us free puppies and chocolate milk shakes at the same time.

He unzips Pavlova's bag and she hops out onto the sidewalk and looks up at us in a very *WTF* kind of way.

"Sorry, Pav," Jack says.

"Yeah," I say. "Lots of drama. Thank god I wasn't wearing a hospital gown." I bend down to pet my dog. "I feel a little guilty about running out on Dr. Sara, but I couldn't stay there for one more minute." I grin. "I'll send her a really good thank-you note."

I pull my phone from my bag. There's a text from my brother, a selfie he took just now, apparently, in front of a sign that says his name.

"Oh my god. Everett," I say. "I forgot. He's here. In DC."
"Where?"

I squint at the picture. "Georgetown, I think." I look up. "He says he's speaking tonight."

Jack smiles. He's so even-tempered, so dependable, but at the same time he makes my electrons spin.

"Well," he says, "I guess we know where we're going."

Seeing Stories

WHEN WE GET TO THE auditorium, Everett is sitting behind a table on the low stage. He's talking to the woman sitting next to him, who has spiky pink hair. She's smiling at him.

The room is filling, but I go straight to the front. I don't want to go up on the stage but I stand at the foot of it, right in front of my brother. It takes him a moment to notice, but when he does, it's like he's seen a ghost.

"Sylvie," he says, coming around the table and hopping off the stage. He crushes me into a hug. "What the hell are you doing here? Aren't you supposed to be at camp?" He lets me go then and looks into my face.

I open my mouth. Then I close it again. I want to tell him the whole story—I will someday—but for now, I can only manage the end. And even then, I feel close to tears in the middle of this auditorium.

"Julia sent me a map," I say. "Or at least I thought it was a map, but it wasn't. I thought she wanted me to find her."

"Okay," Everett says. His voice is careful.

"I thought she was in trouble," I say. "I thought she needed me to save her."

"What happened?"

"I was wrong." I press my hands together. "She's here, in DC, but she didn't need me. Didn't want me to come."

"Oh, Syl," Everett says. "You were always seeing stories in your head. Heroes and villains and victims who need saving." He's smiling, but his eyes are sad. I see my mother's happy-sad face in his. "I don't mean to play Wise Old Brother here, but you can't—"

My tattoo twinges. "Yeah, I understand that now."

Everett is watching my face. "She's here, though?"

I nod. He shakes his head like he's shaking thoughts out of his mind.

"Listen, I have to do my panel. You can sit in the front." He points. "We'll talk more afterward."

When it's Everett's turn to talk, he goes to the podium. Behind him on the screen is a sketch from the first issue of *The Square*.

"Hey, everybody. I have to tell you, I'm a little rattled." He runs his hand through his hair. "My sister's here." There's some tittering in the crowd and someone says, "Uh-oh!"

"No," Everett says, putting up a stop-sign hand. "I love my sister. Actually, I love both of them. But this particular sister is sixteen and I didn't expect her to show up here tonight." He looks at me, like he's talking just to me at this moment. "Though I'm happy she did, because she's going to make an appearance on here." He points his thumb at the screen behind him.

"I've been working on this series for three years," he says. "The story has to evolve or it dies. So tonight, you all will be the first ones to meet my new characters."

There's a smattering of applause. I feel nervous for some reason, and then Everett clicks to the next picture.

"I just drew this a few days ago," Everett says. "They're practically brand-new. These two are Theo's sisters." Theo is one of his *Square* characters, the one I always thought was most like him. I didn't know Theo had sisters.

It's us. Julia and me. She's in a leotard and leg warmers, the tattered remains of a tutu hanging from her waist. She's standing in the middle of an iridescent oil spill, and I'm standing right by her side in pointe shoes and leggings. You can see the reflection of our legs in the oil. We look strong.

"They're ballerinas," he says. "And sisters. Like mine. I spent hours and hours at their recitals when I was younger, so I thought I might as well put it to use." People laugh. "But that's not all I've put to use. We're supposed to talk about where we get our ideas. I mean, usually I make things up. This is a dystopian series, right? Manhattan's not uninhabitable . . . yet." More laughter. "But I did take something from my life here. This is a story line about what it feels like to lose someone. What it feels like to get them back."

There's a catch in my breath and before I realize it, I'm crying. I don't wipe the tears away. I just listen to my brother.

"I have a point," Everett says, "and this is it: you can use the bad things that happen to you. You can make something out of them."

The auditorium is totally silent, and I can imagine that everyone here is trying to think of what they can make out of the bad things, the sadness they can't let go. As for me, I put it into my dancing, for sure, but I also put it into this trip. I put it into finding Julia, letting the world break my heart. And somehow I'm still here.

"In all seriousness"—Everett is looking at me again now—"ballet dancers are superheroes. They go through some major pain to make something beautiful." I swipe the back of my hand across my eyes and it comes away wet. "What I'm saying is, if the apocalypse happens, you want a ballerina on your side."

I'm pretty sure I'm still crying, but I'm also smiling so big I feel like my face might fall off.

There is a throng of people—fans!—waiting to talk to my brother. When they finish, I notice his sketch pad sitting at the edge of the table. I sift through it and find half a dozen versions of the ballerina sisters—Julia and me.

"Can I have a couple of these?" I say.

He nods. "Of course. You like them?"

I gather them up and slip them into my bag. "I love them."

"I was worried you wouldn't. Or you wouldn't want me putting our story in my book, in whatever form." He smiles. "It just sort of came to me the other day. Which is weird, since you were out looking for Jules right then."

There are enough weird things in the world that I'm willing to accept one more.

"I think it's perfect," I say. I lower my voice. "Are you going to go see her?"

He waits. Then he shakes his head. "No." But the way he says it tells me that some part of him wishes he could, even if he knows it's not the right choice.

"You should call Grace," I say.

His face brightens when I say her name. I see the light in his eyes.

"Why?" he asks.

"Because you can't just send a girl drawings of her in the mail with no explanation. It's not polite."

A slow smile spreads across his face.

"Makes sense," he says.

Later, after Jack and I eat burritos with Everett and send him back to the Georgetown dorms, we stand on the sidewalk next to the Volvo. The sky above us is wide and dark, and even though I can't see Ursa Major very well with the city lights shining, I know she's up there.

"Now what?" I ask.

"Now we go to Richmond."

"What?" My eyes are wide.

Jack shrugs. "Someone I trust made a case that it's the right thing to do."

"Can we make one stop first?"

"I told you," Jack says, smiling. "You're the one sailing this ship."

Look

THE WHOLE RESTAURANT IS LIT up gold. The neon sign still buzzes bright blue. Jack and I sit in the Volvo, parked on the street out front. We're both watching the window.

I don't know whether she'll still be there, but after a few moments I see her, walking from the kitchen with a tray. I pick up the fairy tale book. If I give it back to her, what will happen? I'm not sure she'd even want it. And if I'm honest, I don't want to give it up.

I put the book down. I pick up Everett's sketch instead. I get out of the car.

She's still on the same shift, but for me, this has been the longest day. It might as well have been an entire week. It's bright in there and dark outside, but there's a streetlamp right out front, so the sidewalk is illuminated. When I stand there, step into its circle of light, so am I. I can see my sister through the window, putting dishes on a table. I can see myself too, the ghost of my reflection. I see it in the glass, but I know that I'm real, out here on the sidewalk.

Jules steps away from the table and turns my way. She sees me. She stops, lowering the empty tray to her side.

I smile. I wave. It means

hello

and

goodbye

and

you are who you are and that's okay.

She waves back. I don't know what her wave means, but I'll take it. It's something.

There's a bunch of flyers taped to the outside of the window, band shows and lost cats and apartments for rent. I take a piece of tape from the bottom of a flyer for a band called Hashtag Witch Hunt and I use it to attach one of Everett's folded-up sketches to the window. Julia stands in the middle of the aisle, watching me. I take a step back and this is when I see it again: my reflection in the glass, over Julia. We are not the same. We are two different people. We always will be.

I walk back to the car and get in. Pavlova hops into my lap.

"You ready?" Jack asks.

I take a breath.

We're going to drive to Richmond. Jack's going to talk to his dad and I'm going to have to tell Sadie that I've been kissing her brother. And then when I get home, I'm going to tell my mother that I'm not sure about Level Seven. That I need to take a break and figure that out.

I think she'll understand.

When we leave, when she has a chance, my sister will come out and get Everett's sketch from the window. She'll know that we love her—that he loves her enough to have drawn it, that I love her enough to have brought it here. That's going to have to be enough for now.

I look in the rearview mirror. I half expect to see butterflies, owls, bluebirds, twisting vines covering the restaurant. Every Girl in Trouble lined up on the sidewalk. But I think we've crossed into the Ever After. It's time.

I look at Jack. "I'm ready," I say.

Jack smiles at me, and then he pulls away from the curb. I pick up Jack's phone. I'm looking for a Stevie song.

Acknowledgments

I'm sure you know this by now, but there're all sorts of magic in the world. I'm going to take a moment here to thank all the people who've brought it to this book and my life.

I'm so grateful for my team at William Morris Endeavor: my agent Jay Mandel, who is kind and funny and generally fantastic; Lauren Shonkoff, who cheers for me silently during conference calls; Laura Bonner, who handles the whole rest of the world (that's big); Janine Kamouh for her fantastic insight; and Flora Hackett, who's helped take things cinematic. You guys are the best, and I'm so lucky to have you on my side.

At HarperCollins, I'm so happy to work again with my editor Kristen Pettit, who is supportive and insightful and fun. Elizabeth Lynch's enthusiasm always peps me up. Jenna Stempel has designed another beautiful cover, with the help of Hsaio-Ron Cheng and her gorgeous illustrations. Thanks to the rest of the team at Harper too: Jessica Berg, Bess Braswell, Tyler Breitfeller, Jacqueline Hornberger, Laura Kaplan, and Kimberly Stella.

Thanks to the following friends, who've been kind and generous in all sorts of ways: Brian Castner, Barbara Cole, Anne Marie Comaratta, Julie Eshbaugh, Michael Estes, Noah Falck, Laurie Elizabeth Flynn, Kami Garcia, Jeff Giles, Heidi Heilig, Bridget Hodder, Lucy Keating, Jessi Kirby, Kerry Kletter, Nina LaCour, Meg Leder, Jen Maschari, Shannon Parker, Deanna Pavone, Lygia Day Peñaflor, Riley Redgate, Marisa Reichardt, Dee Romito, Rob Selkowitz (scientist-on-call), Laura Shonan, Amber Smith, Eric Smith (who also named my bakery), Courtney Smyton, Janet Butler Taylor, Sherry Taylor, Rachelle Toarmino, Alison Umminger, Kali Wallace, Lauren Willett-Benson, Jeff Zentner, and Missy Zgliczynski. Kathleen Glasgow, for being there for me every day. Harriet Reuter Hapgood and her floor-length tutus. Katie Kennedy, who gave me a pep talk when I really needed it, and great notes. Emily Henry, for her notes and her sparkle. Aryanna Falkner and Gaby Weiss, who answered the call of the BookBat Signal in the sky. Diana Goetsch (and her committee) for the great untaken band name. Denise Zdon Bitar, who talked tattoos with me. Joe Murray, for handing out copies of my book to rock stars when necessary. Jaime Sampson, who named my diner. Symon Mink and his long-ago Volvo. Jodi Bryon and Brett Essler, who are among my favorite humans. Jon and Martha Welch and everyone at my favorite independent bookstore, Talking Leaves Books. Canisius College and my students and colleagues there, who make my job a pleasure, especially Mick Cochrane and Eric Gansworth, the very best mentors turned friends. My professors from the MFA program at the University of Notre Dame: Valerie Sayers, Sonia Gernes, William O'Rourke, and Steve Tomasula, plus my talented cohort there. The teachers and staff at my daughters' dance studio, the Fit Physique, especially Candice Cavanaugh and Kandi Braun. Janet McNally (the other one), otherwise known as Janet of the North, who is the best name doppelgänger a girl could ask for. Janie Killewald for her moonflowers. New York Foundation for the Arts, for awarding me fellowships in fiction twice: I truly appreciate your support. To the Sweet Sixteens, who are supportive and kind. To the Fight Me Club: I'm so happy to be one of you. To Erin, who came back: I'm so proud of you.

Thanks to Misty Copeland, whom I saw at JFK airport when I was doubting this book. Like Sylvie would have, I saw that as a sign. Thanks, too, to Fleetwood Mac, who gave Sylvie and Jack their road-trip soundtrack. When I began this book I wasn't even a Fleetwood Mac superfan (gasp!), but I've come to love these songs, and I sure love Stevie Nicks.

Thanks to my mother, for all her love and support. To my brother Pat, who buys stacks of my books and forgets to give them to his friends. I mean, eventually he remembers, but we get to laugh about it in the meantime. To my sister-in-law Mary, best one I could ask for, and to Peggy McNally, one of my favorite adults. To my daughters: I hope you'll go to the ends of the earth for each other if you need to. To Jesse, who has loved me for such a long time. I love you too.

I lost my dad when I was finishing this novel, and I miss him every day. He used to forward me emails from the International Space Station until I finally signed up myself. Now, whenever I get one, and when I watch its bright dot cross the sky above me, I think of him. Thank you, Dad. I love you.

Resources

If you love someone who is addicted to alcohol or drugs, my heart is with you. There are many amazing organizations working to improve the lives of people suffering from addiction, as well as their families and friends. Some of these organizations are listed below. While all efforts have been made to ensure the accuracy of the information in the following sections as of the date this book was published, it is for informational purposes only. It is not intended to be complete or exhaustive, or a substitute for the advice of a qualified expert or professional.

The National Council on Alcoholism and Drug Dependency has a web page for family and friends of those who are addicted to alcohol or drugs.

www.ncadd.org/family-friends

Alcoholics Anonymous is a support group for those addicted to alcohol and/or drugs.

www.aa.org

Al-Anon is a support group for families of alcoholics and addicts.

al-anon.org

Alateen is an Al-Anon support group especially for teens.

al-anon.org/newcomers/teen-corner-alateen/